Books by Charles Kipps

Out of Focus

Cop Without a Badge

Hell's Kitchen Homicide

CRYSTAL DEATH

A Conor Bard Mystery

CHARLES KIPPS

SCRIBNER

New York   London   Toronto   Sydney

SCRIBNER
A Division of Simon & Schuster, Inc.
1230 Avenue of the Americas
New York, NY 10020

Designed by Carla Jayne Jones

Manufactured in the United States of America

10 9 8 7 6 5 4 3 2 1

Library of Congress Control Number: 2010018472

ISBN 978-1-4391-3995-0
ISBN 978-1-4391-4116-8 (ebook)

For Elaine

CRYSTAL DEATH

Chapter One

It had been two months since Conor Bard had taken to the stage at the Rhythm Bar so he found it comforting that the joint was packed. It didn't matter whether people were there to see him perform after his long absence or just seeking refuge from the torrential rain that had transformed the streets of New York City into whitewater rapids. He had a lively, appreciative audience and his adrenaline was flowing.

Even though the place was a dive, it was still a venue. And to Conor, each venue was a step on the way to achieving his dream: signing with a major record label. So why *hadn't* he been up there jamming for the past eight weeks?

It's my own fault. I should just quit the job.

The job was NYPD. Conor was a cop, a detective in the precinct that encompassed the most high-profile sectors of Manhattan. Times Square. Fashion Avenue. The Diamond District. All the Broadway theaters. Hell's Kitchen, which despite its recent gentrification still harbored remnants of its violent past. So there wasn't much time to pursue a dream when every day someone else's dream bled out on the pavement.

Conor strummed the nickel-plated strings of his electric guitar, a vintage Fender Stratocaster, then stepped up to the microphone and belted out the opening verse of the Temptations classic "I Wish It Would Rain."

"Sunshine, blue skies, please go away . . ."

Now *there* was a song that struck an emotional chord—about a man so miserable he wouldn't leave his house. *When was the last time I was really happy? Maybe never.*

Conor was forty-three. A hard forty-three. The crevices in his craggy face were growing deeper by the day and his brown hair was in a constant battle with encroaching strands of gray. But he didn't dwell on these things. Instead, he spent most of his late nights in hollow hours of denial. Denial about getting older. Denial about his chances of actually making it as a singer. Denial about his aversion to romantic commitment. Denial about his drinking, which was becoming a real problem. Whenever someone asked him where he lived, he was always tempted to say, *Where do I live? I live in denial.*

"I wish it would rain . . ."

The crowd roared its approval at the irony inherent in his decision to sing that particular tune, considering the downpour that had lasted all day. As he soaked up the collective praise, he scanned the faces in the crowd. Many of them were familiar, particularly a pretty thirty-something blond woman he had met the last time he played there. He struggled to recall her name. *Ingrid.* Yes, that was it. Ingrid. *She plays viola. Or is it violin? Something in the string section.* He had intended to get her number that night but for some reason, he couldn't remember why, he never did. *Maybe I was drunk. Maybe it was because she was a musician. Musicians are fucked-up. What the hell? Maybe tonight I'll get her number.*

The door swung open, momentarily allowing the pelting rain to provide an appropriate, percussive accompaniment to the music. Conor was surprised to see Sergeant Amanda Pitts entering the bar. Amanda hadn't been to see him play for two years. But he didn't take it personally. She was always on the job, working twelve, fourteen hours a day, and when she wasn't at the precinct she was likely passed out from exhaustion. *Sarge looks different tonight,* Conor thought.

Then again, he usually saw her under the harsh fluorescent bulbs in the office, which tended to accentuate the worst of her thirty-eight years. *That's what bar lighting will do.* Even though no one would ever call Amanda sexy, in the perpetual twilight of the Rhythm Bar, she was a contender.

Conor made eye contact with Amanda. She nodded an acknowledgment then moved her hand across her throat in a slicing motion as if to say: *Cut!*

Amanda drifted to the back of the bar and disappeared into the darkness where he could no longer see her. He finished the song but because he knew she was there and could feel her staring at him, his performance suffered. The paying customers didn't notice, however, and lavished applause as Conor hit the final chord, then swung the long neck of the guitar upward with a flourish.

Conor leaned into the mike. "We're going to take a short break. But we'll be right back."

That was the signal for Susie the bartender to trigger the iPod plugged into the sound system. She did this at the end of every set, to keep the energy level in the room from plummeting. But the band wasn't due to break for another twenty minutes, so she had been caught off guard. After a few seconds of confused hesitation, Susie lunged for the Play button. Johnnie Taylor's rendition of "Still Crazy" vibrated out of the speakers.

"Starting all over . . . I've got to find what's left of my life . . ."

Conor looked at the band. "Sorry, guys."

And he was. How many shows had he canceled because of the job? It wasn't fair to the other musicians, especially not to Richard Shorter, the piano player. Conor and Richard had gone to high school together. Richard had stuck with him ever since, never complaining about the uncertainty of their schedule. Peter the drummer, who was a veteran known as the "Human Metronome," and Gordon the bass player, a twenty-two-year-old African American who brought a youthful energy to the group, were recent additions to the quartet. But how long would they stick around without a steady or, more to the point, reliable flow of gigs?

3

Conor climbed from the stage and made his way to the back of the room, where he found Amanda propped against the bar.

"Hey, Sarge. Glad you could make it."

"You were in great form tonight."

"Thanks."

"We've got a homicide," she said abruptly. "And you're up."

He motioned to the stage. "I'm in the middle—"

"No problem. The house is full of detectives playing cards. I'll give it to one of them. I just thought you might want this one."

"Why?" Conor asked before he could stop himself.

"The victim's name is Zivah Gavish."

"Sorry. Doesn't ring a bell."

"She's Israeli. One of the biggest dealers in the world for something *you'll* never buy."

"And what's that?"

"Diamonds."

Conor grinned. "Maybe you're right about the diamonds."

"A Stanley Silberman called nine-one-one a half hour ago, at eight thirty. Owns one of those jewelry stores on Forty-seventh Street, in the Diamond District. According to Silberman, Zivah Gavish was supposed to meet him at the annual diamond dealers' dinner tonight. When she didn't show up at the hotel, I guess he was worried enough to phone it in."

Conor rubbed the back of his neck. No way he was going to let the job pull him from the stage. Not this time. *I've got a show to finish. Let her give this to someone else.*

"S-A-P-S is already at the scene," she continued, pronouncing each letter of the acronym.

"SAPS?"

"South African Police Service."

"What's their angle?"

"I don't know. The victim's a diamond dealer. South Africa produces diamonds."

Conor felt himself being reeled in, which he knew was precisely what Amanda intended and something he was definitely trying to avoid. If he was going to get back on the stage, now was the moment. But his legs were like stakes driven firmly into the ground.

Amanda shrugged. "A dead diamond dealer? South African cops? As far as cases go, it doesn't get any better than that." She motioned toward the stage. "Anyway, you should get back up there. Don't want to keep your fans waiting." She started walking away.

"Sarge," he called out.

She stopped, turned slowly.

"Meet you in front?" she asked, although she already knew the answer.

Chapter Two

Conor gave a brief explanation to John, the owner of the Rhythm Bar. John was not thrilled but neither was he surprised. Conor had left in the middle of a set before. Now Conor owed John a favor and having a marker due from a cop wasn't such a bad thing.

Richard would take over and finish the night. While Conor's song list was heavy with R&B and seasoned with a touch of rock 'n' roll, Richard's repertoire spanned all genres. And unlike Conor, who had his own unique style, Richard was a mimic who could capture the voice and inflection of every singer you could name, as if they all resided inside him. Was there a Richard in there too? Maybe. But Richard preferred not to call attention to himself. He was quite content playing the piano and occasionally showing off his ability as a vocal impressionist, then heading across the Hudson River to his job as manager of the largest tire store in Bergen County, New Jersey.

Amanda was waiting in her car. Conor braved the downpour and climbed into the passenger seat, drenched from the quick dash to the curb.

"The patrol boss notified CSU," Amanda said as she steered the car away from the curb. "Turns out the unit was in the area so they should already be there."

"Where's 'there'?" Conor wanted to know.

"That old yarn factory on Forty-fourth they made into condos."

Conor had read an article about the building. It had been purchased by a developer and converted to luxury lofts. Six thousand square feet each, something like that. His one-bedroom brownstone apartment was five hundred and ninety-one square feet, if you could believe the floor plan they gave him when he moved in.

"This is going to be a big crime scene," he noted.

"You're right. With the South Africans showing up."

"No. I meant the size of the place. But now that you mention it, how did non-NYPD personnel gain access to the scene?"

"Good question," she said. "Talk to Sayer and Wasiak. They were the first officers."

"This guy, Silberman. He called in a missing persons report, right? You could've waited before sending a unit over there."

"Yeah. But I had a hunch on this one."

"You were right."

"I'm always right."

"Bring Silberman in." Conor was already plotting the course of the investigation. "Let's see what he knows."

"Will do. And I alerted the homicide squad. They're on the way."

Despite their name, the homicide squad did not generally investigate homicides of their own. Instead, the squad of detectives provided support to the detective who caught the case. Conor wasn't always happy to have them around. Depending on who showed up, the squad could offer valuable assistance. Just as often they could create tension by attempting to wrest control of the case.

Normally, Conor would have roused his partner at this point, but he was without one. His long-term partner, Ralph Kurtz, had retired last year. Steven Clyde, the baby-faced, freshly minted detective who had succeeded Ralph, couldn't take the pressure of Midtown and had recently gotten himself transferred to Missing Persons.

"By the way, Sarge. When am I getting a new partner?"

"Feeling lonely, Bard?"

"As a matter of fact, I am."

"Should have somebody for you soon."

"No rush."

Amanda pulled in front of the building and stopped the car.

"You coming?" he asked.

"Later."

Conor climbed out of the car and looked skyward. The monsoon had abated, giving way to a fog of misty droplets. As he headed toward the entrance to the apartment building, he passed five police cruisers, an ambulance, and the mobile field lab, which wasn't unusual. There also was a black Cadillac Escalade parked ominously in the middle of the street. You only saw those vehicles at a hip-hop event or a federal investigation.

"Where's the party?" Conor asked as he walked up to Logan, a uniformed officer.

"Top floor," Logan replied. "Just press the button marked PH."

Conor stopped in front of the building. A pair of glass doors were flanked on the right by a single metal door, which he assumed was the service entrance. "Listen, Logan. Anybody other than us comes out of here, hang on to them."

"You got it."

The lobby was rather modest given the fact that the lofts started at seven million. There was a reception desk off to the left side. On the right, a couch, a coffee table, two chairs, and a large plant sat against a wall that was unadorned except for a camera mounted near the ceiling.

The concierge identified himself as Bill. A slim man in his thirties, he was clearly rattled by all the police activity but managed to tell Conor that Zivah Gavish had arrived home around five and had not had any visitors.

"What about the other tenants?"

"Owners," Bill corrected him. "We had our first closings a month ago. So far, the only two owners who have moved in are Ms. Gavish and Mr. Morton. And Mr. Morton is away."

"You have a superintendent? Maintenance workers?"

"Super starts tomorrow. Management is hiring porters and handy-men now."

"What do you do when you need to take a break?"

"I lock the door."

"What about the service entrance?"

"Until we're fully staffed, management doesn't want it used. We keep it locked."

"There's no other way into the building?"

"No."

"And you're sure no one entered after five?"

"Just cops."

"How do you know they were cops?"

"They had badges."

Conor almost laughed. Badges? You could buy them in a toy store.

"Did anyone enter the building *before* five?"

"Not while I was here," Bill replied. "I came on at four. You'll have to ask Larry. He's got the day shift. But yeah, usually we do have people in and out."

"Like who?"

"Plumbers. Electricians. Carpenters. There's a lot of work to do in this place. And then there's the real estate agents. They're in here all the time."

Conor was becoming frustrated. "All right. Let me put it this way. Did everyone who entered the building *leave* before five?"

"I think so . . ." He squinted. "I don't remember anyone leaving after Ms. Gavish arrived."

"You said Ms. Gavish returned at five?" Conor asked, just to be certain.

"Yes. And then she left about five thirty."

Conor reacted. "She *left*?"

Bill nodded. "She came back a few minutes later."

"How many minutes?"

"Three or four. She went upstairs. And then . . ."

Conor pointed to the camera. "I'll need the security video."

Bill's eyes blinked nervously. "I have to talk to the manager."

"Do it. I'll be right back."

Conor took the elevator to the penthouse level on the ninth floor. The doors opened directly into an expansive apartment with twenty-foot-high ceilings. He ventured into the foyer and spotted CSU Officer Brian Cobb standing amid a team of crime scene investigators. Brian was hard to miss. He was six feet four inches tall and wore a New York City–born-and-bred attitude on his forty-six-year-old face.

"This is one for the books," Brian said as Conor approached.

"What's the matter, Brian? I thought you'd seen it all."

Brian reached over with a latex glove–clad hand and tapped a CSU investigator on the shoulder. "Could you step aside and let Detective Bard have a look?"

Lying on a red Oriental carpet was a stunningly beautiful woman in a revealing black silk dress and black high-heel shoes. She appeared to be about thirty. Long, black hair framed her ebony eyes and her full lips were covered with dark red gloss. If it weren't for the thin crimson line across her elegantly long neck, one might think she had playfully positioned herself on the floor. But what really jolted Conor's sensibilities were the diamonds. Dozens of them. Scattered across her body and spilling out around her like a galaxy of stars in a night sky.

"Diamonds are a girl's best friend," Brian said.

"Not tonight," Conor observed.

Chapter Three

As Conor slowly circled Zivah Gavish's lifeless form, her eyes seemed to follow him. Even though he had stood over murder victims many times before, the illusion that she was watching his every move created a hypnotic effect and Conor felt caught within her gaze.

Brian dropped to one knee and closed Zivah's lids with two fingers. "Sorry. I was preoccupied with the body. And I don't mean the corpse."

Brian had no respect for the dead. Of course, he saw so much death he had to maintain an emotional distance or he'd go crazy. If necrophilic humor could get him through the night, so what? It wasn't like the recently departed could object.

"Murder weapon?" Conor asked.

Brian examined the wound on Zivah's neck. "Something very sharp."

"Kitchen knife?"

"Could be." He moved his hand slowly, just above the thin line of blood. "But if you ask me, I'd say this appears to be more consistent with an injury from a razor."

Conor looked around the room. It was cluttered with shipping cartons and shopping bags and packing material.

"Or a box cutter," Conor suggested. He knew from experience that when the murder weapon was missing from the scene, it usually indicated that the killer had brought it with him. With a weapon of opportunity—a kitchen knife, a paperweight, or some other household object—perpetrators tend to wipe the prints and leave the weapon next to the body. Sometimes they aren't even smart enough to wipe the prints. The dozens of cardboard boxes strewn about were likely opened with a box cutter. "You find a box cutter in here?"

"No," Brian replied.

So where was it? Conor wondered. *Did the killer take it with him?*

"Any sign of sexual assault?" Conor asked.

Brian lifted the hem of her dress. "Panties still on." He dropped the hem. "But I'll leave the final determination to the medical examiner."

Brian walked to an open wall safe. The floor around it was littered with cash and jewelry. "Looks like the killer was interrupted. Who's going to leave this stuff behind?"

Conor stared at the safe. "It's open. Why is it open?"

"Maybe she doesn't keep it locked," Brian suggested.

"Then why bother to have it?"

"Maybe the intruder forced her to open it."

"Or"—Conor pushed the safe door slightly, revealing the knob of a combination lock—"the killer knew the combination." He bent over to get a closer look at the knob. "Can you get prints off this?"

"I doubt it. The grip has ridges. Had a burglary a couple months ago, same kind of mechanism—"

"Maybe robbery wasn't the motive." Conor's eyes wandered over the cascade of gems sparkling like sequins on Zivah's black silk dress. "All those diamonds? Could be somebody's trying to send a message."

A man around forty stepped up next to them, the scent of stale cigar smoke announcing his arrival. Closely cropped blond hair. Steel gray eyes. Blue suit with a muted yellow tie. He exuded the aura of a cop. But not a local cop. Not even a federal cop. There was a certain worldliness about him.

"One of the diamonds is missing," the man noted, speaking with a distinct accent.

"You're with the South African police." Conor phrased the question more like a statement of fact.

"That's right."

"Detective Conor Bard."

"Inspector Hendrik Kruger."

Conor's eyes were drawn to a small metallic scorpion attached to Kruger's lapel, appearing to cling to the fabric. It was an odd adornment, he thought, certainly more attention-grabbing than the Detectives' Endowment Association pin that often graced his own jackets. "Nice scorpion."

"Thanks."

Kruger offered no explanation as to its significance. Which made Conor think the tiny arachnid was more than a mere accessory.

"Did you say one of the diamonds is missing?" Conor asked.

"Yes."

"They all look the same to me. How can you tell there's one missing?"

"This stone is red." Kruger cast an icy stare at Zivah. "The color of her lips."

"I didn't think they came in red."

"They do. And *when* they do, they are priceless." Kruger grimaced, as if he wished he could take back the words he had just uttered. "I must ask you both, Detective Bard and . . ." He looked at Brian.

"Brian Cobb. CSU."

"And you, Officer Cobb, to be discreet about what I have just told you."

Conor began to feel uneasy. *Something's wrong here.* What was a member of the South African Police Service doing at the scene and why was he so concerned about a missing diamond? Was he involved in the murder? Was he really who he claimed to be?

"Inspector Kruger. If you don't mind, may I see your ID, please?"

Kruger appeared vaguely irritated by the request but complied, removing his identification wallet and handing it to Conor. Since Conor had never seen a South African police ID or shield, he had no idea whether it was authentic. He returned it to Kruger.

13

"I'm going to need you to stick around for a while," Conor said politely.

Kruger slid the ID wallet back into his jacket pocket. "I'm afraid I can't do that."

"That wasn't a request," Conor shot back, riled by Kruger's dismissive response.

"I understand your concerns," Kruger countered, his tone now condescending. "But it's quite urgent that I file a report immediately. However, I will arrange to meet with you as soon as possible."

Conor wondered why Kruger seemed bent on forcing a confrontation. Wouldn't it be easier to simply cooperate? Was Kruger trying to buy time before making a statement? If Kruger was a representative of South African law enforcement, he might have another agenda. *But this isn't Johannesburg,* Conor reasoned. No way he could let Kruger just walk out the door.

Kruger turned to leave. Conor stepped in front of him, blocking his path.

"Inspector Kruger . . ."

"I am not at liberty to say anything until I've spoken with my superiors," Kruger insisted. "So it appears we're at an impasse."

"No, actually we're not."

Conor looked into the foyer, where two uniformed cops were positioned at either side of the elevator. "Officers, please escort Inspector Kruger to the squad."

Kruger was unmoved. "You *are* aware that I possess diplomatic immunity."

"Do you need it?"

"It can be helpful on occasion," Kruger replied sardonically. He glanced at the officers now flanking him. "I suppose you should read me my rights."

"You're not being charged with anything. I'm detaining you under the material witness statute."

"But it appears I *am* in a custodial situation."

Kruger had a point. Being formally charged with a crime and subsequently placed under arrest was not the only requirement for

reading the Miranda warning. Whenever someone was in police custody for any reason, if they were not free to leave, the law specified
they be apprised of their right to remain silent and their right to an
attorney.

"Why don't we start over," Conor offered, trying his best to cool
off. "If you'd just answer a few questions . . ."

"Perhaps tomorrow," Kruger said coldly.

Conor contemplated his next move. There was really only one
option. "Officers."

One of the cops touched Kruger's elbow. "Sir?"

Kruger yanked his arm away and glared at Conor. "I could have
your badge for this."

Conor shrugged. "Go for it. You'd be doing me a favor."

They squared off silently for a tense moment, then Kruger walked
with the cops into the elevator.

"And I thought the *Feds* were bad," Brian said.

"It's just the accent, that's all." But as Conor watched the elevator doors slowly slide shut, he wondered if he had overreacted, even
though Kruger had given him little choice.

Chapter Four

Conor approached Sayer and Wasiak, the two officers who were the first to respond. They were fresh from the academy. Twenty-one. On the job less than six months.

"How'd that guy get in here?" Conor asked as he approached them.

Sayer swallowed. "He said he was South African police."

"What's that got to do with NYPD?"

"Nothing, sir," Sayer replied.

Conor was annoyed but this wasn't the place to conduct a class on crime scene integrity. "When did he arrive?"

"A couple minutes after we did," Wasiak offered.

A couple minutes? What had Kruger been doing? Lurking around in front of the building? Was he there to meet Zivah? Did someone call him and tip him off to the murder?

"Any sign of forced entry?"

"No, sir," Sayer responded.

"How'd you gain access?"

"The concierge unlocked the elevator for this floor," Wasiak explained.

Conor rubbed his temples, processing what he had just heard. "I want your full report when we get back to the house."

The contrite duo hurried away.

Conor shook off the notion that he might have handled Kruger with more finesse and focused his attention on the crime scene again. Open boxes and discarded shopping bags strewn all over the room indicated that the victim was in the process of moving in. Conor looked into one of the boxes and saw a small, decorative cushion that had been sent via Federal Express. There was a receipt taped to the box: eight hundred dollars. *Damn. I wouldn't pay that for a whole couch.* He carefully pulled out the cushion. A network of diamonds had been embroidered across the cotton fabric. As he moved through the loft, he spotted several other items adorned with diamond motifs—a lamp, a blanket, a tablecloth. *Guess she liked diamonds.* A set of French doors, one of which was ajar, caught his attention. "What's over there?"

"A patio," Brian replied.

Conor followed Brian across the room and out onto a large terrace. A round teak table surrounded by four chairs and three evergreens filled the outdoor space. Conor edged around the potted trees and looked down. About five feet below was the roof of another building. He spotted a rusted metal door, hanging by one hinge, and assumed that led to a stairwell. A bare lightbulb, attached to a dangling socket, offered a modicum of illumination.

"Abandoned tenement," Brian explained. "We've got a team in there now."

This was a neighborhood in transition so the stark juxtaposition of these two structures wasn't unexpected. Luxury apartments wedged between boarded-up shells waiting to be demolished were a common occurrence in Manhattan's ever-expanding real estate market. And that proximity represented a fatal flaw, certainly in Zivah Gavish's case, because access to her loft could not be totally controlled. No need for a visitor to be announced by the concierge when the adjoining building offered a less formal way inside.

Conor raised a leg over the low brick wall of the terrace, hoisted himself onto it, then dropped heavily onto the roof of the tenement.

"What are you doing?" Brian asked, alarmed.

"Just wanted to see how hard it was to get from here"—Conor

reached up and grabbed the edge of the wall with both hands, then vaulted back onto the terrace—"to here." He winced in pain as he landed next to Brian.

"You okay?"

"Rotator cuff. Been bothering me for a while."

"You should get that checked out."

As Conor massaged his aching shoulder, he looked up at the exterior wall of the converted yarn factory rising twenty-five feet above him. A camera was pointing down.

"You see what I see?" Conor asked.

"Yeah," Brian replied. "A one-eyed witness."

Conor returned to the lobby, where Clifford Stevens, the manager of the building, had arrived and was pacing back and forth. Stevens, dressed in a deep purple designer jogging suit and wearing what looked to be a very expensive chronograph watch, was trying to project an ultrachic persona. Conor wasn't impressed. He felt an immediate dislike for Stevens, whom he imagined to be a soulless sycophant doing the bidding of an equally soulless real estate mogul.

"The developer has spent a great deal of money on state-of-the-art security," Stevens insisted, clearly concerned about the adverse effect a dead body could have on the sales price of the unoccupied lofts. "I wouldn't want potential buyers to get the idea this building isn't safe."

"Tell that to Zivah Gavish."

"Will this be in the newspapers?" Stevens asked, wincing.

Conor wasn't sure what psychological demons made him want to torture Stevens. He only knew he wanted to see Stevens squirm.

"Newspapers? Front page. Definitely front page."

Stevens trembled slightly. "My God."

"I wouldn't be surprised if they made the story into a movie," Conor added enthusiastically.

Stevens blanched. "I'm sure you can understand that I must do everything possible to mitigate the fallout from this unfortunate incident." His eyes pleaded with Conor. "Is there anything *you* can do to—"

"Sorry. You know the media."

"The media," Stevens repeated, panic overtaking him. But then he snapped his fingers, a man who had suddenly found a way out of a tight spot by shifting responsibility. "You know what? Our public relations firm is very good at damage control."

"You better call them."

"Yes. You're right." Stevens pulled a cell phone from his pocket.

"I'll need the tapes." Conor pointed to the camera mounted on the wall.

"We don't use tapes." Stevens was smug. "We record to a hard drive. Our video system is extremely high-tech."

"Then I guess I'll need the hard drive." Conor was losing patience. "Especially the one from the camera covering the penthouse terrace."

Stevens and Bill the concierge exchanged a nervous glance.

"What's the matter?" Conor asked.

"We're a new conversion," Stevens replied. "We only opened three weeks ago."

"So what does that mean?"

"We had a problem with that particular camera. It's scheduled for maintenance tomorrow."

Conor sighed, frustrated. *A day late and a diamond short.*

Chapter Five

Conor made his way back to the loft.

"You get the tapes?" Brian asked as Conor entered.

"They don't use tapes."

"Hard drive?"

"Yeah. But the camera over the terrace wasn't hooked up."

"They never are." Brian surveyed the cavernous room. "You see how big this place is? We'll be here all night. Taking prints, collecting fibers. Cataloguing diamonds."

"You sure?"

"About what?"

"That every one of those diamonds will make it into evidence."

"Of course not. I need a birthday present for my girlfriend."

"So one of the diamonds . . ."

"Two."

"Earrings?"

Brian nodded.

Conor's cell phone rang. He flipped it open. "Bard."

"Detective." Amanda always called him Detective when she was pissed. "I spoke with the South African Consulate General. This guy you detained? He's exactly who he says he is." She sighed. "I put you on this to *prevent* an international incident, not *start* one."

Conor snapped the phone shut. He hadn't started anything. But he *was* going to finish it. And no set of foreign credentials was going to stop him.

Kruger was the real deal. So what? This was a homicide investigation. Nobody was above suspicion. Certainly not someone who happened to arrive at the scene in lockstep with the first responders.

Conor asked Brian to secure the hard drive containing the security camera video then caught a ride to the precinct in a squad car waiting out front. He went directly to Amanda's office.

"Where's James Bond?" Conor asked.

Amanda stood, edged around her desk. "Apparently, the South African consulate doesn't find it amusing when one of their inspectors is detained. A vice consul showed up demanding Kruger be released."

"So you just let him walk?"

"There wasn't a hell of a lot I could do." She held her arms open wide, palms up. "Material witness? *That* was a reach."

"He refused to answer questions. Plus, he shouldn't have been there in the first place."

"You're right on that one. I'll talk to Sayer and Wasiak. Give them a refresher course on NYPD's velvet rope policy. But back to Kruger. He showed you his ID, right?"

Conor nodded. "But I couldn't confirm his identity. I've never seen a South African Police Service ID. Have you?"

"Spent the night with someone from SAPS once. International law enforcement convention in London." She looked off. "I *think* he was from SAPS. Anyway, never saw his ID. Saw everything else but, no, not his ID."

"Listen, Sarge, there are some things I just don't need to know."

"You want to speak with Kruger, I'll have to check protocol. My guess is we file an official request with the South African government. In the meantime, we located Stanley Silberman for you. See what he has to say."

*   *   *

Conor, carrying two plastic bottles of water, entered the conference room. He held one of the bottles by the screw cap, pinching it between his thumb and forefinger.

Silberman, a slightly built man in a conservative black suit, was standing against a wall, staring at the floor.

"Mr. Silberman?"

Silberman looked up, startled. "Yes?"

"I'm Detective Conor Bard."

Silberman appeared to be in his midfifties. His hair, what was left of it, was more salt than pepper.

"Thank you for coming in." Conor motioned to a chair. "Why don't we sit down?"

Conor decided not to mention the missing red diamond. Until he had determined exactly who knew about the valuable little piece of crimson ice, he would keep that detail to himself.

"Would you like some water?" Conor asked, holding out a bottle by the screw cap.

Silberman took the water. "Thank you."

Conor placed a notebook and pen on the table. "I understand you knew Zivah Gavish."

"Yes. We were business associates."

Silberman's eyes were puffy and red. His shoulders were hunched forward. His hands trembled. *Does someone get this devastated over the death of a "business associate"?* Conor wondered. Silberman's palpable grief was more consistent with the way friends, lovers, and relatives handled such bad news.

"We'll need to notify the next of kin," Conor said. "Does she have relatives in the city?"

"No. Her parents are in Tel Aviv. That's where Zivah lives."

"The apartment on Forty-fourth Street?"

"Her pied-à-terre in the city."

Conor almost laughed. *Six-thousand-foot pied-à-terre? I should get into the diamond business.*

Silberman shifted nervously in his seat. "She must be buried as soon as possible."

Conor had dealt with this situation before. When the deceased was Jewish, religious law dictated a speedy interment. But when a homicide was involved, a thorough autopsy was required. Although Jewish law provided for delays due to legal reasons, the transport of the body, travel to the funeral by relatives, and avoidance of a burial on holy days, any postponement should be only as long as absolutely necessary.

"I can speak with my rabbi," Silberman offered. "I invited Zivah to come to temple with me a couple of times. Rabbi Burstein was very fond of her. He could notify Zivah's parents and help make the necessary arrangements."

Conor mulled over Silberman's proposition.

"All right," Conor finally said. "If you don't mind."

"It's the least I can do."

Silberman suddenly grabbed his right wrist with his left hand and held it tightly, his arms now positioned awkwardly across his stomach. Conor thought that was odd but chalked it up to Silberman's anxiety.

"I suppose there's going to be an autopsy," Silberman said.

"In a case like this, of course."

"We consider an autopsy desecration of the body."

In past cases, Conor recalled that the solution had always been to have a rabbi present.

"Why don't we let your rabbi handle that?" Conor suggested.

Silberman nodded. "Okay."

Conor got the interview back on track. "You called nine-one-one at eight thirty? Is that correct, Mr. Silberman?"

"Yes. I called because Zivah wasn't there and I couldn't reach her on her cell phone. Cocktails were at six. And the dinner started at seven."

"When someone's an hour or so late, people don't usually call police."

"I felt responsible," Silberman countered. "She was my date."

Conor picked up the pen and flipped open the notebook. He would have no trouble remembering what Silberman had just said but the word *date* was an interesting way to begin his written chronicle of the case.

Chapter Six

Conor scribbled *date* at the top of the page then looked up at Silberman. "Sounds like you and Ms. Gavish were more than business associates."

Silberman didn't respond right away. When he did, his voice was a whisper, barely audible. "No." And then his eyes finished the sentence: *Oh, how I wish there had been more.*

"But you said she was your *date.*"

"Not really," Silberman admitted sadly. "When she stopped by my shop a couple days ago, to show me some loose gems, she asked me to escort her to the diamond dealers' dinner at the Crowne Plaza." He smiled for the first time. "I was thrilled to do it."

"So you and Ms. Gavish were not romantically involved?"

"Oh, no!" Silberman responded quickly, overstating it in a manner that further betrayed his infatuation.

"Why didn't you pick her up, take her to the dinner?"

"I was on my way to her apartment. But then she called and said she was running late and asked me to meet her at the hotel."

"When did she call?"

Silberman rubbed his eyes. "Let's see. I left the shop around five thirty, caught a cab."

"Where's your shop?"

"Silberman Jewelry. Forty-seventh between Fifth and Sixth."

"Okay, you took a cab . . ."

"Yes. Got all the way to Forty-second and Ninth before she called. I'm really not sure what time it was."

"Check received calls on your cell phone. That'll show the exact time."

Silberman removed his cell phone, tapped a couple keys. "Five twenty-eight."

"What time did you arrive at the Crowne Plaza?"

"Just after six. The cocktail party had already started."

"Must've been a lot of traffic," Conor observed dryly. "Half an hour to go from Forty-second to Forty-eighth?"

"Actually, I got out and walked."

Conor recalled that, according to the concierge, Zivah arrived home at approximately five o'clock and didn't have any visitors after that. She was last seen alive around 5:35. Silberman had placed himself a short distance from Zivah's building at 5:28. Could Silberman have climbed the stairs in the abandoned building, hoisted himself onto the terrace, killed Zivah, then arrived at the Crowne Plaza on Broadway and Forty-ninth by six? If so, he would have had about a thirty-minute window. Was that enough time? Did Silberman actually get to the Crowne Plaza at six or was it later?

"Had you and Ms. Gavish gone out together before?"

Silberman shook his head. "I would see her when she came into my shop. And sometimes I'd run into her at parties." He paused. "We did have lunch once. Last spring. After I purchased several pieces from her we went to the Evergreen, a diner down the street. It was raining. I bought her one of those three-dollar umbrellas." He was suddenly swimming dreamily in a brief encounter that had surely meant nothing to Zivah Gavish.

"Mr. Silberman?"

"Yes?" Silberman lost his tenuous grip on the past and came tumbling back to the present.

"I was wondering. A woman as beautiful as Ms. Gavish, I wouldn't think she'd have a problem getting a date. I mean, you said there was nothing between the two of you . . ."

"Zivah could have any man she wanted." Silberman's lip curled slightly.

"Have you ever been to Ms. Gavish's residence?"

Silberman shifted in his chair. "Why are you asking me these things?"

"Just routine," Conor assured him. *Did I just sound like Columbo? Or did I sound like my old partner Ralph sounding like Columbo?*

Silberman took a sip of water before responding. "No. I have never been to Zivah's apartment."

Conor made a note—*never on the premises.* An obvious declaration of innocence offered by Silberman.

"Do you know anyone who would want to harm Ms. Gavish?" Conor asked.

Silberman's eyes misted. "Zivah? No, not Zivah. She was the most wonderful woman I have ever met."

Conor looked at Silberman. *Poor bastard. In love with a woman way out of his league.* Did Silberman, the suitor, kill Zivah because he couldn't have her? Did he become enraged when Zivah said she didn't want him to pick her up? Even the most unlikely person was capable of irrational acts when emotions were in play. And throughout history, unrequited love had been motive enough for murder.

Chapter Seven

"**H**ow'd it go with Silberman?" Amanda asked as Conor entered her office carrying a bottle of water by the screw cap.

"I locked him into a story."

Which was all Conor really wanted to do at this point. If there were discrepancies later on, at least he would know Silberman was lying about something.

"One thing is clear," Conor added. "He was in love with the victim."

"So what does that mean?"

"Nothing, really. Just is what it is." Conor held up the bottle of water. "Silberman's prints and DNA. Just in case."

"I don't want to know," Amanda snapped.

Conor lowered the bottle. Of course she didn't want to know. Collecting prints or DNA without consent was a slippery slope. There were privacy issues to be considered. And unless Silberman developed into a viable suspect, placing such data about Silberman in the system was questionable.

"You heading back to the loft?" Amanda asked.

"Yeah. You coming?"

This was a homicide, which meant a "full response" from the precinct was in order. The regulations required that "the Precinct Squad Sergeant *and/or* the Squad Commander (Lieutenant)" be at the scene. Since Amanda preferred to remain ensconced in her office, she always interpreted the clause in the language to mean that her presence wasn't specified as long as the squad commander made an appearance.

"No need for me to come," she pointed out. "Lieutenant Rooney's on his way over there now."

Conor turned to leave.

"Oh, and Bard. I think I have somebody for you."

"What do you mean?"

"A partner." Her phone rang. She waved him out the door. "We'll talk about it later."

Conor placed the bottle of water he had given Silberman into a plastic evidence bag and then into a large manila envelope. He tucked the envelope under his arm and, since he didn't feel like driving, found a uniformed cop to drop him on Forty-fourth Street.

As he headed into the building, he was ambushed by Lew Michaels, a wiry little man who looked like a human Gumby. Michaels worked the crime beat for the *New York Post*.

"Detective," Michaels demanded. "What's going on in there?"

"Wish I could tell you, Lew, but I'm not authorized to comment."

"Come on, Conor, give me *something*."

"Sorry, Lew. Not now. Maybe later."

Conor entered the loft and spotted Lieutenant Jay Rooney, standing, arms crossed, watching the drama unfolding before him. Rooney was fifty-two. Full head of auburn hair. Six feet two inches tall and in top physical condition.

Conor stopped next to him. "Hey, Lieutenant."

Squad Commander Rooney ran a tight ship but gave detectives a great deal of latitude, which engendered loyalty and respect among the troops.

"Poor girl," Rooney said as a team from the medical examiner's office transported Zivah's body out of the loft. "Beautiful. Israeli. *Diamond* dealer, for Christ's sake. South African cops." He looked at Conor. "It's a helluva case."

There was a wistfulness in Rooney's voice. Unlike Amanda, who had opted for sergeant as soon as she was eligible, Rooney had avoided promotions. Detective work, the grittiness of it, was in his blood. Extremely efficient and frequently decorated, Rooney was one of the best who ever wore a gold shield. But his excellence eventually betrayed him, and he found himself being swept higher and higher in rank. Now perched well above the action, he felt more of an observer than a player.

"I better get going." Rooney checked his watch. "Got a long drive home."

Soon after becoming lieutenant, Rooney had married and moved with his pregnant wife to Spring Valley, New York, thirty miles north of Midtown. But when Rooney was a detective he was single and lived in Manhattan on Thirty-seventh Street. Conor was a rookie then, walking the beat. Once in a while he would hang out with Rooney after work and stagger home at dawn wondering how the hell he was going to make his shift the next day. What he learned during those nights of conversation, drinking, and chasing women with Rooney represented all Conor knew about being a detective.

Never overestimate the criminal mind, Rooney would intone as he clutched yet another glass of whiskey on the rocks. At the time, Conor thought Rooney meant never *underestimate* the criminal mind. But once, when he finally asked Rooney if that was what he had intended to say, Rooney ranted on and on about the fact that criminals weren't the geniuses they thought they were. *They're all stupid,* Rooney had insisted. *Don't give them so much credit. They always make mistakes.* Over the years, Conor had come to realize that the crux of any investigation, when broken down to its lowest common denominator, was deceptively simple: find that one mistake.

Rooney left. Conor walked over to Brian Cobb and handed him the manila envelope.

"What's this?"

"A bottle of water. You'll find a set of prints. I want to know if you can match the prints on the bottle with prints in the loft."

Brian opened the envelope and pulled out the evidence bag. He eyed the bottle with suspicion. "Where did this come from?"

"I don't recall," Conor answered. "But if you find matching prints in the apartment, that might jog my memory."

The revolving door of the crime scene began spinning faster: just after Rooney left, Tony Kingston from the homicide squad showed up. Conor was relieved it was Kingston instead of certain other guys on the squad. He had worked with Kingston in the past when Kingston was assigned to the Eighteenth Precinct.

African American, five feet ten inches tall, forty-seven years old, Kingston looked nothing like a detective. Maybe that was because he was really an accountant. At least that's what he was planning to be in three years, when he retired. He had become a certified public accountant and was the go-to guy for all the cops during tax season.

"This is *your* fault, huh, Bard? I was in dreamland when they called."

"Sorry about that."

Kingston's affinity for numbers gave him the tolerance to endure the minutiae of police work—particularly in the gathering and cataloging of evidence—and made him an ideal candidate for the homicide squad.

"So what's the deal?" Kingston asked.

Conor filled him in.

Kingston scratched the back of his head. "Let me see the terrace."

They pushed through the French doors and peered down at the tenement roof.

"Doesn't look like it'd be hard to climb up here," Kingston observed.

"It's not. Just did it myself." Conor rubbed his shoulder.

"What's the matter?"

"Old football injury. I must've aggravated it climbing over the railing."

"Better have somebody look at it," Kingston suggested.

"Yeah. I know."

They headed back into the loft.

"Guess we ought to check out other buildings around here," Kingston began. "Look for any cameras in the vicinity. And I'll do a pawnshop canvass." He glanced at his watch. "Won't make much headway at this hour. I'll get a few of the guys on it first thing in the morning."

Conor walked with Kingston to the elevator.

"And I'll work the neighborhood," Kingston added. "Maybe there was a witness who saw someone enter the tenement."

"Thanks."

"You got a big problem with the roof," Kingston pointed out. "Ten million people in the city. Any one of them could have crawled up onto that terrace."

Ten million people in the Naked City. Conor already knew that. And he was beginning to think those were the odds of finding Zivah Gavish's killer. One in ten million.

Chapter Eight

Conor wandered to the open, spacious kitchen at the back of the loft, where Brian was bent over the marble counter sniffing a cocktail glass that contained a small residue of amber liquid. "Scotch. Glenfiddich. Single malt. Twenty-one years old."

Conor frowned. "You can tell all that just by smelling it?"

"Yeah."

"I'm impressed."

"And also by observing the label." Brian pointed to a bottle of Glenfiddich on the counter next to the sink.

"You shouldn't have told me that. Now I'm disappointed."

Brian rotated the glass half a turn. "Hand-painted." He laughed.

Conor didn't get the joke until he took a closer look. An elegant hand, wearing a diamond ring, had been expertly painted onto the side of the glass. "Hand-painted. Very funny."

Brian rotated the glass again. "Probably cost a fortune, just like everything else in this place."

"Where'd you find it?"

"In the sink. Got some good prints on it."

"You get the hard drive?" Conor asked.

Brian motioned toward a young man sitting at a large wooden dining table, a hard drive and laptop computer in front of him. "TARU is transferring the video files to DVD as we speak."

TARU, the Technical Assistance Response Unit, specialized in retrieving data. The unit had become increasingly vital to all investigations given the continuing advances in technology.

Conor spotted a cell phone lying on the coffee table. He walked over, reached down to pick it up.

"Whoa," Brian boomed. "I haven't processed it yet."

"I want to see who she's been calling."

"All right, but at least wear these." Brian reached into a leather bag, produced a pair of latex gloves, then stepped over and handed them to Conor.

Conor stretched the latex, forcing his hands into them. "I hate these things." He picked up the cell phone. *An iPhone. Visual voice mail. I ought to get one of these things.*

He slid the arrow to activate the home screen, tapped the phone icon. There were four voice mails. Three had not been played. At 4:17, Zivah had received the first voice mail, from a woman named Valentina, informing Zivah that her armoire was ready for delivery. The other three were from Stanley Silberman wondering where she was. He sounded more and more concerned with each message. The first was at 7:13, the last one at 8:27, just before he called 911. *Was Silberman really that concerned about Zivah? Or were the calls intended to later substantiate Silberman's claim that he did not know Zivah was dead?*

Conor walked back to the kitchen. "She have a computer?"

"A laptop," Brian replied. "Soon as I dust it, swab for blood, it's all yours."

Conor started for the elevator.

"Hold on," Brian called out. "Where are you going with that cell phone? Don't you need a warrant to remove it from the scene?"

"It's lost property. You don't need a warrant to remove lost property."

Brian half laughed. "Lost property?"

"Somebody left it on the coffee table. So it's lost property." Conor slid the phone into his jacket pocket, then pulled off the latex gloves. "They make my hands sweat."

"Yeah? Well now your sweaty prints are going to be all over the phone."

"Come on, Brian, a few elimination prints aren't going to kill you."

Elimination prints were fingerprints one would expect to find— those of the NYPD personnel who responded to the scene.

"Send that DVD over to the house when it's ready," Conor instructed as he continued into the elevator.

As Conor exited the building, he heard the sound of a bell coming from inside his pocket. He removed Zivah Gavish's cell phone and saw a text message. According to the header, it was sent by someone named Kenneth Madison.

Hey, Zee. I'm beat. Drank way too much at Bobby's party. Going to crash in a little while. Hope you're enjoying the dinner. Call you when I get up.

Conor located Madison's phone number in the iPhone's address book. Madison picked up on the second ring.

"Hello?"

"Mr. Madison? Kenneth Madison?"

"Yes. Who is this?"

"Mr. Madison. I'm Detective Conor Bard. And I need to—"

"*Detective?* What's going on?"

"You're an acquaintance of Ms. Zivah Gavish?"

"Zivah? Yes, I know Zivah. Is she okay? Has something happened?"

Conor drew in a breath. It was never easy breaking this kind of news. "Mr. Madison. I'm sorry to inform you that Ms. Gavish has been the victim of a homicide."

"That can't be. I just spoke with her this afternoon—"

"Mr. Madison. I'm sorry."

"Oh my God! How? Where?"

"I'm sorry, sir, but we cannot release any information at this time. I hope you understand."

"I'm driving back to the city right now," Madison insisted. "I'm—"

"Mr. Madison. Where are you, sir?"

"I'm in the Hamptons. I drove out yesterday afternoon."

The Hamptons. Playground of the rich, just a hundred miles from Manhattan. Conor had been there a couple of times as a guest of an ex-girlfriend.

"I can be in the city in two hours," Madison offered.

Conor recalled Madison's text message. *Drank way too much at Bobby's party.* No way Conor wanted a drunk driver on the road. "There's nothing you can do tonight, Mr. Madison. And maybe you've been drinking. Have you, sir?"

Madison didn't respond.

"You shouldn't be driving this late at night, especially when you're upset. I think it would be best if you came back in the morning."

There was a long silence. "Okay," Madison finally said.

Before hanging up, Conor had to ask the obligatory question. "Mr. Madison. Do you know anyone who would want to harm Ms. Gavish? Ex-boyfriend, business partner, anybody like that?"

"Hurt Zivah? Absolutely not."

Conor decided that instead of having Madison come by the precinct, where the surroundings always put someone on guard, he'd arrange to meet Madison at his home or office. They agreed to meet at his apartment in Trump Tower, on Fifth Avenue and Fifty-sixth, a building that contained some of the most expensive residences in the city.

"I'll be there at eight," Madison offered.

Conor had intended to walk back to the precinct, so he'd have some time to think about his next move, but the rain had suddenly returned with a vengeance. As Conor scanned the area for a cruiser to run him up to Fifty-fourth Street, a black Cadillac Escalade pulled to the curb. The passenger side window slowly slid down.

"Need a ride, Detective?" Kruger was behind the wheel, a cigar clenched between his teeth.

Chapter Nine

Conor hesitated, then decided he'd forget about the earlier confrontation with his South African counterpart and start all over. He climbed inside the SUV. "Thanks."

Kruger brushed a piece of tobacco off his lip, exhaled a cloud of smoke. "Got a Hoya in the glove box. You want it?"

Although Conor sometimes enjoyed a cigar, he declined. "No thanks."

Kruger hit the gas and pointed the SUV down Forty-fourth Street. "I've spoken with my superiors. And I am prepared to answer some of your questions."

Some? Conor wanted to come back at him hard, explain that *all* answers were mandatory. But that would be counterproductive. Better just take whatever he could get. For now.

Kruger brought the car to a stop at Tenth Avenue. "So what do you want to know?"

As Conor contemplated where to begin, he noticed that the scorpion pin was missing from Kruger's lapel. "What happened to the scorpion?"

Kruger puffed furiously on his cigar. "I'm afraid I'll need a drink to answer *that* one."

Conor mulled over Kruger's proposition. A drink? Why not? If he was going to conduct an interview with a foreign law enforcement officer, it might as well be over a cocktail.

"Sure," Conor said, "I wouldn't mind a little something."

"What I'd really like is a glass of Groot Constantia pinotage. One of the vice consuls at the consulate told me there's a South African wine bar somewhere around here."

"Yeah. I know it. It's called Xai Xai. Fifty-first Street. Make a left."

"Xai Xai. That's a small town in Mozambique."

"Well, this Xai Xai is a South African wine bar. Owned by an Indian woman named Tanya."

Kruger made a left onto Tenth Avenue. "South African wine bar just around the corner. That's a stroke of luck."

"It's not luck, it's geography. You forget where you are, Inspector Kruger."

"Please. Call me Hendrik."

"You're in New York, Hendrik. You can get anything you want here."

"Even a South African wine bar owned by an Indian woman."

"Exactly."

Kruger glided the Escalade to a stop on Fifty-first Street between Eighth and Ninth avenues. He reached under his seat and produced a metal plaque the size of a license plate. It read *South African Consulate—Official Business*. He tossed it onto the dashboard.

Tanya, an attractive American-born Indian woman in her early thirties, greeted them when they entered the bar. She was also the proprietor of a South African restaurant down the block called Braai. Conor would stop by both places on occasion.

"Hendrik is looking for a Groot something or other," Conor explained. "I hope you have it."

"Groot Constantia," Kruger elaborated. "Pinotage."

"We have a wide selection of pinotage," Tanya said. "Let me check with Thabiso, our sommelier."

Conor and Kruger sat at a table near the window.

"Would you like a glass of pinotage as well, Conor? May I call you Conor?"

"Yes to both questions."

Thabiso, a young black man, approached. "You were asking for a Groot Constantia pinotage?" He spoke with the same accent as Kruger.

"*Ja,*" Kruger replied.

Thabiso took the cue and addressed Kruger in their shared native tongue. Kruger looked at him, an intense stare, then spoke in Afrikaans. His tone was more a demand than a request.

Conor's ear wasn't accustomed to the language so he wondered if he was imagining the edge in Kruger's voice. But there was no mistaking the narrowing of Kruger's eyes. *Guess he has a problem with sommeliers,* Conor mused.

Thabiso drifted away.

"Allow me to explain my reticence to be candid earlier this evening," Kruger began.

"It's okay," Conor countered. "I could have handled it better myself."

"I understand. You had no way of knowing that you walked into the middle of our investigation."

"Really?" Conor tempered his response. "I thought it was the other way around."

A waiter delivered two glasses of pinotage.

Kruger waited until the waiter was out of earshot. "Have you ever heard of Robert Mouawad?"

"No."

"He's a Lebanese diamond dealer." Kruger raised his glass. "*Gesondheid.*"

"*Gesondheid,*" Conor repeated. "Which means I can now say cheers in about twelve languages." He took a sip of wine, savored the taste. "What does Mouawad have to do with the diamond stolen from Zivah Gavish's apartment?"

"Nothing at all. I am merely trying to give you a frame of reference." Kruger held the glass under his nose and inhaled. "Robert Mouawad's diamond collection is spectacular. Some stones are even named after him. Like the Mouawad Lilac. Twenty-four carats. Emerald cut. Worth over twenty million dollars. The Mouawad Pink, twenty-one carats. Radiant cut. Valued at twelve million."

"So the missing diamond—"

"Is rather small by those standards. Only eleven carats. But weight alone does not determine value, it is also the color." Kruger took another sip of pinotage. "On Friday, we intercepted an e-mail sent by Zivah Gavish to Sulaiman Aziz, a billionaire gem collector from Abu Dhabi. A JPEG image of a diamond was attached." He reached into his pocket and produced a four-by-six photo. "A deep-red-colored gem unlike any I have ever seen."

Kruger regarded the photo admiringly then handed it to Conor. Although Conor knew nothing about diamonds, it didn't take an expert to see that there was something special about the sparkling red gem in the photo. He looked up at Kruger. "Can I keep this?"

Kruger nodded, then continued. "According to the e-mail, the stone had been cut and polished by a firm in India. Unfortunately we have been unable to determine who exactly cut the rough stone."

"Are there a lot of diamond cutters in India?" Conor asked.

"It's the diamond-cutting center of the world," Kruger replied. "In any event, Zivah Gavish indicated to Aziz that she had received delivery of the diamond and was looking forward to his arrival in New York on Monday."

"Delivery? How? By international courier?"

"We don't know. But we are certain that Aziz is the buyer. There are not many people in the world with both the strong desire and the nearly unlimited means to acquire such a stone."

"Why is this red diamond the business of the South African Police Service?"

"It is our business because we believe the rough stone was smuggled out of South Africa by a man named Wouter Marwala." Kruger sneered. "A blue-eyed black."

Chapter Ten

Conor wanted to ask what Kruger meant by "blue-eyed black." Was it some genetic anomaly? Someone with a mixed heritage? A derisive term of some sort used in South Africa? He decided not to press the issue. Wouter Marwala was a smuggler of illegal contraband. Which was only of importance to Conor if Marwala's activities had a direct bearing on the homicide investigation.

"Do you think Wouter Marwala might have had something to do with Zivah Gavish's murder?" Conor asked.

"With Marwala, anything is possible."

"Where is he now?"

"In Johannesburg. But he does have many known associates in New York."

"Many?"

"Marwala doesn't just move diamonds," Kruger explained. "He does a brisk trade in drugs as well. Counterfeit currency. It all flows through the same pipeline. We have been able to identify at least fifty people in the U.S. who do business with Marwala."

Fifty? Conor didn't like that number. If Marwala wanted to kill Zivah Gavish he would have no difficulty finding an assassin among his compatriots on American soil.

"Can I have a copy of that list?" Conor asked.

"Of course. I'll e-mail you the documents tomorrow morning."

Conor took a long sip of wine. "Connect the dots for me, Hendrik."

"Between Wouter Marwala and Zivah Gavish?"

"Yes."

"Our theory is that Marwala, or someone known to Marwala, engaged Zivah Gavish to find a discreet buyer for the red diamond. "

"Wait a minute," Conor said. "If Marwala sought out Zivah Gavish to sell this diamond, which he may have smuggled out of South Africa, why would he kill her?"

"Why? He is a psychopath. If he had already been paid for the diamond, maybe he wanted it back. Then he would have both the diamond and the money."

"Having his cake and eating it too," Conor said.

"Quite a nice piece of cake," Kruger noted.

It occurred to Conor that the diamond, appropriately red, might be what is called a "blood diamond"—mined and sold for the purpose of supporting rebels or even global terrorism.

"Is this a blood diamond?" Conor asked.

"The only cause Marwala funds is his own. He lives in a compound outside of Johannesburg. Has a private army." Kruger clenched both fists. "We haven't been able to touch him. Twice we arrested him but he was able to beat the charges. Plausible deniability, that's Marwala's strong suit. He rarely places himself in a position where he can be directly linked to the criminal activity of his empire."

As Kruger went on about Marwala, Conor sensed that in Marwala, Kruger, like Sherlock Holmes, had found his archenemy, his Professor Moriarty.

"So how did Marwala get his hands on this diamond to begin with?" Conor asked, interrupting Kruger's diatribe.

"That's a very good question. Unearthing such a rare diamond would have made headlines. But Marwala uses several methods to control the mine workers. Bribes. Threats. Once, a miner had the courage to come to us about Marwala's activities. The miner was dead an hour after he left our office."

"The rough diamond was dug out by a miner on Marwala's payroll?"

"That's what we believe," Kruger replied. "Perhaps it was unearthed in a remote region of our country. Where the guards are also in Marwala's employ."

"So it's possible Zivah Gavish's killer was after the diamond."

"Since very few people knew of its existence," Kruger said, "it is quite likely the stone was the objective." He drew in a deep breath. "I must ask you to keep all this to yourself."

"Look, Hendrik. You're working an international smuggling case. I'm working a homicide. We have different agendas, but it's to my benefit as well not to broadcast the fact that the red diamond is missing."

"Good. Maybe if we work together, it will be helpful to both of us."

"I agree." But Conor knew that Kruger's suggestion was an effort to keep himself in the NYPD loop. How much information would flow from SAPS remained to be seen.

While Conor found all this very interesting, there was another question he wanted Kruger to answer, and it wasn't about diamonds. "You mind telling me why you were at the scene so soon after our units got there?"

Kruger picked up his glass, swirled the wine around. "My plane arrived from Johannesburg at fifteen hundred hours. I retrieved my luggage and took a car into the city. I stopped by the consulate, dropped my bag, then proceeded directly to the Crowne Plaza Hotel, where the diamond dealers' dinner was to take place. The consulate had arranged a ticket for me. I arrived at seventeen fifty-six. I planned to observe Zivah Gavish during the event then question her."

"But she never showed up."

"No. So I initiated contact with the man who was sitting next to her empty seat."

"Stanley Silberman."

"That's right. Mr. Silberman confirmed to me that Zivah Gavish was supposed to be on her way. He was extremely concerned, distraught, one could say. So I decided to proceed to Zivah Gavish's apartment building on Forty-fourth Street and investigate."

The timeline sounded rehearsed to Conor, more like a carefully crafted story than an actual account of events.

"Sulaiman Aziz was also at the dinner tonight," Kruger said. "He appeared quite concerned, kept checking his watch. So, from what I observed, if Aziz *is* the buyer, he did not have the merchandise. Perhaps he was expecting Zivah to attend the dinner with the red diamond in her pocketbook."

"Rather cavalier way to transport something so valuable."

"But a perfectly reasonable way to transport something so small," Kruger pointed out, "especially if it is illegal."

Conor began to wonder what he had stumbled into. Israeli diamond dealer, South African Police Service, Abu Dhabi billionaire.

"If you intend to question him," Kruger began, "Sulaiman Aziz is staying at the Waldorf-Astoria. The Presidential Suite."

Conor's instincts told him it was time to end the conversation, assimilate what Kruger had divulged so far, then come back at him the next day.

"Okay, Hendrik. What about the scorpion?"

Chapter Eleven

"I took it off before the vice consul arrived."

Kruger pulled the small scorpion pin from a jacket pocket and began reattaching it to his lapel.

"I was an officer with the Scorpions, a special police unit. Our motto was: Loved by the people, feared by the criminals, respected by peers. We were extremely effective. And that's what did us in."

"How so?"

"The Scorpions were formed to do two things: shut down smuggling operations and expose government corruption. Unfortunately, the officials we identified as corrupt were powerful enough to legislate the disbandment of the unit."

Kruger described how the African National Congress, South Africa's ruling party, had dismantled the Scorpions two years ago during the unit's investigation into the financial dealings of six influential ANC members. As a result, the Scorpions were merged with the South African Police Service, ending the elite squad's ability to act autonomously.

As Kruger spoke, a South African song wafted out of the speakers, a bluesy melody floating over a jazzy rhythm. Conor cocked his head. He found himself suddenly lost in the composition, deciphering the chord structure, admiring the ebb and flow of the tonal waves.

"How can you fight corruption," Kruger concluded, "when you *report* to those who are corrupt?"

Conor was only half listening now. Which was not the best way to gather information. But this song was interesting, unexpected. He was caught by its unique sound.

"We did what we had to do," Kruger continued. "By any means necessary."

Given the unmistakable disdain Kruger had shown for the sommelier and for "blue-eyed black" Marwala, Conor wondered if Kruger, who didn't appear to be the most accepting person when it came to skin color, realized he was quoting Malcolm X. Apparently not. So there was a certain irony inherent in the words Kruger had chosen to sum up the Scorpions.

"Just curious," Conor said, "but were any of the Scorpions black?"

"Of course." A thin smile formed on Kruger's lips. "Apartheid no longer exists. We are all South Africans now."

When the check arrived, Kruger insisting on paying. "Don't worry, it's on the ANC, the bastards who brought down the Scorpions." He pulled out a credit card. "I love spending ANC money."

The rain had stopped so Conor declined Kruger's offer of a ride and instead walked the three blocks to the precinct. The South African song filled his head again, providing an appropriate soundtrack as he reviewed the conversation at Xai Xai.

At the least, Kruger was an interesting character. At the most, he was somehow involved in the murder of Zivah Gavish. A rogue cop for sure, Kruger now was forced to operate within the system. But that wouldn't last. Kruger was too accustomed to playing by his own rules to start toeing the line. That made Kruger unpredictable and potentially dangerous. Just because he was under the yoke of bureaucracy didn't mean he had transformed into an obedient soldier.

Since Kruger could conceivably impact the investigation, Conor wanted to know more about his background, specifically the nature of the Scorpions. To that end, he would contact Ross Marks at the FBI.

Marks was a veritable encyclopedia when it came to foreign governments and their machinations.

What about Sulaiman Aziz? A billionaire from Abu Dhabi certainly had the wherewithal to arrange a murder. But that didn't make sense. Rare gems likely meant much more to Aziz than money, so why would he kill a source of future rarities? Conor checked his watch. It was almost two A.M., too late to visit Aziz at the Waldorf. He'd wait, stop by early in the morning.

So what had he accomplished by meeting with Kruger? For one thing, he had fifty more suspects—Marwala associates in the U.S. And it now appeared likely that Zivah Gavish had become embroiled in some sort of political intrigue. But whatever her role, she didn't deserve to die lying on the floor wearing a blood necklace.

Conor did a quick assessment of the case. Brian was still collecting evidence and would be on the scene the remainder of the night. The techie was working on the DVD of the security video. The medical examiner wouldn't issue a time of death until tomorrow. The sweep of the yarn factory and tenement must not have turned up anything, or he would have been notified. Kingston and his team would canvass the neighborhood the next morning. *Better grab a little rest now while I have the chance.* But Conor was too wired for that.

The Rhythm Bar still had a respectable crowd considering it was Monday night and the band had finished its last set an hour ago. "Angel," by Sarah McLachlan, spilled from the speakers.

". . . oh, this glorious sadness . . . that brings me to my knees . . ."

Susie must've broken up with her boyfriend, Conor guessed. Whenever Susie had a problem in a relationship, which had seemed like once a week during her three years as bartender, she'd fire up the iPod with mournful ballads—always female vocalists, always heart-wrenching lyrics.

As Conor passed the bar, Susie jammed a straw into a vodka tonic like a samurai delivering a death blow. *I knew it,* Conor thought.

Richard was packing up equipment in the small dressing room off to the left of the stage.

"Sorry I had to split," Conor said as he entered.

Richard picked up a cable and began winding it into a tight ball. "Can't mess with your day job."

"How'd it go after I left?"

"You're not going to believe this," Richard replied.

"Believe what?"

"Guess who came in tonight?"

"Who?"

Richard continued to wind the cable.

"Come on, Richard. Who?"

Conor assumed it was some ex-girlfriend he'd been avoiding. Which was an occasional downside of performing in public: your past would sometimes take a seat in the front row.

"Alan Woodcliff," Richard finally said.

Conor cocked his head. "Alan Woodcliff?"

Alan Woodcliff was the hottest rocker to come out of the Jersey shore since Bruce Springsteen.

"He stopped by the tire store this morning," Richard explained. "That's the thing about tires: *everybody* needs them." Richard stuffed the cable into a duffel bag. "So I mentioned we were playing at the Rhythm Bar and he said he'd try to make it but I didn't think he'd actually show up. Then, halfway through the second set, in walks Alan Woodcliff with two hot chicks. It was like: Elvis is in the house. He comes backstage after the show—really nice guy. Signs autographs, poses for pictures. Told me he liked the band. Said I had a great voice."

"You should follow up with Woodcliff. Maybe . . ."

Richard laughed. "Just because I can sound like anybody, people always say: 'You have a great voice.' Yeah, I do. I have a lot of great voices. Willie Nelson. Billy Joel. I can do them all. And so can a million other guys playing weddings and bar mitzvahs. But you, you've got your own style. If we ever get anywhere, it's on you. That's why I gave him a copy of the CD we made. If he likes it, maybe he can get it to his record company."

Another ray of hope, Conor thought. Years ago, the rays of hope were blinding, like spotlights. But this ray was dim, a flashlight with its batteries about to die. Alan Woodcliff? What was he, twenty-three, twenty-four? *Hell, I could be his father.* As much as Conor wanted to make it in the music business, he just couldn't bring himself to start thinking that some kid, albeit an extremely popular and successful kid, was going to really help him get there.

"Good thing Alan Woodcliff needed tires," Conor said, trying hard to muster some excitement.

Chapter Twelve

Conor's apartment, on the second floor of an aging brownstone on Forty-eighth Street between Eighth and Ninth avenues, felt like a walk-in closet compared to the loft at the yarn factory. But what could he do? Win the lottery? Not likely. Score a major recording contract? Twenty years ago, he was certain that would happen. These days it was getting harder to believe.

He stopped in the kitchen, pulled a bottle of vodka from the freezer, poured some into a water glass, then continued into the living room. It occurred to Conor that it might be a very long time before he was back onstage at the Rhythm Bar. *Sarge gave me a choice, right? Why didn't I tell her no and finish the set? Hell, why didn't I just resign a year ago?*

He was a breath away from doing just that. But he stayed on the job for one reason—to apprehend the son of a bitch who killed Besa Kodra.

Images began playing across his mind. Monica, the beautiful Albanian woman he had met a year ago. It had started well with her, an attraction, a genuine affection, and for the first time he had found himself in a world full of possibilities. But that was last year, the distant past. Monica was home now, in Albania. Their story was over. Forever.

In the end, Monica was part of a painful episode in Conor's life, one that almost cost him his job, and he was still haunted by it. Haunted by *him* really. John Hicks had raped and murdered Besa, Monica's sister, seven years ago. Suddenly, a horrific slide show of crime scene photos played across Conor's mind. When he first dug into the cold case files and learned the details of the crime, it filled him with rage. The rape, the torture, the disfigurement. It made him sick even though Monica was well out of his life.

That's all Monica left me, Conor thought, an intense hatred of a fugitive killer. The only way to put it all behind him was to apprehend John Hicks.

Conor had contacted Fred Schroeder at the cold case squad and asked Schroeder to put Hicks on the front burner. And Conor had spoken with Detective Edward Maher, the detective who had originally caught the Hicks case. Maher had promised Conor he would be more proactive in seeking to apprehend Hicks.

Still not content, Conor had been in touch with Operation Intercept, a fugitive task force maintained by the United States Marshals Service, and had obtained a federal warrant against Hicks for unlawful flight to avoid prosecution. But there were so many fugitives in the U.S., hundreds of thousands. When a recent nationwide sweep by Operation FALCON (Federal and Local Cops Organized Nationally, a cooperative effort involving the U.S. Marshals Service and local law enforcement) snared more than 35,000 fugitives, John Hicks was not among those apprehended. In fact, it had been years since there had been any sign of Hicks. When Conor ran Hicks's DNA through the national DNA database, his genetic profile had been found at the scene of two more rapes, one in Massachusetts five years ago and one in Pennsylvania a year after that. Then the trail had gone cold. He realized that this was probably an exercise in futility. Hicks could be anywhere in the country, or even the world.

But Conor hadn't given up. He was regularly paying confidential informants in all five boroughs of New York City, hoping against hope that one of them would spot Hicks. The sick bastard had killed Besa in the Bronx and was living in Washington Heights at the time.

In Conor's experience, perps always came home to roost, like predators who stalked the same feeding ground season after season. Which made a CI named Jimmy important to Conor. Washington Heights was Jimmy's neighborhood. A fugitive like Hicks couldn't just reappear in the Heights without seeking help from a friend or relative. He would need money, a place to stay. There would be whispers on the block if Hicks returned. And Jimmy was getting paid to listen.

Still, apprehending Hicks was a long shot. Getting longer every day. *Maybe I should have retired.*

A forty-three-year-old ex-cop could land a decent job at a security firm or as an investigator for an insurance company. So he was a viable entity in the private sector. On the other hand, he knew dozens of fifty-year-old ex-cops walking around, knocking on doors, getting nowhere. Not that fifty was ancient, it was just that the world of corporate security was youth oriented. So the longer Conor stayed on the job, the lower his value on the open market. *If the music thing didn't work out—* He stopped himself in midthought, laughed out loud. What industry was more youth oriented than the music business?

He grabbed his acoustic guitar, a Martin D-35, which was propped up against the wall, settled in on the couch, and found himself strumming the melody of a Beatles song.

"Zivah in the sky with diamonds . . ."

He stopped singing. *No, not* Zivah, *Lucy.*

Once again, a case had invaded the music hemisphere of his brain. He placed the guitar on the couch, in no mood to play anymore, downed the entire glass of vodka, then stood and walked out the door.

Chapter Thirteen

The precinct was eerily quiet. No perps screaming about police brutality. No EDPs—emotionally disturbed persons—ranting and raving. Even Amanda had finally left for the day.

Conor found an envelope on his desk. Inside was a DVD with an accompanying note explaining that the previous week's surveillance footage from Zivah's building had been edited into seven twenty-four-hour segments, midnight to midnight. The camera was set to shoot one frame a second instead of the standard thirty frames of full-motion video. So each twenty-four-hour period was represented by forty-eight minutes of images, about four and a half hours total.

Conor slid the DVD into the slot on the side of his computer. The monitor flashed to life, displaying a menu. He grabbed the mouse, navigated to the file labeled MONDAY, and clicked Play. The time code at the bottom of the screen read 24:00:00, then 00:00:30, then 00:01:00, advancing one second of video time for each thirty seconds of real time. The image was sharp and in color.

Just an empty lobby until time code 07:41:00, when a fat man with a huge belly was captured walking into the lobby carrying some sort of toolkit. After speaking with the concierge, he disappeared from view. Conor slid a piece of paper in front of him, picked up a pen, and wrote, *Jabba the Hutt*—because the fat man brought the *Star Wars* character to mind—*arrived 7:41 A.M.*

Two workers appeared at 10:17. He dubbed them Beavis and Butthead. So now there were three men in the building. The question was, when did they leave?

Two deliverymen arrived at 12:10 with an extremely large box—probably a piece of furniture. They walked back through the lobby and exited after twenty minutes. A woman swept in at 1:15. Barbie, he called her, because her blond locks looked more like wispy rayon filament than hair, and her cheeks were the creamy color of a doll's molded plastic face. She was back in the lobby an hour later and out the door. A young dark-haired woman, who he surmised was a real estate agent, arrived with a couple at 2:36. They were in and out in ten minutes. *Must not have liked the price tag,* he mused. A middle-aged woman—likely another real estate agent—entered with two young men. They stayed forty-five minutes. Then, a delivery that appeared to be machine parts. At 3:12 a wiry little man entered, picked up the machine parts, and carried them out of sight. He left at 3:32. Jabba the Hutt followed ten minutes later. Beavis and Butthead right after that. So everyone who had entered earlier was now out of the building.

Bill took over as concierge at four. UPS delivered several packages. No one else until five past five, when Zivah Gavish, dressed in a blue pantsuit, entered carrying a large shopping bag. At 5:32, she swept back through the lobby in the black dress she was wearing when she was found sprawled out on the floor. She returned to the building at 5:36, hurrying through the lobby and into the elevator. *Did she forget something?*

Nothing more—just Bill the concierge and empty lobby—until 8:42, when Sayer and Wasiak got there.

Conor fell heavily back into his chair. *Jesus. She was out the door. If she hadn't come back . . .*

So who was there waiting for her? Had they seen her leave? It occurred to Conor that any number of deliverymen could have been in the loft, figured out how easy it would be to gain access, then come back later to loot the place. They would have seen Zivah exit, climbed the stairs of the tenement, entered the apartment. But then Zivah would have returned and caught them in the act. Unfortunately, the camera covering the terrace had not been functional. So there was no video to identify the intruder.

Conor formed an image in his mind of the loft. Boxes everywhere. Which meant deliveries may have been arriving all week. He put the video labeled FRIDAY into the computer. Zivah in and out a couple of times. Several deliveries. A well-dressed Indian man, perhaps a potential buyer. Thursday, more deliveries. Wednesday, the trees on the terrace were delivered by two burly men. One in particular grabbed his attention. His face was mean, angry. If ever there was someone who looked like a perp, this was the guy. When he brought the trees out to the terrace he must have noticed the proximity of the tenement next door, the easy point of entry it provided. Could the tree delivery guy have cased the loft, noticed the safe, and come back later to kill Zivah Gavish? *Add him to list of suspects. Ten million and counting.* Conor feared that whoever killed Zivah Gavish had a good chance of getting away with it. Unless they had made that one mistake Rooney was always talking about.

Conor checked his watch. It was twenty to four. Already well on his way to an all-nighter, there was no sense sleeping at this point. He wandered down the hall to the small kitchen used by the detective squad, where he found a woman rummaging around in the refrigerator. She was obviously a hooker—microskirt, fishnet stockings, halter top, extreme high heels. Around thirty. Perfect body. Smooth, cocoa skin.

She glanced at Conor. "Hope you don't mind, but I'm starving." She went back to sifting through the contents of the refrigerator. "Pudding. Cookies. Cake. There's nothing but sugar in here. Where's the protein?" She shut the refrigerator door, then spun around and looked at him. "Not even a piece of cheese."

"Who brought you in?" Conor demanded.

She gave him a quizzical look, then laughed. "Oh, *this*." She motioned to her skimpy outfit. "I work Vice." She picked up a folder that was lying on the table. "Just stopped by to get my transfer papers."

"You transferring in *here*?"

"Yeah. I spoke with Sergeant Pitts. She told me she might partner me with a detective named Bard. You know him?"

Chapter Fourteen

"*I'm* Conor Bard."

"Rosita Rubio. Nice to meet you." She headed out of the room. "Can we talk about this over breakfast?"

Conor stood there, stunned. *Am I dreaming? Did I fall asleep on the couch?*

Rosita reappeared at the door. "Really. I'm starving. And I get really cranky when I don't eat."

There was a new diner on Tenth Avenue and Forty-ninth Street Conor had been meaning to try ever since he saw the sign that read: Open 24 Hours. Twenty-four hours was a good thing. Especially for a cop.

Twenty-four-hour diners had always fascinated Conor and God knows he'd seen plenty of them. This one didn't disappoint. The place was full of well-heeled clubgoers winding down, morning deliverymen gearing up, cabdrivers in midshift, drug dealers, whores, hip-hoppers, muggers, and all manner of Darwinian species brought incongruously together in search of sustenance, cautiously quenching their thirst at a Hell's Kitchen watering hole.

Rosita slipped the trench coat off her shoulders, stood in full hooker regalia for a moment, then slithered into a booth across from Conor.

Conor looked around the room. "They think—"

"I know what they think," Rosita cut in. "They think you're a pimp."

He laughed, flagged down a waiter.

"What can I get you?" the waiter asked, his delivery jaded.

"I'll have a Bloody Mary," Rosita said.

Conor looked at her. *A Bloody Mary?* He was beginning to like her.

"I'm sorry," the waiter said. "It's after four. I can't serve alcohol."

"And give me a lumberjack special with sausage," she continued, ignoring the pronouncement of the time. "Eggs over easy. Side order of bacon. White toast. Can they butter the toast in the kitchen?"

"The lumberjack special comes with pancakes," the waiter said drolly, "not toast."

"*Side* order of white toast," she countered. "Can they butter it in the kitchen?"

"If you like."

"And not too spicy with that Bloody Mary."

The waiter drew in a breath. "Miss. I already told you—"

"It's three fifty-nine," Conor insisted. "Bring the Bloody Mary."

The waiter glanced toward a wall clock. "It's four oh five."

"Your clock is fast," Conor shot back. "Bring the Bloody Mary. And I'll have a Ketel One on the rocks. Hamburger. Medium."

The waiter put his hands on his hips. "It's after four. I don't want to get in trouble."

Conor looked across the table at Rosita. "He won't get in trouble, will he, Detective Rubio?"

"I don't think so, Detective Bard."

"You two on the job?" the waiter asked, not convinced.

Conor didn't respond.

"Better get your drinks," the waiter said as he hurried away. "It's almost four."

Conor gave Rosita a bemused look. "A lumberjack with sausage? *And* a side of bacon."

"That's why I'm in the gym six days a week. Not because I like working out. Because I like to eat. Side order of bacon? I'll do an extra twenty minutes on the treadmill. That'll cancel out the calories."

His hand involuntarily slid down to his stomach. It felt like a couch cushion. *I've got to get back in shape. I'm turning into mush.* He used to hit the gym at least three times a week. Lately it was more like three times a year.

"Do me a favor," she said.

"What's that?"

"If we do partner up, just treat me like you would any of the guys. Okay?"

"Okay. You're just one of the guys." *With great tits.*

"I know what you're thinking."

"You do?" *Was I that obvious?*

"You're thinking that a woman can't hold her own if the going gets tough. You know, in a physical confrontation. That's what all male cops think. But let me tell you something, that's total bullshit." She crossed her arms. "Now, I won't mention names but one of the detectives I was working with tonight, totally out of shape, had a belly the size of a hot air balloon. I could kick his ass. No problem. Matter of fact, I could kick the ass of every one of the dicks on the squad." She raised her arms above her head, rotated her shoulders. "Just so you know, I have a black belt in karate." She lowered her arms. "The point is, my whole life I've had to go out of my way to prove I was good enough just because I'm a woman. I'm tired of it. So, if you can accept me as one of the guys, we're golden. Otherwise, guess you better find yourself another partner."

He couldn't deny she had a point. Most of the talk around the squad about women's shortcomings in the physicality department came from men who couldn't run half a block without wheezing and couldn't bench-press a broomstick.

He looked at her tight abs then patted his stomach again. *She probably could kick* my *ass.*

Chapter Fifteen

The drinks arrived. Conor held up his glass. "*Salud.*"

Rosita tapped his glass with hers. "*Cheers* in Spanish? Nice."

"I'm multilingual. I can say *cheers* in twelve languages."

"*Salud.*" She took a sip.

"So how'd you like working Vice?" he asked.

"Well, the best part is that sometimes I get to dress up like a whore. Every woman's fantasy, right?"

"Not *every* woman. You don't know what I have to go through to get most women to put on a garter belt and stilettos once in a while."

Rosita laughed. "Anyway, to answer your question, I'm glad to be out of it. There's a certain hypocrisy, you know? I mean, a guy hires a prostitute, gets caught, he pays a fine. *She* goes to jail."

"Double standard."

"Yeah. And another thing. You take the same guy, same pross, only this time they're making a porn film and he's paying her to have sex on camera. *Now* it's legal. Does that make any sense to you?"

"Maybe somebody should tell the johns to bring a camcorder when they go cruising for a hooker."

"Right." She held her arms open wide. "The guy's a filmmaker now, not a john? And she's not a whore, she's an actress?"

Conor laughed. "So where'd you grow up?"

"Spanish Harlem. My father's Cuban and my mother is African American."

"Sister? Brother?"

"An older sister. Her name's Candida. The Tony Orlando song was a hit when she was born."

Conor began singing. "Oh, my Candida . . . just take my hand and I'll lead ya."

"Yeah. That's what everyone used to do when they met her. So now she calls herself Candy. Which my mother hates. 'Candida' is still my mother's favorite song."

"When did you come on the job?"

"I was twenty-two. Working as a cashier at a deli on a Hundred and Sixteenth Street. One night some guy comes in, pulls a gun, demands all the money in the register. I probably should have just given it to him but something about him pissed me off. So, I opened the register with one hand and grabbed a can of string beans somebody left on the counter with the other. Bashed the shit out of him. He was still out cold when the cops got there. I said to myself: 'That was fun. I should knock these scum out for a living.' After the Academy, my first assignment was the Two Five. Then transferred to Vice to get my shield."

Now it was Conor's turn. He grew up on the Jersey shore, a town called Toms River. His mother still lived there. Father had passed away almost twelve years ago. A brother living in Pennsylvania, sister in New Jersey.

"I played football in high school."

"Were you the star quarterback?"

"Something like that. Anyway, I went to community college for a couple years. Then I formed a band. My big plan was to be discovered. We appeared in clubs all over Jersey, but we never really got anywhere. So I took the exam and joined the force."

"A band?"

"I sing. And play guitar."

"Still?"

Her question stung him somehow. *Still?* What did she mean, *still?* Did he look too old to be performing? Age was his Achilles' heel, the thing he found hardest to keep in check with denial. He was forty-three. Looked more like fifty. Although he could lie to himself about how old he appeared, the mirror always told the truth. Which meant time was running out on his chances of having a music career. Unless he was planning a geriatric collection of songs somewhere down the line. *Will you still need me, will you still feed me, when I'm sixty-four?*

"Yeah. I'm *still* singing."

"I'd love to see you perform sometime."

"No problem. As soon as we solve this case."

She grinned. "Does that mean . . ."

"What the hell? Let's give it a shot."

He filled her in on the basic details. Woman found in her loft, throat slit. No sign of forced entry. Missing red diamond. His encounter with Kruger, his interview with Silberman, his conversation with Madison.

"The security video didn't show anyone in the building after five," he told her. "So I'm thinking the killer gained access from the roof of the abandoned tenement next door to the yarn factory."

"Shells like that? Always full of addicts, dealers, homeless. When I was on the beat in Harlem, we had those buildings on every block. So, from what you're telling me, this could be a simple burglary gone wrong. Some doper climbs onto the terrace and walks into the loft. The victim's standing in front of an open safe. Hard to resist."

"I'd agree. Except the only thing taken was the red diamond." Conor retrieved the photo of the diamond and handed it to Rosita.

Rosita whistled. "Now *that* would look good on my finger."

"There were dozens of other diamonds all over the floor," Conor continued. "And I don't know how much cash. It appears the killer was looking for that one thing."

"So you're thinking, because the diamond was from South Africa, it could be some kind of international conspiracy?"

"I'm not thinking anything. Just telling you what I know."

She handed the photo back to Conor. "Not bad for my first homicide."

"You're a virgin?"

"Yeah. Only not necessarily in the biblical sense."

Conor raised his arm and motioned for the check.

"What are you doing?" she asked.

"Getting the check."

"What? We on a date?"

"No problem. I got it."

"You buy the guys breakfast?" She reached into her halter top and produced a twenty. "We'll split it."

"Okay." He grimaced as he lowered his arm.

"What's the matter?"

"Ah, it's my shoulder. I think I might have a torn rotator cuff."

She stood, stepped behind him, started massaging his shoulder. "Don't worry. I'm a paramedic."

"Really? You took the course?"

"Yeah. Like I said, I've always had to prove I was as good as a man at this job. Raise your arm."

He did as she asked.

"Now move it in a circle."

"Okay." He gritted his teeth.

"That hurt?"

"Yeah."

"Now move your arm up and down."

He complied.

"I don't think it's a rotator cuff injury," she said.

"Then what is it?"

"I'd say it's shoulder impingement syndrome."

"Really?"

"Yeah." She kneaded his shoulder with both hands. "That's when the tendons lose their resiliency and can no longer hold the ball joint in the socket. It's common among aging adults."

"Thanks a lot."

"Hey, it's a better diagnosis than rotator cuff tear."

63

As she continued to massage his shoulder, he noticed that everyone in the place was staring at them.

"We've got an audience," he observed.

"You want happy ending?" she asked shrilly, her voice rising to a crescendo.

Chapter Sixteen

Conor and Rosita walked up Tenth Avenue laughing.

"You see the look on that guy's face?" she asked.

"I think he was reaching for his wallet."

"I probably could have made more in the diner bathroom in twenty minutes than I'll ever make working an eight-hour shift."

He looked at her. "Well?"

"Well, what?"

"Where's my happy ending?"

"You got me as a partner. That's your happy ending."

"Yeah. You're right."

"You've worked a lot of homicides?" she asked.

"Caught eleven. Assisted on, oh, I don't know, ten, twelve."

"Did you solve them all?"

"A couple of them went cold. But most of them were wrapped up in a few hours."

"How?"

"Sometimes there was a witness and we got a good ID. A few confessed when we went to interview them." He recalled Rooney's assessment. "Killers always make mistakes. They aren't the smartest people in the world."

"How does this case compare?" she asked.

"This one isn't going to be easy. Too many wild cards. Take Kruger, for example. The guy doesn't seem like a cop. He comes across more like a spy. With his own agenda." Conor yawned. "Although I haven't figured out exactly what that agenda is."

"You must be tired," she said.

"You could say that."

"Why don't you go home, grab a couple hours." Her voice was soothing. "I've been on midnight to eight for the past couple of weeks. I'm used to it. I'll go get out of this outfit and—"

"You mean you don't dress like that all the time?"

"Very funny. Anyway, get some rest. Let's meet at the precinct tomorrow morning—"

"*This* morning."

"Right. This morning. Seven o'clock. I'll hang with you as long as I can tomorrow," she offered. "Then I'll go catch some sleep. That way, one of us will always be on the job. Couple days we'll both be on the same schedule."

"All right, Rosita, see you tomorrow."

"Don't call me Rosita."

"Isn't that your name?"

"Yeah. But I don't use Rosita on the job."

"What am I supposed to call you?"

"Rubio. Just call me Rubio. That sounds like a cop's name."

"Okay, Rubio. See you tomorrow."

"And I want to call you Bard, okay?"

"Sure. Why not? Bard and Rubio. It's kind of got a ring to it."

A suffocating silence greeted Conor when he stepped into his apartment. He stopped and stood just inside the door, allowing echoes of past lovers to fill the void. Had he held them in his arms ten minutes ago or ten years ago? The melody of the Gilbert O'Sullivan song "Alone Again (Naturally)" came to mind.

I truly am indeed . . . alone again, naturally . . .

Conor considered having his usual nightcap—half a water glass full of vodka—but thought better of it, given the fact it was quarter to five and he wanted to be back at the precinct in two hours. Instead, he went to bed and almost immediately fell into a deep sleep, which was interrupted at six thirty by Eric Clapton's bluesy "Early in the Morning" blasting out of the speakers of his iPod-equipped alarm clock. He liked to set the "wake to music" option, choosing the tune to reflect his frame of mind or correspond with what was happening in his life. One night recently he felt really in a rut and set the song to Sonny and Cher's "I Got You Babe" because that's what Bill Murray's character woke to in the movie *Groundhog Day* as he lived the same day over and over. This morning, it was Eric Clapton urging him to get up.

"Want to see me hug my pillow where my baby used to lay?"

Conor hit the snooze button and silenced Clapton's mournful refrain. Then he got up and staggered into the kitchen to make coffee. *Better get moving.* Homicide investigation. Day one. It's murder.

Chapter Seventeen

Conor passed a newsstand on Eighth Avenue. The *New York Post* headline blared: *Diamond Dealer Dead.* He stopped, bought a copy, then continued down the street. The byline on the article was Lew Michaels and the victim was identified as Zivah Gavish. *How the hell did Lew get the name of the victim?* Probably from Bill the concierge. At least there were no details about the nature of the homicide.

Rosita was on the phone when Conor arrived at his desk. Her hooker apparel had been replaced by a conservative blue skirt and matching jacket. White shirt buttoned to the collar. With much more of her covered, she appeared somehow far sexier to Conor than the night before. *What am I thinking? She's my partner for Christ's sake. Just one of the guys.*

"He just walked in." Rosita spoke into the phone. "I'll let him know." She hung up, looked at Conor. "Kingston from the homicide squad. He's got a team over on Forty-fourth Street. He'll call back when he has something."

He dropped the *Post* in front of her. "You see this?"

"Yeah." She pushed the paper aside. "You get some sleep?"

"A solid eighty minutes. Who needs more than that?" His eyes wandered to a vase on her desk, containing a single yellow flower. "What's that?"

"A flower." She touched the petals. "I was going to buy a whole arrangement but I didn't want to freak you out."

Amanda, carrying a brass plaque, walked up to them. Conor looked at the plaque. "Cop of the month?"

She nodded. "Barry from Alpha Engraving just dropped it off."

"Who's the lucky guy?"

"Girl," Amanda replied. "Heidi Spangler." She tilted the plaque so Conor could see the inscription. "You ever get one of these?"

"Not even close."

"Didn't think so." Amanda looked at Rosita. "I see you've met Detective Rubio."

"You mean my new partner?" Conor asked.

Amanda offered a half smile, somewhere between sweet and sarcastic. "That's what I like about you, Bard. You never labor over your decisions."

"Better that way, Sarge. Whenever I think something over, I make a mistake."

Conor and Rosita rode the elevator to the thirty-seventh floor of Trump Tower, inner sanctum of the ridiculously rich, and approached the door of Kenneth Madison's apartment.

"I'm thinking of moving down from a Hundred and Tenth Street," Rosita said in mock earnest. "I should check out an apartment in this building."

Conor rang the doorbell. "The way the economy is going, you could probably pick one up for four or five million."

The door swung open and there was Kenneth Madison. Tall, maybe six-five, full head of wavy black hair. His chiseled body was barely concealed by the silk kimono he was wearing. "Detective Bard?"

"Yes," Conor replied. "This is my partner, Detective Rubio."

"Nice to meet you," Rosita offered.

"My pleasure." Madison stood aside, motioned for them to come

CHARLES KIPPS

in. He tugged on the collar of his robe. "Sorry. I just got out of the shower. Will you excuse me for a moment?"

"Sure," Conor said.

Madison pointed to a couch. "Please. Have a seat. I'll be right back." He disappeared down a hall.

Conor looked around. The apartment was spectacular. Not like Zivah's loft was spectacular. Madison's home was more uptown, upscale. Both places were far beyond his means, unattainable even in the most outrageous, expansive manifestations of his imagination. When he daydreamed about stardom as a major recording artist, he didn't even dare envision anything as grand as this.

"Short walk to the precinct. Nice view of the city." Rosita sat on the couch. "I could live here."

Conor sat next to her. "Yeah, you could. All you've got to do is seduce Madison and move right in."

"Not a bad idea." Rosita moved her shoulders back slightly, which had the effect of accentuating her breasts, then moistened her lips with her tongue and brushed a stray strand of hair away from her cheek.

Conor looked at her and frowned. "What are you doing?"

"Getting ready to conduct an interview. What do you think I'm doing?"

Chapter Eighteen

Madison strode into the room. "Sorry to keep you waiting." He was now dressed in a charcoal suit, clearly custom tailored. "Can I get you a coffee?"

"No thanks," Conor replied.

Madison looked at Rosita.

"I'm fine," Rosita said.

Madison handed each of them a business card then eased into a chair. "This all feels like a nightmare. I just can't believe Zivah is gone." He looked at Conor. "Can you tell me what happened?"

"I'm sorry, Mr. Madison. Like I said on the phone last night, we can't release any details at this stage of the investigation."

Rosita pulled a notebook and pen from her purse. "May I ask the nature of your relationship with Ms. Gavish?"

"We were seeing each other. Just started dating actually. I met Zivah six months ago at a charity event." Madison smiled. "She was one of the most generous people I ever met. In fact, the only time we ever argued was because of her generosity."

"What do you mean?" Conor wanted to know.

"Some bum on the street would walk up with his hand out. Zivah would stop, open her pocketbook. And the whole time I'm thinking the guy is going to grab her wallet and take off." Madison shook his head. "I guess you've got to be a New Yorker to understand you shouldn't be dangling an open purse in front of a homeless guy. Why do you think so many tourists get mugged?"

Tell me about it, Conor thought. In his first year on the job it seemed like all he did was listen to tales of woe from out-of-towners who didn't have sense enough to keep moving when approached by Times Square predators.

"I'm heartbroken," Madison sighed. "Just heartbroken. Zivah was incredible." He looked off for a moment. "I should clear up one thing. Zivah and I were not in an exclusive relationship. We were just getting to know each other. But I think it could have led somewhere. I really do."

"Mr. Madison," Conor began, "you told me on the phone that you couldn't think of anyone who would have wanted to harm her."

"No. No one."

"No ex-boyfriends?" Rosita asked.

"She never mentioned any problem with a former lover," Madison replied.

"How about a business associate?" Conor pressed.

"Zivah was the most ethical person I know," Madison insisted. "Anyone who dealt with her came away satisfied. But if you're asking me who might have killed Zivah, I *can* answer that question. When I bought the apartment—"

Conor was caught off guard. "You own it?"

"Yes," Madison confirmed. "It's one of my investments. I was planning to either flip it or rent it."

Rosita crossed her legs, allowing her skirt to edge into her lap. Conor noticed.

"How did Ms. Gavish come to live there?" Rosita asked.

"Zivah went with me to take a look at the place before all the renovation," Madison explained. "It was a mess. But I knew it was a fabulous space, a fantastic investment opportunity. Well, Zivah fell in love with the space too, just fell in love with it. She told me she would rent it from me if I decided to buy it. We went out onto what would eventually become the terrace to discuss it. I saw the abandoned building next door and realized it represented a risk. I told Zivah I was going to buy the loft but I didn't think it was the right apartment for her. She wouldn't listen." He paused, exhaled. "And then, after she moved in, I was sorry I ever gave her the keys. I mean, once, when we were out on the terrace, someone was on the roof of the building next door, staring up at us."

"Can you describe this person?" Conor asked.

Madison squinted, trying to remember. "Not really. I suppose I was . . . wait a minute. He had a white streak."

Conor was interested. "A white streak?"

"Yes," Madison replied. "I don't know. Maybe it was the light. His hair was dark but it looked like he had a strip of white hair across the top of his head." Madison sneered. "Like a skunk." He stood, paced. "I should have never let her move in. I should have insisted that she find another place." He stopped pacing, pointed a finger at Conor. "Somebody climbed from the roof of that building, some drug addict. She probably even gave money to the guy at some point. That's who killed Zivah."

Conor couldn't argue with the scenario. The moment he had stepped onto the terrace himself it was obvious that the roof of the abandoned tenement represented a possible point of entry to the loft.

"When was the last time you saw Ms. Gavish?" Conor asked.

"Sunday," Madison replied. "We had a wonderful brunch and then I drove out to the Hamptons." His jaw tightened. "The thought that some animal is walking the streets . . ." Something occurred to him. "Her parents need to be notified."

"Have you met them?" Conor asked.

"No. But they have to be told. I could do it but—"

"A business associate is taking care of that," Conor said.

"Who?"

"A man by the name of Stanley Silberman," Rosita replied.

Madison looked at Rosita. "Stanley Silberman?"

"Is there some problem with Mr. Silberman?" Conor asked.

"Problem? No, not really. It's just that Zivah told me he was always asking her out. Yesterday, when I talked to her, she said Silberman had insisted on picking her up and taking her to the dinner. I told her, 'If you feel uncomfortable, call him and just say it would be better to meet at the hotel.' That was the last time I spoke with her." Madison stared forlornly at the floor. "I've never known anybody who was murdered. It doesn't seem real."

Rosita produced a business card and a pen. She wrote something on the back of the card then handed it to Madison. "I have a friend who does grief counseling. My cell phone number's on the back. If you feel you need it, give me a call and I'll put you in touch with her."

Madison glanced at the card then looked at Rosita. "Thank you, Detective Rubio."

"You're welcome," Rosita said, flashing a warm smile.

Conor and Rosita exited Trump Tower and eased down Fifth Avenue.

"Let's leave the car where it is," Conor suggested, "and walk to the Waldorf."

"Sounds good to me," Rosita replied.

They turned onto Fifty-fifth Street, headed east toward Park Avenue.

"You really *do* want to live in that apartment, don't you, Rubio?"

"What are you talking about?"

"Grief counseling?" Conor laughed. "Didn't you listen to what he was saying? Not exclusive. That's how he put it. He's probably got ten women like Zivah around the city. Sure, he must be upset. One of his girlfriends turns up dead. But I guarantee you he doesn't need grief counseling."

"Hey, he's a nice guy. Perfect life. Something like this? He could use a little professional help."

"Nice guy? Be careful now, Rubio. At this stage of the investigation he could be considered a person of interest."

"Yeah," Rosita said breathily, "he's a person of interest all right."

Conor shot her a look.

"Come on, Bard. I'm just fooling around."

"Well, something about him bothered me," Conor countered.

"Hell-oh! He's young. Amazingly good-looking. Got the male model thing going on. Plus, he's totally rich. If I was a man, I'd be jealous too."

"I'm not jealous."

"Okay. *You're* not jealous. But when I see some gorgeous rich bitch, I get jealous. Like what the fuck? She's got everything. And I've got nada."

"You're not so bad."

"Wow," she replied with a laugh. "You're a real charmer."

"Me? I'd say *you're* the charmer."

"What? You mean with Madison?"

Conor didn't respond.

"So what? Let him fantasize. It could be useful to us down the line." Rosita shrugged. "Maybe I've been working Vice too long."

Conor looked at her. His partner using sexuality as a weapon? *Hey, why not?* Ralph could never have pulled *that* off.

Chapter Nineteen

Conor and Rosita entered the lobby of the Waldorf-Astoria. Conor picked up the house phone.

"Waldorf-Astoria," the operator barked. "How may I direct your call?"

"Sulaiman Aziz."

"I'm sorry," the operator said. "Mr. Aziz has a block on that room. May I take a message?"

"This is Detective Bard. NYPD. I need to speak with Mr. Aziz immediately. It's urgent."

"Hold, please."

Conor stood there, phone pressed to his ear for at least five minutes. "Now I'm getting pissed."

Conor hung up the phone and walked to the front desk.

"Sulaiman Aziz's room number, please."

A dispassionate clerk blinked at Conor. "I'm sorry but—"

"Now!" Conor whipped out his badge.

The clerk eyed the gold shield for a moment, then picked up a receiver and dialed a number. "Mr. Carter. There's a detective here to see Mr. Aziz."

The clerk hung up and looked at Conor. "Mr. Carter is our head of security. He'll be here in a moment."

Conor and Rosita stepped a few feet away.

"I love a forceful man." Rosita patted her hair demurely.

"So you *can* be a girl when you want to."

She dropped her hand. "Don't tell anybody."

"Detective Bard?"

Conor turned to see a man dressed in a dark suit approaching him.

"Yes."

"Ed Carter. Head of security. How may I assist you?"

Conor could tell immediately that Carter had once been on the job. Erect posture, alert expression, polite tone in his voice. After a brief discussion in which Carter confirmed he was a retired detective, Carter called the suite and informed Aziz that Conor and Rosita were coming upstairs.

When they stepped off the elevator on the top floor, a door swung open to reveal a man dressed in a flowing white robe, the traditional garb in Abu Dhabi.

"I am Sulaiman Aziz. Please. Come in."

The sprawling Presidential Suite was aptly named. The rooms had double-height ceilings and the plush furnishings were indeed fit for a president. As Aziz led them to a sitting area near a window, Conor spotted two other men, also dressed in white robes, standing guard at opposite ends of the room.

Conor, Rosita, and Aziz sat in three chairs grouped around a low table. There was a demitasse of thick Turkish coffee in front of Aziz as well as a slice of mango. "Would you like something?" Aziz asked.

"No, thank you," Conor replied.

"You're here about Zivah Gavish," Aziz stated without emotion, a man completely at ease, above the law.

Conor was surprised that Aziz didn't ask how it was that NYPD came knocking on his hotel door, how cops even knew he was connected to the case at all.

"I prefer to get right to the point," Aziz said evenly. "What is it you want to know?"

"You are aware that Zivah Gavish was murdered last night," Conor said.

"Unfortunately, well aware."

"When was the last time you saw Ms. Gavish?" Rosita asked.

"In Abu Dhabi. Last month."

"I thought I read somewhere that Israelis weren't allowed in the country," Conor noted.

"We have no official policy in that regard, Detective." Aziz smiled wryly. "Is there anything else you'd like to know? Or are you done? Because when you are finished there are matters I would like to discuss."

"Have you ever been in Zivah Gavish's apartment?" Rosita asked.

"The loft? No. She told me about it when she was in Abu Dhabi. If I'm not mistaken, it was under construction."

Conor nodded in acknowledgment. "May I ask why you are in New York?"

"To attend the diamond dealers' dinner."

"That's a long trip just for hotel food," Rosita observed.

Aziz was not amused. He sliced off a piece of mango with a knife, then speared the chunk of fruit with a fork. "As I'm sure you are already aware—or I don't think you'd be here speaking with me right now—I came to New York to conclude a transaction with Ms. Gavish. In fact, I have wired a substantial amount of money into the escrow account of an attorney acting as intermediary." Aziz held up the fork with the impaled mango still in place. "However, Ms. Gavish's untimely death prevented me from acquiring the merchandise. You may check with the attorney. His name is Seymour Kramer. I'll be happy to provide you with his address and phone number."

"Would you mind telling me what it was that you were purchasing from Ms. Gavish?" Conor asked.

"Yes, I do mind," Aziz answered quickly. "My transactions are always confidential. But under the circumstances I find myself in a position where it is necessary to describe the item." He finally ate the morsel of mango. "A red diamond of extraordinary beauty." He placed the fork on the table. "I can only assume that you or one of your agencies have examined Zivah's e-mails. One of her e-mails is to me, with a photo of the red diamond attached. Since I must return to Abu Dhabi soon, I would like to conclude my transaction at this time and ask your assistance in—"

"The red diamond you described," Conor interrupted, "was not recovered from Ms. Gavish's loft."

Aziz grimaced slightly, cast his gaze out the window. Obviously this was not good news to a rare-gem collector.

"If you do happen to determine who killed my friend Ms. Gavish," Aziz said evenly, his eyes fixed on the New York skyline, "and recover the property stolen from her loft, I would request that I be notified."

"Okay," Conor replied. "But I do have one question."

Aziz turned and faced Conor. "And what is that, Detective?"

"This red diamond we're talking about. Is it legal?"

"All my transactions are legal. And I must say, I resent the implication." Aziz picked up the demitasse. "I always require proof of provenance from the seller."

"And if the paperwork is forged?" Conor asked.

"I am an expert in gems, Detective." Aziz took a sip of coffee. "Not documents."

Chapter Twenty

Conor and Rosita exited the Waldorf and walked west toward Fifth Avenue.

"I think we can eliminate Aziz as a suspect," Conor said. "The way he reacted when I told him the red diamond was missing . . ."

"Could've been an act."

"Too subtle. Besides, all that money? Why kill? No, Rubio, I don't think Aziz is our guy. But we'll check out the lawyer later. See where that leads."

Conor and Rosita stopped at the car, Conor on the driver's side, Rosita on the passenger side, and stared across the hood at each other.

"I've got to tell you, Rubio, I hate to drive."

"You want *me* to drive?"

"Yeah."

"I don't like to drive either."

"Sorry, but I'm the senior partner."

They both started around the front of the car.

"Okay," she said as they crossed, "but you should know something."

"What's that?"

"Seems like every time I get behind a wheel, I have an accident."

"I'll be sure to wear my seat belt."

When they got back to the precinct, Conor dropped Madison's business card on his desk. "Madison International Properties."

"He must be doing well," Rosita noted. "Living in Trump Tower."

"Let's find out." Conor entered Madison International Properties in a Google search box. A list of articles filled the screen. "Madison International announces plans for Virginia resort."

Rosita walked over and stood behind Conor. "Kenneth Madison," Conor continued, reading from the screen, "CEO of Madison International Properties, revealed today that the company would be breaking ground on a superluxury resort complex near Virginia Beach next summer. Chase Manhattan Bank will provide financing for the four-hundred-million-dollar project."

Rosita whistled. "Four hundred million!"

The collection of Internet articles detailed a multitude of holdings owned by Madison International. No doubt about it, Madison was well-heeled.

Rosita struck an exaggerated pose and flicked her hair. "You think he liked me?"

"*Liked* you? I think we should stop by the post office so you can fill out a change-of-address card."

Conor alerted the squad that a possible suspect had a streak of white in his hair—as Madison had described it—then called Kingston and imparted the same bit of information.

"Got it," Kingston said. "Streak of white."

A uniformed officer approached Conor.

"Lieutenant Rooney would like to see you," the uni said.

Conor grimaced.

"What's the matter?" Rosita asked.

"When the lieutenant wants to talk to you," Conor explained, "it's never good news."

Charles Kipps

They strode into Rooney's office.

"Hey, Lu," Conor said. "You meet my new partner, Detective Rosita Rubio?"

"Good to see you." His tone was not particularly welcoming, which could be attributed to his old-school mentality. A woman detective? A woman of color? Probably hard for him to fathom. Still, as squad commander, he must have signed off on Rosita or she wouldn't have been standing in his office.

"I hate to put pressure on you two," Rooney began, "but I just got a call from the chief of detectives."

"How's the chief doing?" Conor asked.

"Not good. The developer of the building where your victim was killed is the mayor's best buddy. As in, hey, buddy, how much money will you contribute to the campaign?" Rooney held up a copy of the *Post*. "This is going to get a lot of attention."

"Money always does," Conor agreed.

Which is why the bodies of a hundred murder victims found in a cramped Bronx apartment would never generate the heat of one cold corpse discovered in a six-thousand-square-foot loft. And although every detective wants to solve every homicide, being rich or famous or powerful got you special treatment, even in death.

Rooney looked at Conor. "We're part of the political system, whether we like it or not. The chief of detectives loves going to those big parties at Gracie Mansion. Wants to stay on the guest list. So when the mayor whispers in his ear, the chief turns around and shouts at us. You've been on the job long enough to know the drill."

"Yes," Conor replied. "I have."

"Then do us all a favor," Rooney concluded. "Find the dumb bastard who killed that girl." He paused. "Pronto."

Amanda intercepted Conor and Rosita as they left Rooney's office.

"Medical examiner just called," Amanda said. "You ready for a little blood and guts?"

In every homicide, especially one as high-profile as the murder of an Israeli diamond dealer, the presence of the detective who caught the case was required at the autopsy. If questions arose regarding the crime scene, there wasn't time for the ME to pause, scalpel in hand, and make a phone call.

Conor looked at Rosita. "Ever been to an autopsy?"

"No. But it sounds like fun."

Chapter Twenty-one

Zivah Gavish was laid out naked on a metal examination table. Harold Selzer, the medical examiner, hovered over her.

"Beautiful girl," Selzer remarked as he jotted something down on a clipboard. "Don't get too many lookers in here."

Selzer, fifty-seven, five-nine, dark brown hair, had been with the ME's office since he graduated college. Conor had seen him often over the years, too often. Rosita had met him once, at a lecture Selzer gave about toxicology.

"You just missed Rabbi Burstein," Selzer said. "He asked me to do only what was absolutely necessary, release the body as soon as possible. Some guy named Stanley Silberman was with him."

Conor raised an eyebrow. "Silberman?"

"Yeah. Apparently Silberman insisted the rabbi make an appearance even though the victim wasn't Orthodox. Go figure."

Conor did figure. He figured Silberman didn't want to let go without seeing Zivah Gavish one more time. Naked. On a slab. *Creepy,* Conor thought.

"I told the rabbi I'd do my best to get her out of here this afternoon. Unless you have a problem with that."

"You're the ME," Conor said. "If you're satisfied, so am I."

"Any sign of sexual assault?" Rosita asked cautiously.

"Doesn't appear to be," Selzer said. He turned his attention back to the corpse. "I'd put the time of death between five and eight."

"She returned to the apartment at five thirty-six," Conor noted. "So if you're right about the brackets, she was killed during the three hours and six minutes between five thirty-six and eight forty-two when patrol got there."

"Of course I'm right about the brackets," Selzer fired back. "I'll have the toxicology report in a couple weeks. But cause of death is rather obvious." He leaned over, his face only a few inches above Zivah's neck. "There's an odd coagulation pattern, some mottling on the skin, at several points along the wound. Also, some kind of fine powder."

"What does that mean?" Conor asked.

"Don't know." Selzer straightened up. "I've taken samples. Let's see what the lab says."

Conor and Rosita exited the ME's office. She was uncharacteristically quiet.

He looked at her. "Well?"

"Well what?"

"Your first autopsy."

She looked away. "I don't want to think about it."

"Can't take the sight of blood?"

"Blood doesn't bother me."

"So what's wrong?" he asked.

"I'm too young to think about mortality."

"So am I," Conor countered as he opened the car door. "Give me the keys. *I'll* drive."

Seymour Kramer was in his midseventies, a distinguished man at home in his oak-paneled office overlooking West Fifty-seventh Street. His

85

desk was huge and polished to a high shine. A wall of leather-bound books dominated the room.

"I spoke with Mr. Aziz," Kramer said, "and he has authorized me to provide you with certain information."

"According to Mr. Aziz," Conor began, "he was in New York to conclude a business deal with a diamond dealer named Zivah Gavish."

"That's correct," Kramer confirmed.

Conor waited for more but Kramer did not elaborate.

"Have Mr. Aziz and Ms. Gavish often done business together?" Rosita asked.

"Yes."

Again, silence. Conor realized Kramer had no intention of elaborating without being prompted.

"Did this business happen to involve a rare and valuable red diamond?" Conor asked.

"Yes," Kramer replied.

"Is this diamond a legal diamond, Mr. Kramer?"

"I would assume so," Kramer replied, sounding disinterested.

"You don't know?" Conor pressed.

"It's not my business to know. I simply act as an intermediary for a transaction. The parties involved exchange the requisite documentation among themselves." Kramer cleared his throat, waited for the next question. Conor obliged.

"Now that Ms. Gavish is deceased and the diamond is missing, what happens to the money that Mr. Aziz . . ."

"If the diamond is not recovered," Kramer said impatiently, "the funds will be returned to Mr. Aziz, of course."

"Can you explain to me how this works?" Conor asked. "I mean, who gets what first? The money or the diamond?"

"I am designated to arrange for delivery and payment in a manner satisfactory to both parties," Kramer explained.

"Kind of like PayPal?" Rosita asked.

Kramer was unamused. "Something like that."

"So I have a diamond," Conor said, "and I am selling it to someone for a great deal of money . . ."

"You engage me, as does the other party," Kramer replied. "When I receive the money from your buyer, I notify you. Once you deliver the item in question and I have confirmed that with the buyer, I disburse the funds to your account."

"How much do you charge for that kind of service?" Rosita wondered.

"It depends." Kramer smiled for the first time. "I *do* receive a modest fee for my services. When you're ready for such a transaction, please let me know."

Conor and Rosita walked along Fifty-seventh Street.

He looked at her. "PayPal?"

"Well, it's the same thing, isn't it?"

Conor laughed. "Yeah, I suppose you're right."

"You know what I find interesting?"

"What?"

"Aziz, an Arab, in business with an Israeli and hiring a Jewish lawyer."

"Just goes to show you, Rubio, religion is for the poor. Rich people can't afford to practice it."

Chapter Twenty-two

When Conor and Rosita got back to the precinct, Conor checked his e-mail and found a message from Kruger with a PDF file attached.

"Hey, Rubio. Look at this."

Rosita walked behind him and peered over his shoulder at the screen. "What is it?"

"Marwala's known associates in America."

"How many are there?"

"Kruger said there were fifty."

"So what do we do? Interview all of them?"

Conor recognized several of the names. A few were small-time hoods. A couple were mobbed up. "No. For now, we just add them to the guest list." His cell phone rang.

"Bard."

"Conor. It's Brian. I just transferred a ton of evidence from the loft to the crime lab."

"On my way." He snapped his phone shut and looked at Rosita. "Let's go."

"Where we going?"

Conor stood. "To look for a needle in a haystack."

*   *   *

Conor and Rosita entered the crime lab to find Brian standing in front of a long table. Hundreds of items were spread out in front of him, most of them tucked into plastic evidence bags.

"Jesus, Brian," Conor said, "you look like death warmed over."

"Yeah? Well, I won't be sleeping any time soon. I've *still* got a crew over there." He looked at Rosita. "Who are you?"

"Rosita Rubio."

"*Detective* Rosita Rubio," Conor pointed out. "She's my new partner."

"Boy, did you get lucky, Bard."

"That's what *I* told him," Rosita agreed.

"Brian Cobb. Nice to meet you."

"Same here."

"Find anything interesting?" Conor asked.

Brian flipped open a file folder. "There are a lot of prints in the tenement and the loft. *That's* good. I even got a palm print off the terrace wall."

Conor was surprised. "You can get prints off brick?"

"It's not easy but it can be done." Brian held up the palm print. "If the killer came over that wall, this is his palm." He looked at Conor. "Unless it's yours." He turned toward Rosita. "He tell you he climbed over the wall?"

"Yeah," she replied.

"Almost ripped his arm out of the socket," Brian added.

"That's all right," Rosita said. "I gave him a nice shoulder massage."

Brian looked at Conor then back at Rosita. "I'm leaving that one alone." He placed the palm print on the table. "The position of the print, the angle of it, I'd say it was made by someone reaching up from the tenement roof." He looked down his nose at Conor. "Like you did."

"Sorry," Conor said. "You want my palm print for comparison?"

"I do." Brian opened a drawer, took out a sheet of clear plastic, and placed it on the table. "Press down on this."

Conor placed his palm on the plastic.

"So," Brian continued, "unless the palm print is yours, or the killer wore gloves, whoever he is—"

"Or whoever *she* is," Rosita interjected.

"A woman?" Brian shrugged. "Why not? Women kill. Not as often as men, but women do kill."

"Am I done?" Conor asked impatiently, his palm pressed against the plastic.

"Yeah."

Conor lifted his hand.

Brian opened another drawer and pulled out a small jar of powder and a brush, then began spreading the powder on the plastic sheet. He compared the plastic sheet with the palm print taken from the terrace wall. He held up the plastic sheet. "You will marry a dark-haired woman and have three kids."

Conor leaned over and squinted at his palm print. "Really?"

"How the hell should I know?" Brian placed the plastic sheet back on the counter. "I'm not a palm reader."

"Well?" Conor asked. "Do they match?"

"Not even close."

"So I'm in the clear?" Conor wanted to know.

"This time. Just try not to contaminate any more crime scenes."

"I'll do my best."

"The problem is, there's no extensive database of palm prints. On the other hand . . ." Brian pointed to the hand that was painted on the cocktail glass found in the sink at the scene. He laughed. "On the other *hand*. Get it?"

"Don't quit your day job," Conor advised.

"Anyway," Brian continued, "got two good sets of prints off that glass. Matched one set to the victim. The other belongs to a Kenneth Madison."

Conor was surprised. "Criminal database?"

"No. Gun permit. Madison registered a gun in the Hamptons a few years ago. As far as the other prints at the scene, must be about fifty distinct patterns, I'll start running them through this afternoon."

Brian picked up a piece of paper. "Oh, and your water bottle? Matched the prints to a set in the loft."

Silberman's prints in the loft? Conor was surprised. Given Silberman's adamant denial that he had ever been in Zivah's apartment, Conor really hadn't expected to find evidence to the contrary. But Silberman's fingerprints now made him a liar. And maybe a killer.

Chapter Twenty-three

Manhattan streets, whether they are framed by brownstones or canyons of monolithic skyscrapers, can appear indistinguishable. Not so with the block of West Forty-seventh Street between Fifth and Sixth avenues, known as the Diamond District.

At either end of the block, the streetlights are topped with diamond-shaped glass rather than globes. Hasidic men, in their long black coats, black hats, untrimmed beards, and side curls known as *payot*, prowl the pavement in search of a transaction. Signs abound, proclaiming that a merchant buys and/or sells diamonds and gold. Tourists scurry past the cacophonous swirl of activity like frightened seals in shark-infested waters. It is a street that is often chaotic, always colorful.

Conor and Rosita parked the car on Sixth Avenue then walked down Forty-seventh Street.

"Why are there so many Hasidic men in the jewelry business?" Rosita wondered aloud.

"Why are there so many Amish farmers?" Conor countered.

"You don't know, do you?"

"Why there are so many Hasidim on Forty-seventh Street? Of course I do."

Actually, Conor did know why the diamond industry was populated with Hasidim. His old partner Ralph, faced with long, lonely nights after his wife, Laura, had died three years ago, spent hours on the computer researching just about everything. So the first time they caught a case in the Diamond District, Ralph was ready with a thorough history. According to Ralph, Orthodox Jews began emigrating to Antwerp, Belgium, in 1261 and, after being persecuted for centuries, finally established themselves as a community in the seventeen hundreds, eventually winding up controlling the diamond trade.

"In 1940," Conor explained, "the Nazis invaded the Netherlands so the Orthodox Jews left Belgium and came to New York, bringing the diamond business with them." Conor waved his arm in a broad arc. "Ninety percent of all diamonds in America pass through this one block, processed by more than twenty-five hundred diamond-related businesses."

"You know what, Bard? When you retire from the job, you could get work as a tour guide."

They stopped in front of Silberman Jewelry.

Rosita stared through the glass. "*That's* Silberman?"

"That's Silberman," Conor replied.

"There's your killer right there," she said. "Didn't have a date for the prom. Never got over it."

"A lot of guys didn't have a date for the prom," Conor noted. "Doesn't make them killers."

"True. But conversely, every killer sat home on prom night."

"Really? You sure about that?"

"Yeah. Check it out. I bet I'm right. High school can really mess up your head."

Conor shrugged. "I had a great time in high school. Guess that's why I'm a cop and not a killer."

"Me too. Must've been asked to the prom by at least twenty guys. They all thought that if they took me to the prom they could fuck me."

"Did they?"

"Buy me a corsage," Rosita said without missing a beat. "Let's see what happens."

Conor smiled. Rosita could spar. He liked that. Not as well as Ralph, who was heavyweight champion when it came to quick comebacks, but adeptly enough to make her a worthy opponent.

Conor rang the buzzer. Silberman looked up, squinted, then jumped when he realized who was standing outside his window. He reached under the counter and pressed the lock release.

"How are you today, Mr. Silberman?" Conor asked as he entered.

"I'm fine," Silberman replied, his eyes drifting to Rosita.

"Meet my partner, Detective Rubio."

Conor noticed that Silberman's left wrist was bandaged. *Very interesting.* The night of the murder, Silberman had held his wrist at one point during the interview. So how had he hurt it? Climbing onto the terrace?

"We need to ask you a few questions," Conor said. "Just to make sure we've got the facts straight."

Silberman nodded cautiously. "Okay."

"You told me you had never been in Ms. Gavish's loft," Conor began. "Is that correct, Mr. Silberman?"

"Yes."

"So how come we found your fingerprints there?" Conor asked pointedly.

Silberman's lip quivered slightly. "I . . . I . . . don't know."

"You don't *know?*" Rosita was incredulous. She looked at Conor. "His prints found in the loft of a dead woman and he doesn't know?"

"I was never there," Silberman insisted. "I swear to you, I was never there!"

"Who are we supposed to believe?" Conor asked. "You? Or forensics?"

Silberman rubbed his forehead with both hands, then suddenly grabbed his bandaged right wrist with his left hand.

Conor feigned concern. "Hurt your wrist, Mr. Silberman?"

"Oh!" Silberman released the grip on his wrist. "Just a minor strain."

"How'd you do that?" Conor wanted to know. *Climbing onto the terrace?*

"I . . . I . . ." Silberman stammered. "I sprained it. There was a pothole. I tripped and fell on the street over by—"

"Okay," Conor interrupted, "back to your fingerprints being in the loft. We need to resolve that, Mr. Silberman."

"There must be some mistake." Silberman squinted, concentrating. "Wait a minute! The only thing it could be . . ."

"What could it be, Mr. Silberman?" Rosita asked.

"Her birthday is coming up," Silberman said, exhaling audibly. "I sent her a jewelry box as a gift. Is that where you found my fingerprints?"

"We're not at liberty to divulge that information," Rosita stated officially.

"Thanks for your time," Conor said abruptly. "We'll be in touch."

Conor and Rosita started toward the door. Conor stopped, turned, and looked at Silberman's bandaged wrist.

"Next time," Conor suggested pointedly, "watch where you walk. The city's full of potholes."

Silberman's face drained of color.

Conor and Rosita walked down Forty-seventh Street.

"Poor guy." Rosita laughed. "He turned completely white."

"And so it was later," Conor sang, "as the detective told his tale . . . that his face at first just ghostly, turned a whiter shade of pale."

"Wow," Rosita said, surprised. "You have a nice voice."

"Thanks, Rubio."

"But hey, I didn't expect the investigation to turn into a Broadway musical."

They arrived at the car.

"Give me the keys," Rosita said. "A star shouldn't be driving himself around."

They climbed into the car, Rosita behind the wheel.

She started the engine. "If the jewelry box is the only place we find Silberman's prints—"

"Then, assuming he can prove he sent her the jewelry box, we have no case against Silberman based solely on the prints."

"What about his wrist?" Rosita asked.

"Anybody can fall down."

"So what you're telling me is . . ."

"We're nowhere with Silberman. At least not now." Conor rubbed his chin. "Let's go back to the lab. See what else Brian turned up."

Chapter Twenty-four

Conor and Rosita walked along a table laden with evidence. Cigarette butts, beer bottles, whiskey bottles, fast-food wrappers, empty cans, all manner of garbage was neatly laid out and marked with an identifying tag.

"You running a dump here or what?" Conor asked.

Brian picked up an evidence bag containing a cigarette butt. "Tenement next door." He placed the bag back on the table and picked up another. "Crack vial. Found dozens of these things." He put the bag down. "Needles. Razor blades. Baggies full of cocaine residue."

Rosita pointed to an evidence bag. "Is that a bidi?"

"That's what it is," Brian confirmed.

Conor took a closer look. "What? Those little Indian cigarettes?"

"Yeah," Brian replied.

"Where'd you find it?" Conor asked.

Brian read the number off the tag and then picked up a list. He ran his finger down the entries. "It was removed from the planter on the terrace."

Conor looked at Rosita. "When was the last time you saw one of those?"

"When I was growing up," Rosita replied, "there was a newsstand near my house run by an Indian family. We used to buy bidis all the time. They were cheap. And you could get different flavors, which appealed to kids. Now they're banned in New York. To keep kids from buying them like we did."

Conor studied the tiny brown cylinder. A bidi. Not a commercially produced American cigarette smoked by the millions.

Who smokes bidis? Who killed Zivah Gavish?

The answer to both questions could be the same.

A bidi was certainly an unusual piece of evidence. Whoever smoked bidis had been on Zivah's terrace as recently as Wednesday, when the trees arrived. Unless, of course, one of the deliverymen smoked bidis. Or the bidi was crushed out in the planter before it was delivered to the loft.

"Where's the victim's laptop?" Conor asked Brian. "I thought you were going to send it over to the house."

"I was just about to." Brian pointed to a desk near a window. "It's over there."

Conor pulled up two chairs. He and Rosita sat side by side in front of the laptop computer. He flipped it open and hit the power button. "Let's check her contact list for Indians."

"Isn't that profiling?" Rosita held up the back of her hand. "I'm a little sensitive in that area, know what I mean?"

"Yeah. Me too."

"Since when do white males have to worry about profiling?"

"Suppose we were looking for a white male who drank martinis. I'd be on that list."

"That's different."

"Who smokes bidis?" he asked.

"A lot of people," she insisted.

Conor looked over his shoulder at Brian. "You know anyone who smokes bidis?"

"Just Indian people," Brian replied.

The laptop finished starting up. A screen with icons appeared.

"So what do you want to do?" Conor asked Rosita as he brought up Zivah's address book. "Eight hundred and seventy-nine contacts.

Want to do this alphabetically? Just to make sure we're not profiling."

Rosita reached over, typed *India* in the search box, then hit return.

Twenty-one names appeared on the screen. Most were Indian companies. Only a few had a local New York number listed in addition to their Indian phone and address. Conor pulled Zivah's iPhone from his jacket, navigated to recent calls. He scrolled slowly, comparing the list on the computer screen with the list on the iPhone.

"Tasha Sen," he said. "Zivah Gavish called someone named Tasha Sen last Sunday." He pulled out his own cell phone. "Better call on mine. If Tasha Sen saw the *Post* this morning, getting a call from the late Zivah Gavish might be a little disconcerting." He punched in the number.

"Hello?" A woman's voice flowed softly from the phone.

Chapter Twenty-five

Conor and Rosita climbed out of the car in front of the Ritz Plaza, a high-rise rental building on Forty-eighth Street between Eighth Avenue and Broadway. The doorman announced them and they took the elevator to the twenty-eighth floor. Rosita rang the doorbell. After a moment, the door swung open to reveal a beautiful Indian woman wearing a pastel green cotton dress. She was in her midthirties, around five-six, and had light brown skin. *Sienna* was the word that popped into Conor's mind, although he wondered how he had managed to dredge up the name of such an obscure color.

"Ms. Sen, I'm Detective Bard. And this is my partner, Detective Rubio."

"Please," Tasha said. "Come in."

Conor and Rosita entered the apartment, a one-bedroom corner unit—comfortable, not extravagant—with a great view of the Hudson River.

"I couldn't believe it when I saw the paper this morning," Tasha said with a sigh.

Conor nodded empathetically. "You mentioned on the phone that you and Ms. Gavish have done business together in the past."

"Yes. That's right. I represent a small gem-cutting company in Mumbai. Zivah has purchased some of our diamonds."

"How long have you known her?" Rosita asked.

Tasha stared off. "Let's see . . . a year and a half."

"Did you know her well?" Rosita wanted to know.

"Not very. I'm only in Manhattan five or six times a year. Zivah was often traveling. South Africa, Brussels. Or she was home in Tel Aviv."

Conor was content to let Rosita conduct the interview. That gave him an opportunity to take in all of Tasha. Sexy. Exotic. *Something in the way she moves, attracts me like no other lover.*

"When was the last time you saw Ms. Gavish?"

"Oh, I haven't seen her for quite a while. We were supposed to get together on Sunday night for drinks but she canceled."

"Did she ever mention anyone who had threatened her?"

Tasha shook her head. "No."

"Did she ever express concern about anyone, business associate, friend, whatever?"

"No. But as I told you before, I didn't know her that well."

"We're neighbors," Conor interjected. He walked to the window and pointed down at Forty-eighth Street. "I live on the next block."

"Then we should have a neighborly cocktail one of these days," Tasha said, embracing Conor with her eyes.

Rosita seemed vaguely annoyed by the flirtation between them. "Ms. Sen. Do you smoke bidis?"

"Bidis? No one smokes bidis anymore."

"So you don't know anyone who smokes them?" Rosita pressed.

"Why? Because I'm Indian I should know people who smoke bidis?"

Rosita and Tasha squared off silently. Conor almost stepped in but thought better of it. *Two women? Two minorities? Let them figure it out.*

Rosita didn't take the bait. "If you don't mind, Ms. Sen, please answer the question."

"Okay. But why is that important?"

"We're not at liberty to say," Rosita replied.

"About the only person I know who smokes bidis is Arun Punjabi. It's hard to find them in New York so whenever Arun goes back to India, he brings a suitcase full of them."

"Do you have his address?" Rosita asked.

"Sure. Bombay Sawing. He has an office in the Diamond District." Tasha retrieved Arun Punjabi's information.

"Thanks for all your help," Conor said.

"Any time," Tasha replied, extending an unmistakable invitation.

Conor and Rosita exited the Ritz Plaza.

"Well," Conor said, "we've got a good lead."

"Maybe two leads."

"Two?"

"Yeah. One lead in the case and the other in your love life." She looked at him. "So you like dark meat?"

"Dark meat, white meat, doesn't matter. When I eat a chicken I enjoy every single part of it. The legs." He paused for effect. "The thighs." He paused again. "The *breasts*."

Rosita shot him a look.

"You *were* talking about chicken, weren't you?" Conor laughed. "Speaking of chicken, I'm starving."

They settled in at the Café Edison on Forty-seventh Street.

"How you holding up?" Conor asked.

Rosita was hunched over a cup of coffee. "Fading. But the coffee helps."

"You want to go home?"

"Not yet. The best way to turn a tour around is to hang in as long as possible." She took a sip of coffee. "So where are we?"

"Well, we've got bidi-smoking, diamond-cutting Arun Punjabi. Silberman, the lovesick admirer with a sprained wrist. Kruger, the

South African Scorpion. Then there's the tenement roof where anybody could've gotten into the loft."

"What's your guess?"

"My guess? Don't really have one."

"But if you had to guess. Who would it be?"

"I'm thinking it's becoming more and more obvious that whoever killed Zivah Gavish gained access from the tenement roof."

"Some crackhead."

"Maybe," Conor said. "Or Kruger."

"Kruger?"

"Sure. He's a rogue cop. Once a rogue, always a rogue. Plus, to be part of a unit like the Scorpions, he's got to be highly trained. Remember the police academy? The obstacle courses. Scaling walls, rappelling off buildings. I'd bet Kruger went through a lot worse. So climbing onto the terrace from the roof would be nothing to Kruger." He paused, replayed something in his head. "The only problem is the camera. Kruger had no way of knowing it wasn't working and he was too smart to have missed it hanging above him."

"Maybe he wore a mask."

"Possible. But that would mean he brought a mask with him."

"Be prepared. Isn't that the Boy Scout motto?"

"Kruger's no Boy Scout, that much I'm sure of."

Conor rubbed his eyes, thinking. When he had viewed the security video from the loft, an Indian man had visited the building on the Friday before Zivah Gavish was killed. Could it have been Punjabi?

"What?" Rosita wanted to know.

"Arun Punjabi."

Rosita snapped her fingers. "Arun Punjabi smokes bidis. A bidi was found in a planter on the victim's roof. So maybe we can connect him to the scene."

"That depends."

"On what?"

"Arun Punjabi's answer to one simple question."

Chapter Twenty-six

"**H**ave I ever been to Zivah Gavish's apartment?" Arun Punjabi repeated. "Why, yes. I have."

His response rendered the little bidi, which upon its discovery had promised so much as a piece of evidence, nothing more than an Indian cigarette discarded by someone who admitted being there.

"I stopped by to show her some new pieces we had just cut. On Friday I believe it was."

Arun Punjabi was an elegant man. Medium height, brown skin, intense eyes. He was impeccably dressed in a tailored gray plaid suit, English cut. His office, in a high-rise building on Forty-seventh Street near Fifth Avenue, was small and somewhat claustrophobic, divided into two rooms. Punjabi conducted business in one room, from behind a cluttered desk. The other contained a long bench lined with several diamond-cutting devices, each made up of a viselike grip to hold the stone and a spinning disk that actually cut the gem. A young Indian man was staring intently at one of the machines.

Given the value of the inventory, gaining access to the office was a two-step process. First a visitor was buzzed into a tiny vestibule. Then, in order for someone to actually enter the office, the outer door had to be shut and locked. Only then would the inner door open.

"I must say," Punjabi said, "I am shocked by what happened."

"Do you smoke bidis?" Conor asked abruptly.

Punjabi was mildly surprised. "That's an odd question, Detective." He stared down at his desk, as if he was formulating a careful response. "Yes, I do smoke bidis." He looked up at Conor. "It's a terrible habit. One I cannot seem to break."

"When you visited Ms. Gavish," Rosita began, "did you happen to smoke one?"

Punjabi once again stared down at his desk before answering. "Yes. She got a phone call so I went out onto the terrace to give her privacy. And also to smoke a bidi." He held up two fingers, pantomiming smoking a cigarette. "When I finished, I was going to toss it on the street but there were people walking by so I went to the side and looked down onto the roof of a building. There was a man on the roof. So I just crushed the butt out in the planter."

Punjabi's story felt contrived, Conor thought, too detailed. The people on the street, the man on the roof, putting the bidi out in the planter. All Rosita had asked him was if he had smoked a bidi at Zivah's apartment, not how or where he had extinguished it. But by being so specific, Punjabi had inadvertently acknowledged that he was aware of the abandoned tenement and therefore also aware that it represented a potential entry into the loft via the terrace.

Rosita followed up with another question. "Can you describe the man you saw on the roof?"

"No. I'm sorry. I was unable to get a good look at him."

Conor decided to up the stakes. "Mr. Punjabi. May I ask where you were last night?"

Punjabi appeared taken aback. "You want to know where I was last night?" His eyelids fluttered nervously. "Surely you don't think—"

"No," Conor assured him. "We're just gathering information, filling in the blanks. So, if you don't mind . . ."

"I was attending the diamond dealers' dinner. At the Crowne Plaza. I arrived just before six and left at nine thirty."

"And between five and six?" Conor pressed.

"I was here, in the office, until quarter to six. Then I walked to the Crowne Plaza."

Rosita wandered into the other room. The young Indian man looked up at her.

"That's interesting." Rosita leaned over and examined one of the cutting machines. A spinning metal disk, attached to the end of a thin metal arm, periodically made incremental cuts into the rough stone. This caused a cascade of fine powder to rain down into a small dish-like container.

"Your diamond cutter will confirm that?" Conor asked Punjabi.

"No. He leaves at five." Punjabi was now concerned. "Should I call a lawyer, Detective?"

"If you feel you need one," Conor replied as he walked into the diamond-cutting room.

"I've done nothing wrong," Punjabi insisted as he followed Conor. "But these questions . . ."

"What's that?" Conor asked the young Indian man.

The young Indian man was clearly uncomfortable. He glanced at Punjabi as if to ask what he should say.

"That's a diamond-cutting apparatus," Punjabi answered.

Conor pointed at the trail of fine powder falling away from the rough stone each time the disk made contact. "No, I mean that."

"Diamond dust," Punjabi replied.

"Diamond dust?" Conor frowned. "Isn't that valuable?"

Punjabi nodded at the young Indian man, indicating it was all right to answer.

"Only diamond can cut diamond," the young Indian man said. He picked up a disk that was lying on the bench. "We coat the edge of the metal disk with diamond dust."

Punjabi shifted his feet impatiently. "Detective. I have an appointment in ten—"

"We're done," Conor cut in. "Thank you for your time."

Punjabi ushered them to the door. "If there's anything I can do, please let me know." He was relaxed now, apparently relieved he had survived an interview with police. "Zivah was an absolute delight. I would hate to see her killer not be brought to justice."

Conor and Rosita entered the precinct. Conor found a stack of file folders on his already cluttered desk.

"What are those?" Rosita asked.

"Crime scene photos." Conor fanned the folders out like a deck of cards, then flipped one of them open.

Besides general shots, there were photos of various pieces of evidence, labeled according to the location where the items were found: *Kitchen counter. Coffee table. Contents of kitchen trash can. Terrace. Console table in foyer. Master bathroom.* There looked to be around twenty folders containing hundreds of pages.

Rosita pulled out a chair and slid behind her desk. "So we *can* place Punjabi at the scene. But the question is, when? He says it was just on Friday."

Conor removed his cell phone from his jacket and dialed.

"Are there any developments?" Kruger wanted to know when he heard Conor's voice.

"Actually, no. But I have a question. You told me Zivah Gavish sent an e-mail last Friday with a photo of the red diamond attached. What time was that?"

"Hold on."

Conor could hear computer keys clacking.

"Three forty-one," Kruger said.

"Thanks."

"Why do you want to know?" Kruger asked suspiciously.

"Just trying to build a timeline."

There was a long pause before Kruger spoke. "All right. Keep me posted on your progress."

"I will. Anything on your end?"

"No. Not yet."

Conor dropped into his chair, removed the DVD of security video from a drawer, and slid it into the computer. Rosita got up, walked over, and stood behind him.

Conor chose FRIDAY from the DVD menu. "Let's see when Punjabi got there." As it turned out, Punjabi arrived at three seventeen and left at three thirty-five.

"He didn't stay very long," Rosita noted.

"Eighteen minutes," Conor noted. "Long enough to deliver a red diamond."

Chapter Twenty-seven

Arun Punjabi was shaping up to be a viable suspect, if not in the murder of Zivah Gavish, certainly in the cutting, transport, and sale of a diamond of extraordinary value and dubious provenance.

"Punjabi would be a nice collar," Conor remarked.

"You really think he killed Zivah Gavish?" Rosita asked.

"I meant as a smuggler. We prove he imported the diamond illegally, turn the case over to Customs, and get a nice write-up in the file." He shook a finger at Rosita. "You've got to think about these things, Rubio. You want to make Detective Second Grade one of these days, don't you?"

"Sure." She yawned.

"You're done for the day."

"I'm all right."

"No, you're not." He stood. "I need you to be sharp, Rubio. Come on. I'll drive you home."

Conor's cell phone rang. He checked the caller ID. It was Jimmy, the confidential informant.

"Bard."

"Detective. It's Jimmy. I think I saw that guy."

Conor's heart began to pound. Did he mean Hicks?

"Who are you talking about, Jimmy?"

"That guy! The one in the mug shot you gave me! I think I saw him!"

"You *think*?"

"I don't know," Jimmy whined. "I didn't get a good look at him. But I'm pretty sure it was him."

"Where?"

"On Broadway. Hundred and Seventy-second."

"Is that where you are now?"

"Yeah."

"Stay there. I'm on my way." Conor snapped the cell phone shut, concern written all over his face.

"What happened?" Rosita asked.

Conor removed his wallet and flipped it open. John Hicks's face stared out from behind a clear plastic sleeve.

"You have a *mug* shot in your wallet?" she asked, surprised.

"That's what I asked Ralph our first day. Ralph always carried mug shots in his wallet."

"And now *you* do. How fucked-up is that?" She took a closer look at the photo. "Ugly son of a bitch. Who is it?"

"Name is John Hicks."

"And how did Mr. Hicks earn a spot on the Conor Bard most wanted list?"

How much to tell his new partner? Almost anything he said could lead to a host of questions he didn't really want to answer. "I know the victim's sister."

"Want to tell me about it?" she asked.

"Maybe some other time."

"Give me a copy of the mug shot. I'll stick it in my purse. Okay?"

"Yeah. That would be great. You live uptown, don't you?" Conor started walking away.

"A Hundred and Tenth."

"Good. That's on the way."

"On the way to where?" Rosita asked as she caught up with him.

"That was Jimmy. A CI in Washington Heights. He may have spotted Hicks."

"Really? Then I'm coming with you."

"You're tired."

"You can drop me home after we meet your CI," Rosita insisted. "This guy Hicks? He's dangerous, right?"

Conor laughed. "So you're coming along to protect me?"

"Somebody's got to."

Conor and Rosita found Jimmy pacing nervously on the corner of Broadway and 172nd Street. He was a small man, mixed race, with sticks for arms and legs. It was impossible to guess how old Jimmy was—he once told Conor he was thirty-five—but at times he looked either much older or much younger.

Jimmy frowned at Rosita and then at Conor. "Why'd you bring your girlfriend? This is serious, man. *Serious.*"

"She's not my girlfriend, Jimmy."

"I'm Detective Rubio. You got a problem with that?"

Jimmy shrunk away. "No, no. No problem."

"So what's the deal, Jimmy?" Conor asked.

Jimmy pointed across the street. "I was over at the Western Union. My cousin down in Virginia wired me some money." He glanced at Conor. "Speaking of money . . ."

"Look, Jimmy. I don't have all day. I'm in the middle of a homicide investigation."

Jimmy brightened. "You need help with that?"

"No, I don't. Now tell me about this person you saw."

"Okay, okay. Anyway, I happened to look out the window and there was this guy. I could've sworn it was the guy in the mug shot."

Rosita stepped up close to Jimmy. "Nobody's asking you to swear. Was it our perp or not?"

Jimmy seemed confused, unsure how to play her. "He was walking fast and I—"

Rosita grinned. "So you really don't know *who* it was, do you?"

"It *looked* like him," Jimmy said, now completely intimidated.

"And people say I look like Eva Longoria." Rosita turned toward Conor. "What do you want to do?"

"We came all the way up here. Might as well check it out."

They started walking toward the car. Jimmy ran after them.

"Come on, Detective, how about a little something?"

"I thought you said your cousin just wired you some money," Conor replied.

"Not a lot."

Conor reached into his pocket, pulled out a ten, and handed it to Jimmy.

Jimmy stuffed the cash in his pocket. "I hope that was your guy."

"Yeah," Conor said. "Me too."

Jimmy hurried down the street. Conor and Rosita climbed into the car, Conor behind the wheel.

"You think he really saw Hicks?" Rosita asked.

"Probably not."

"So why'd you give him money?"

Conor started the engine. "To keep him interested."

They cruised the neighborhood for half an hour, grid-style, uptown, across town, downtown, then back across town. No John Hicks. But Conor wasn't really expecting to find Hicks so easily.

"You're on the run long enough," Conor observed, "you can smell cops."

Conor drove to East 110th Street, where Rosita lived. She dozed most of the way downtown.

"So was it good for you?" he asked as she opened the car door.

"Was what good?"

"Your first day as my partner. A little bit of heaven, huh?"

She mockingly blew him a kiss. "You took the words right out of my mouth."

"See you in the morning."

"I can't wait."

As he watched her walk away, he was forced to admit, though he had spent only a few hours with her, she had somehow made the job less routine. He enjoyed having a female around. Even though she was just one of the guys.

Conor contacted Kingston and made arrangements to meet him at the homicide squad. Then he called Ross Marks at the FBI.

"What do you know about Scorpions?" Conor asked.

"I know they have a poison stinger."

"Well, I've got one and I'm wondering just how poisonous he is. Name is Hendrik Kruger. He's with SAPS now."

"I've got a contact at the South African consulate," Marks offered. "I'll check it out."

"Thanks. And see what you can dig up about a man named Wouter Marwala. According to Kruger, he's a smuggler. Gems, dope, whatever."

"I've got bad news and I've got bad news," Kingston said. "Which do you want first?"

"What the hell," Conor replied. "Give me the bad news."

"The bad news is, there are no security cameras on the street covering the tenement."

Why do neighborhoods resist the installation of an NYPD camera? Conor wondered. It would be so much easier to fight crime if there were a video record of it.

"Okay. What's the other bad news?" Conor asked.

"I talked to a lot of people on Forty-fourth Street. Residents. Business owners. The place next door to the yarn factory? Crash pad for a lot of bad guys. Neighborhood board has been trying to get the building torn down for years. We've got the place staked out but so far nobody's shown up."

"Well, if they do, lock them up, trespassing, public drunkenness, aggressive panhandling, whatever it takes to detain them until I can get there."

"Don't worry. Somebody goes in that building, their next stop is a holding cell."

Conor told Kingston about the diamond dealers' dinner at the Crowne Plaza and that Stanley Silberman, Arun Punjabi, Sulaiman Aziz, and Kruger all claimed to have been in attendance.

"I'll contact the Crowne Plaza," Kingston said. "And arrange for you to look at the security video."

Exactly when Silberman, Punjabi, Kruger, and Aziz, for that matter, entered the hotel was important. Zivah had returned to the loft at 5:36. If any of the men had arrived at the Crowne Plaza at six or earlier, it would greatly reduce their window of opportunity and maybe even eliminate them as suspects.

Kingston scratched his head. "I can understand you looking at Silberman, Aziz, and Punjabi. But *Kruger*?"

"I don't know, Tony, there's something about the guy. Everything he tells me feels wrong. Like he's playing some kind of game. This morning he e-mailed me a list of people he claims are Wouter Marwala's known associates. Fifty of them. Are they really possible suspects? Or is the list a diversion?"

"We probably should check out the names anyway."

"Exactly. Kruger knew we wouldn't ignore leads in a case like this, right? That's what I mean. Chasing down information on those fifty people will take manpower. And it shifts the spotlight away from him."

"Could be he's just trying to help," Kingston suggested.

"Maybe. But our agenda is to catch a killer. His agenda is to bring down Marwala. By providing the list of Marwala's contacts he's letting us do the heavy lifting in *his* case."

Kingston nodded an acknowledgment. "All right, let me get going on all this."

"There's more," Conor said. "Several deliverymen were in and out of the loft the day Zivah Gavish was killed."

"You're thinking one of them could have cased the place then gone back in through the tenement?"

"That's precisely what I'm thinking. I'll get you a DVD of the security video from the loft."

"A lot of suspects," Kingston observed.

"I know." Conor looked at Kingston. "By the way, where were you on Monday night between five and eight?"

"I was with Kruger," Kingston quipped.

Chapter Twenty-eight

It was five o'clock and rush-hour traffic clogged the West Side Highway as Conor drove uptown. He truly was wiped out so he decided he'd drop the car off at the precinct then head home. Things were percolating. Kingston and Marks would get back to him the next day. There would be a lot of ground to cover. Better to start fresh.

As he approached the precinct, his cell phone rang. He checked the caller ID—Richard Shorter.

Conor flipped open the phone. "Hey, Richard, what's up?"

"I'm in town. Over at Colony Records picking up some music. What are you doing?"

"Getting ready to call it a day. Or call it two days. Haven't slept much since last night."

"Got time to grab a coffee before I head back to Jersey?"

Conor wanted to decline. But he felt an obligation. Richard hardly ever came to the city except for the gigs.

"Sure," Conor said. "Meet you at Colony in five minutes."

*   *   *

CRYSTAL DEATH

Conor walked to Colony Records on the corner of Forty-ninth Street and Broadway. The Times Square landmark had been there for sixty years. Colony's collection of sheet music was the best in the city and if you were looking for even the most obscure CD, Colony would have it. Their slogan was: I Found It! At the Colony. As he drifted down an aisle, he had a bout of anxiety. *Will I ever have a CD on the shelf? Am I kidding myself?*

Richard, carrying a shopping bag, approached Conor.

"What did you buy?" Conor asked.

"A new fake book," he replied.

Fake books are a musician's bible, containing the music sheets for hundreds of songs and updated periodically to include the latest hits.

Conor and Richard walked out of the store.

"Let's go over there." Conor pointed across the street at Mama Sbarro, a buffet-style eatery that also had pasta and pizza. Whenever he was in a hurry, he'd duck in the place and fill a plate from the buffet. He could have meat loaf, vegetables, potato, salad, the works, all for under ten dollars and in less than ten minutes.

When they walked into Mama Sbarro, Scott, the manager, greeted them. "Hey, Conor. How you doing?"

"Good, Scott. You?"

"Can't complain."

Scott drifted away.

Richard shook his head. "You know what amazes me about you? No matter where we go, you know the owner or the manager."

"Yeah, well, this is my hood."

Conor bought a double espresso. Richard opted for a bottle of sparkling water.

"Gordon's joining another band," Richard said.

Conor wasn't shocked. It was inevitable, given the nature of the situation.

"How about Peter?"

"He's cool for now."

117

The operative words were *for now*. Peter was too good a drummer to hang around without a schedule of gigs.

Conor took a sip of espresso. "Guess you didn't hear from Alan Woodcliff."

"Hey, man, give him time. He'll call."

Yeah. Right. He'll call. Conor felt a sudden rush of reality. His music career was slipping away. Day by day. No, minute by minute. It was getting harder to live in denial.

Chapter Twenty-nine

When Conor got back to the precinct, Amanda waved him into her office. She was on the phone.

"Mr. Silberman, please hold on." She hit the Hold button and looked at Conor. "It's Stanley Silberman. He's pretty upset."

"About what?"

"Zivah Gavish's body. He wants it released."

"I was with the ME this morning," Conor said. "He told me he was going to release the body."

"So what's the holdup?"

"I don't know." Conor started out of the office. "Let me talk to Silberman."

Conor walked to his desk, dropped in his chair, and grabbed the phone. "Mr. Silberman. It's Detective Bard."

"Detective Bard!" Silberman was near hysteria. "What's happening with Zivah's body?"

"Mr. Silberman. The medical examiner indicated to me that he would release the body today."

"I've tried reaching him but he won't return my calls."

"He's a very busy man, Mr. Silberman."

"Please, Detective. Zivah needs to be buried as soon as possible.

Her parents are arriving tonight and they expect to fly back to Israel with their daughter tomorrow."

"I understand," Conor said. "Where can I reach you, Mr. Silberman?"

Silberman gave Conor the number.

"I'll call you right back," Conor assured him.

Conor dialed the ME's office. "It's Detective Bard. I need to speak with Selzer."

The call was transferred. "Hey, Bard. What's up?"

"I just got off the phone with Stanley Silberman."

"Silberman? The guy's a nut job. Left me four messages in the last hour."

"So what's the situation with Zivah Gavish's body?"

"I'm ready to release it but not to Silberman. He's not a relative, not a husband. He has no legal standing. Rabbi Burstein said the parents were flying in. When they arrive, the body will be released to them. Would you please impart that bit of information to Mr. Silberman? And tell him to stop calling me."

Silberman sounded somehow hurt when Conor informed him that the body would not be entrusted to his care.

"I only want to do the right thing by Zivah," Silberman insisted.

Conor finally got Silberman off the phone. *Why is Silberman in such a hurry to get Zivah Gavish's body out of the country?* Was it really just for religious reasons? Or was key evidence in the homicide about to be buried in the desert?

As Conor pushed out of his chair to head home, he looked up and saw Rooney approaching.

"Can I see you a minute?" Rooney asked. "In my office."

"Sure." Conor looked at Rooney's face. Something was wrong.

They started across the room.

"Things are going well with the investigation," Conor said. "I just met with Kingston at the homicide squad and—"

"This is not about the case."

Not about the case? Conor was suddenly concerned. *That doesn't sound so good.*

When they entered the office, Rooney shut the door and got right to the point. "I got a call from IAB a little while ago."

"Internal Affairs? What's their problem this time?"

"*You* are," Rooney replied.

Chapter Thirty

"**M**e? Why?" But Conor knew why. It was only a matter of time before some ambitious IAB cop made a move.

"That bar where you play. It's a licensed establishment."

Conor sighed. Technically, a cop can't work at a place with a liquor license. But Conor never thought of himself as *working* at the Rhythm Bar—he was *performing*.

"Lieutenant, I—"

"Listen, Bard. I don't give a fuck. I got enough problems without trying to figure out which one of you guys is working at a bar."

"Okay. What do I need to do?"

"Talk to Danny Hahn," Rooney replied. "Let him handle this."

Danny Hahn was the union delegate, an elected position within NYPD. He was responsible for mitigating problems among the rank and file.

"All right. I will."

Conor left Rooney's office with a knot in his stomach. The job was sabotaging his music career at every turn.

* * *

As Conor walked from the precinct toward his apartment, his cell phone rang. He smiled when he checked the caller ID. It was Ralph, his ex-partner. He and Ralph had developed a rapport over the nearly twenty years they were together. When Ralph was forced into retirement from the regular police force a year ago, he had gotten a job on the district attorney squad, where they didn't have a mandatory retirement age.

Conor snapped open the phone. "Hey, you old dog, what's up?"

"Heard you caught the diamond dealer case. One of my ADAs told me."

"Yeah."

"How's it going?"

"Moving right along."

"So you're dead in the water?"

"Exactly."

"That's because you will never solve a case without me. Want to have dinner?"

Conor was tired. But he really wanted to see Ralph. And besides, he had to eat. "Where you want to go?"

"How about La Mela?"

La Mela was in Little Italy, just around the corner from Ralph's office. Conor dined there often and knew the owner, Frankie Cee. Ralph, given the proximity of the DA squad, was there almost every night.

"I've got another hour of paperwork," Ralph said. "How about we meet at seven thirty?"

It'll be good to see the old geezer, Conor thought as he snapped the phone shut. But this wasn't going to be simply a reunion dinner. They'd be in a brainstorming session about the case. Plus, he wanted to speak with Ralph about the IAB situation.

It was six o'clock. Conor considered stopping by his apartment but realized that if he lay down on the couch, he'd probably be out for hours. His cell phone rang. It was Rosita.

"Hey, Rubio. Why aren't you asleep?"

"I was. But then I got a call."

"From who?"

"Kenneth Madison."

"I suppose he was looking for grief counseling," Conor said without sparing the sarcasm.

"No. He was looking for you."

"For *me*?"

"Yeah," Rosita said. "Ain't that a bitch. I give a guy *my* cell phone number and he calls me for *your* cell phone number."

"Did he say what he wanted?"

"No. Maybe it's some guy thing. Anyway, I didn't want to give him your cell, so I took down his."

Conor jotted down the number then hung up and dialed Madison.

"Mr. Madison. My partner said you were looking for me."

"Yes," Madison replied. "Do you have time for a drink?"

"Actually, I'm meeting someone for dinner. What did you want to talk about, Mr. Madison?"

"I'd prefer if we spoke in person," Madison countered. "I'm in my car so I can give you a lift wherever you like."

"Okay," Conor said, now intrigued.

Chapter Thirty-one

A custom-built Mercedes limousine glided to a stop at the corner of Forty-eighth and Broadway. A moment later, a chauffeur bounded from the car and opened the rear door.

"Thank you, Detective," Madison said as Conor climbed into the backseat. "I wouldn't have bothered you if it wasn't important."

"No problem."

The chauffeur closed the door and returned to his post behind the wheel. "Where are we going, sir?" the chauffeur wanted to know.

"One six seven Mulberry Street," Conor replied. "Restaurant called La Mela."

"One sixty-seven Mulberry," the chauffeur repeated as he raised the glass partition between the front and back.

"Would you like something to drink?" Madison asked.

Conor shrugged. "Sure. Why not?" He eyed a bottle of Grey Goose. "You don't have ice, do you?"

"Of course." Madison lifted a lid in a center island to reveal a container of ice.

"A little Grey Goose on the rocks would be great," Conor said.

Madison removed a couple of ice cubes, placed them in a cocktail glass, then poured a double shot of vodka. He handed it to

Conor then picked up his own glass, which was filled with amber liquid.

"Cheers," Madison said.

"Cheers," Conor echoed.

"I prefer scotch," Madison noted. "You know what a Scotsman I know says about vodka? Odorless, flavorless liquid consumed by the brainless." Madison patted Conor's shoulder. "I don't mean you, Detective." He studied Conor. "What's your background?"

"Scottish and Irish."

"Well, there you go. You should be drinking scotch." Madison held up his glass. "Glenfiddich twenty-one-year-old. The first thing I did when Zivah moved in was make sure there was a bottle in the house." He smiled sadly. "Zivah preferred wine. Israeli wine. You ever have Israeli wine?"

"No."

Madison shuddered. "It's terrible. Well, it's not terrible really, but if you compare it to a fine Bordeaux or Burgundy . . . Anyway, Zivah loved Israeli wine." His voice trailed off as he drifted back in time.

"So, Mr. Madison . . ."

"Please. Call me Kenneth."

"Okay, Kenneth. Why did you want to see me?"

Madison took a sip of scotch, savored it. "A couple of reasons, actually. Remember I told you about the guy on the roof with the streak of white hair?"

Conor took a deliberate sip of vodka. "Yes."

"I couldn't sleep last night. So I got up and got dressed and was halfway out the door . . ." Madison took a deep breath. "I almost went over to Forty-fourth Street. I was going to stake out the loft, see if that guy turned up and—"

Conor wasn't happy. "Mr. Madison—"

"Kenneth."

"Kenneth. That's not good. You shouldn't even be thinking—"

"I know, I know. That's why I didn't go. But I wanted to find that guy and"—Madison's face contorted—"I can't stand the thought that some monster—"

"Kenneth. Please. Leave the investigation to us. If you start—"

"I can't help it. I feel like I have to do *something*."

Conor and Madison took a moment.

"I'd like to contact Zivah's parents," Madison said, calming down a little. "I want to offer them my plane to fly home with Zivah."

"That's very generous of you," Conor observed.

"The truth is, my plane, it's a Gulfstream Four, is due for maintenance in Switzerland. So it's not a big deal to stop in Israel. I'd do it anyway, fly Zivah home, but the timing happens to work."

"A rabbi named Burstein has been in touch with her parents. I'll ask him to call you." Conor looked at Madison. "You said there were a couple of reasons you wanted to talk to me. Anything else?"

"I want to sell the loft as soon as possible," Madison said. "I don't want anything to do with it. I don't care what I get for it. I'll take a loss. I just"—he clenched his fists—"I wish I'd never bought the damned place . . ."

"How can I help, Kenneth?"

"I have a buyer interested in the loft, and in this market, when you have someone interested, you've got to close the deal. Do you have any idea when I might be able to get in there?"

Releasing a crime scene was up to the detective who caught the case—as long as the Crime Scene Unit and DA concurred it was appropriate.

"I see no reason why we can't release the apartment tomorrow," Conor said.

"Please. Don't get me wrong. Do whatever is necessary. But as long as I hold title—"

"I understand."

"I'm not sure you do," Madison countered. "May I be honest with you?"

Conor nodded.

"I'm a decent-looking guy. I stay in shape. I've never had a problem attracting women. Add a few billion dollars and, well, you get the idea."

"Yes, I do." The Beatles song "Baby, You're a Rich Man" filled Conor's head. *How does it feel to be . . . one of the beautiful people?*

"I love women," Madison continued. "And I have access to the most spectacular women in the world."

Spread the wealth, Conor almost said.

"So I wine and dine them, buy them presents, take them to Rome or Paris for the weekend."

Never mind, Conor thought. *I can barely afford to drive to Rome, New York.*

"In some ways," Madison admitted, "it's a transaction. I want what they have and they want what I have. So when I met Zivah, I wasn't exactly sitting at home pining away. Anyway, Zivah was different from the gold diggers I usually attract. She was making her own money, never asked me for anything. When I did try to buy her something expensive—an Hermès pocketbook—she refused it. Told me to take it back to the store."

"Did you?"

"No. I gave it to a busty brunette who had no problem accepting it as payment for future services." Madison smiled. "But with Zivah, it wasn't just about the sex. She was wonderful to talk to. Funny. Charming. Smart. In fact, I was beginning to worry that I was falling in love. Which wouldn't have been terrible. It's just that I'm thirty-six and have all these possibilities. I didn't want to be in a serious relationship. Maybe when I'm forty I'll feel differently."

Conor almost laughed. The way Madison said *forty*, it sounded ancient. "I'm past forty and I still think like you do."

"So you understand?"

"Definitely."

"You realize, then, with several women in your life, you get several sets of problems."

Conor raised his glass. "I'm with you on that one."

"If I'd never met Zivah," Madison said, "I wouldn't have this sick feeling in my gut right now. But I do. Even though we weren't in a monogamous relationship, there were possibilities. Whoever killed Zivah took away a potential future I might have had with her. It hurts. And there are only two things that will help this ache in me right now: getting rid of the place where Zivah was killed. And seeing whoever did this die on a gurney with needles stuck in his arm."

Madison appeared lost somewhere between rage and sorrow.

Maybe Rubio is right, Conor thought. *Maybe Madison does need some sort of counseling.*

They rode in silence for a few blocks.

"Are you free on Thursday?" Madison asked. "Six o'clock?"

"What's happening on Thursday?"

"I had arranged a birthday party for Zivah. After what happened, my immediate reaction was to cancel it. But I remember one conversation I had with her and she said: 'If anything happens to me, I don't want sadness when I'm remembered. I want a celebration.' So instead of a birthday party, I'm having a memorial service for Zivah. A celebration."

A memorial service? Conor found the prospect of being in the same room with Zivah's friends and associates an appealing one from an investigative standpoint. A chance to observe her inner circle. Madison gave Conor the location, a bar called Le Lounge in the East Village.

The limousine stopped at a traffic light on Mulberry and Grand streets.

"I'll get out here," Conor said. "The restaurant's just down the block."

Madison pressed a button and lowered the glass partition. "David. Detective Bard will be getting out here."

The chauffeur quickly unhooked his seat belt, climbed out of the front seat, and opened the back door.

"So I'll see you Thursday?" Madison asked.

"I'll be there," Conor replied.

Chapter Thirty-two

Ralph Kurtz was waiting when Conor entered La Mela. Sixty-three years old, five feet eleven, a little overweight, Ralph was wearing a suit that looked like he had slept in it. But that was Ralph, definitely no fashionista. He was sitting at a table with Frankie Cee. Frankie, also in his sixties, was the unofficial mayor of Mulberry Street. Anybody who was anybody made it a point to stop into La Mela when they ventured to Little Italy. As a result, the restaurant was often filled with celebrities and others who perhaps would rather not discuss their occupations.

Ralph stood, embraced Conor. "Hey, kid."

Conor was genuinely happy to see Ralph. Since Ralph had retired a year before and started working at the DA squad, they had stayed in touch, gotten together once in a while. But Ralph lived on Staten Island and worked in Lower Manhattan, so despite the best intentions, their weekly get-togethers had quickly become geographically inconvenient. Conor realized that they hadn't seen each other for almost two months.

"You look terrible," Ralph said as they sat down.

"Thanks for noticing."

"He's right," Frankie chimed in. "What's the story? Some woman putting you through the ringer?"

"A *dead* woman," Conor replied. "Caught a helluva case. Haven't slept much the past couple of days."

Ralph looked at Frankie. "Guess that's why he invited me to dinner. He needs my help."

"*I* invited *you* to dinner?" Conor protested. "I thought *you* invited *me* to dinner."

"Yeah, I guess I did," Ralph allowed. "But that's only because I could tell by your voice you desperately needed my help."

Frankie pushed himself away from the table. "I don't care who invited who to dinner. What do you want to eat? Meat? Fish?"

"I'll eat anything," Ralph said.

"How about a salad?" Frankie asked. "And then some codfish."

Ralph brightened. "Yeah, yeah. That's great, Frankie." He looked at Conor. "You ever had Frankie's codfish?"

Conor had. It wasn't on the menu but Frankie cooked up special dishes once in a while for the regulars.

"Martini?" Frankie asked Conor.

"Yeah. Thanks."

Frankie stood and headed into the kitchen.

"Laura says hello," Ralph said.

Ralph and Laura had been married for thirty-six years. When she died three years ago, Ralph seemed to shrink in size. Now, whenever he visited her grave, he had these long conversations with her. And, according to Ralph, Laura always told him to say hello.

Ralph grabbed a stuffed mushroom from a platter of antipasti sitting on the table.

"You know what's funny," Conor began, "my new partner eats just like you do."

"Really?"

"Yeah. The other day we were at a diner and she ordered—"

"*She?*"

"Name's Rosita Rubio."

Ralph grimaced. "And I was hoping they'd give you some bozo so you'd realize how much you miss me."

"I do miss you, Ralph."

"She's not prettier than me, is she?"

"Definitely not."

"So, kid," Ralph said with a flourish, "tell me everything."

Chapter Thirty-three

"**B**efore I get into the case, something happened that really pisses me off." Conor recounted the IAB situation.

"Those bastards," Ralph growled, shaking his head.

"Rooney told me to talk to Danny Hahn."

"Danny's good at these things," Ralph assured him.

"I'll quit the job before I let some jerk tell me I can't play music in a bar."

"Just relax. Let Danny handle it." Ralph popped another stuffed mushroom into his mouth. "So what's up with your case?"

Conor gave Ralph the details, outlined the people involved, then handed him the photo of the red diamond.

Ralph tilted the photo into the light. "Beautiful."

"So I'm wondering if that was the target," Conor said, "or if the diamond just happened to be there."

"It was the target," Ralph offered with conviction. "What did we work? Two homicides in the diamond district involving the theft of gems? It was always about the diamonds. And in both cases, who did it? Somebody on the inside. Your killer was after this diamond. And from what you tell me, very few people knew about it. What you've got to do is find the motive."

"Priceless diamond? That's motive enough."

"Yes and no. This sounds like a setup and Zivah Gavish was the patsy." Ralph pointed his finger at Conor. "No doubt about it, this was a Diamond District death."

Conor stared glumly at Ralph. His old partner was right. It could've been an elaborate scheme to collect tens of millions of dollars and then retrieve the red diamond.

Ralph chuckled. "What's the matter, kid? Lost without me, right?"

Frankie returned to the table. "You guys done talking about business?"

"Yeah," Ralph said. "I was just giving him a refresher course in the Ralph Kurtz method of crime solving."

Conor walked into his apartment at eleven, snapped on the television, and lay down on the couch. At some point he drifted into a deep sleep, waking at four thirty in the morning. *Now what?* His schedule was totally screwed. He showered then made his way to the precinct, arriving at his desk at five fifteen. Rosita was there.

"You're up early," she said.

"Yeah. Fell asleep on the couch. What time you get here?"

"Three. It's going to take me a couple days to get my clock straightened out."

He noticed a bottle of spray cleaner and a roll of paper towels on the floor next to her chair.

"The desk was filthy," she explained. "Didn't your old partner ever clean it?"

"Yeah. I think Ralph cleaned it once about ten years ago. Steven wasn't here long enough to get it dirty." Conor dropped in his chair. "Had dinner with Ralph last night."

She looked up from her desk. "Really? How'd it go?"

"He's the same old smug son of a bitch he always was."

"He came up with something you hadn't thought of."

"Right."

He told her about Ralph's theory regarding a scheme to keep both the money and the diamond.

"Well, that *is* a possibility. He have anything else to say?"

"He wanted to know if you were prettier than he was."

"What'd you tell him?"

"I lied. I said no."

She tossed her hair with both hands. "You think I'm pretty?"

"For one of the guys, you're not bad."

"Thanks." She motioned to the bottle of spray cleaner. "Your desk could use a little of this."

"Caught a ride downtown with your boyfriend," Conor said. "Kenneth Madison. Limousine with a fully stocked bar."

"Sounds like your kind of guy."

"Actually, except for the billions, we're pretty much alike."

"And except for the fact I can't sing, I'm Whitney Houston."

Conor recounted his conversation with Madison.

Rosita was impressed. "Flying the body home on his private jet? That's a nice gesture."

"Yeah. I guess so."

She studied him. "What's wrong?"

"IAB."

She was alarmed. "Internal Affairs?"

He explained the situation.

"How you going to handle it?" she asked.

"I'm meeting with Danny Hahn, the union delegate. See if he can get IAB off my back."

"I'm sure it'll work out. I mean, it's not that big of a deal."

"I hope you're right."

Rosita looked down at a sheet of paper on her desk. "I made a list of a few things we probably should do." She paused. "If you think so, I mean."

"Shoot."

"Phone records on everybody. Zivah Gavish. Silberman. Punjabi."

"And we should take a look at Zivah Gavish's bank and credit card statements," Conor added.

"We already talked about getting Madison's E-ZPass account activity. Just to confirm that he drove to the Hamptons when he said he did. He probably used the Midtown Tunnel, so there would be a record of exactly when he passed through the toll booth."

"Right," he agreed. "I'll call Kingston later and get him working on it."

"And another thing. I was wondering if we should go over the DVD of security video from the victim's building. Not just the day she was killed, but all the footage we have."

"Good idea," Conor said.

They headed toward the media room.

"By the way, Rubio, Kenneth Madison is having a memorial service for Zivah Gavish. Tomorrow night. Six o'clock. At a place called Le Lounge."

"Judging from the name, I'd guess it's a lounge."

"I know. It's a little strange, right? But it was supposed to be her birthday party. Madison feels Zivah would have wanted him to go through with it."

"I'm glad you told me because I don't have a thing to wear to a memorial service at a lounge."

"You better go out and buy something."

"That's what I was thinking."

For the next two hours, they went through the DVD, starting with the oldest file, one week before the homicide. Zivah appeared periodically, always smiling, and every time her graceful image swept through the frame, Conor felt a twinge of emotion he was at a loss to identify. It wasn't sadness or anger, more like a longing for something. For what? To meet her? To get to know her, this woman who was constantly smiling, presumably happy every day? That opportunity would never come. But, no, that wasn't it. He realized his subconscious was dredging up images of Monica's sister, Besa, and the man who murdered her: John Hicks. Still a fugitive, still not brought to justice. Besa dead. Zivah dead. And no one in jail in either case. Yes, that's what he felt when he looked at Zivah. An anxiety that maybe Zivah's killer would not face justice just as John Hicks had not.

Conor moved to the file labeled SATURDAY. Zivah was in and out a couple of times. Madison arrived at eight thirty. He and Zivah left at nine fifteen. They didn't return that evening.

"Guess she spent the night at Trump Tower," Rosita said.

He switched to the SUNDAY file. Madison and Zivah. Three twenty Sunday afternoon. They went upstairs. Madison walked back through the lobby at five past four. Four thirty, Zivah left again. Returned at six thirty carrying shopping bags. Back out at seven forty-five. Home at eleven thirty.

"Where'd she go?" Rosita wondered aloud.

Conor pulled Zivah's iPhone from his pocket and navigated to the calendar. An entry on Sunday night read *8 PM. A.P. Dinner.* "AP? Arun Punjabi?"

If the initials *AP* stood for Arun Punjabi, then why hadn't Punjabi mentioned the fact that he had dinner with Zivah the night before she was killed? A bizarre omission. Unless he was hiding something.

"Want a bidi?" Conor asked. "I know where to find one."

Chapter Thirty-four

Punjabi stood, walked around his desk to where Conor and Rosita were standing. He was visibly shaken. "I suppose I should have mentioned it but I didn't think it was important."

Rosita's face filled with disbelief. "Not important? It was her last supper. And you didn't think it was important?"

"I have a business to run," Punjabi said. "I didn't want to get involved."

"Too late for that," Rosita fired back.

"May I ask how you learned of my dinner with Zivah?"

"You were listed in her appointment book," Conor explained.

Punjabi was clearly unnerved. "We had dinner, that's all. What do you want me to say?"

"I don't *want* you to say anything," Conor replied. "What I want is for you to tell us what happened."

"Nothing happened." Punjabi was alarmed. "What do you mean?"

"You had dinner with her," Conor pointed out. "Why?"

"Why?" Punjabi's mouth twitched. "Why?"

"That's the question, Mr. Punjabi," Rosita chimed in. "Why?"

"No particular reason," Punjabi said, obviously lying.

"So it was a date?" Conor asked.

"A date? Dear me, no. I have a wonderful wife in Mumbai. There was nothing inappropriate between me and Zivah."

"Where'd you go to dinner?" Rosita asked.

"Uccelli."

"That's an expensive place," Conor observed.

"The food is very good."

"It better be," Conor said. "At those prices."

"Who picked up the check?" Rosita wanted to know.

"I did."

Rosita curled her tongue in her cheek. "Just two business associates having dinner on a Sunday night. Is that what you're saying, Mr. Punjabi?"

Punjabi cleared his throat, swallowed. "Yes. That's all it was."

Conor and Rosita walked toward the car.

She looked at him. "Why don't you and me go to Uccelli tonight for dinner?"

"What are we going to do? Split an appetizer?"

They crossed the street and walked past a large store window. Conor stopped and stared through the glass at the collection of jewelry. Velvet trays full of rings. Necklaces hanging inside rectangular displays. Bracelets. Brooches. All manner of diamond-enhanced adornments. Yellow sunlight bounced off the individual stones, creating rainbow bursts of color.

"If you're thinking of getting me a birthday present," Rosita said as she joined Conor at the window, "the necklace on the top left would be perfect."

"I wonder how much that costs?" Conor asked rhetorically.

"Hey, Bard, I was just kidding."

"I know. But what makes one diamond worth more than another?"

"Size matters," she said with a smile.

"Yeah, but it's not just size, it's quality."

"Can't argue with that."

Conor turned and faced Rosita. "You know what would help us with this case? If I could sit down and talk to someone in the diamond business. Get a crash course."

"You know anybody?"

He concentrated hard. Then: "I should call that woman."

"What woman?"

"Tasha Sen. She knew both Punjabi and Zivah. So we could kill two birds with one stone."

Rosita rolled her eyes. Conor removed his phone and dialed.

"Hello?"

"Ms. Sen. It's Detective Conor Bard."

"How are you, Detective?"

"Just fine. I don't want to impose, but I was wondering if I could ask you a few questions about the diamond business."

"Sure. When?"

"Today, if that's possible."

"Oh, I'm sorry. Today isn't good. How about tonight?"

Conor didn't answer immediately. *Tonight? Even better.*

"What time is good for you?" he asked.

"How about eight thirty?"

"Great. I'll pick you up at—"

"Can we meet at the restaurant?"

"Sure." He gave her the address of Joe G's, an Italian restaurant on Fifty-sixth Street between Eighth Avenue and Broadway.

"See you later," she cooed.

Conor snapped the phone shut and looked at Rosita, who was staring straight ahead. "What?"

"Nothing."

"Look, Rubio. We'll sit her down and—"

"Not *we*. You. I'm still trying to turn my clock around. I'm sure you can handle the interview by yourself." She pulled at her hair. "Besides. I'm having a bad hair day."

"For me, every day is a bad hair day."

"You interview Tasha Sen solo."

"Okay, honey."

140

Her head snapped to the right. "What did you say?"

"I said, 'Okay, honey.'"

"You ever call Ralph honey?"

"No. But then again, I never heard him say he was having a bad hair day."

Conor's cell phone rang. It was Amanda.

"Hey, Sarge. What's up?"

"Got somebody here to see you," Amanda said.

"Who?"

"Zivah Gavish's parents."

Chapter Thirty-five

"I'm Detective Bard," Conor said as he and Rosita entered the conference room to find a man and woman, both around sixty, both dressed in black, both of their faces etched in pain. "And this is my partner, Detective Rubio."

The man stood. "I am Chaim Gavish. Zivah's father." Chaim motioned toward the woman. "My wife, Adina."

Conor wasn't sure what to say. "I'm sorry for your loss," he finally offered.

"We stopped by to tell you something," Chaim said. "If you will allow us."

"Of course," Conor replied.

Rosita stood silently, her eyes downcast.

Chaim waited a long moment before continuing. "When Adina and I married, we prayed for a child. And when that blessed day came, and Zivah was given to us, we rejoiced." He looked at Adina. "She was the most wonderful little girl, right, Adina?"

"So beautiful, so precious."

Chaim turned toward Conor again. "She took her first step when she was ten months old, spoke her first word before she was a year old." He reached over and took Adina's hand. "Remember?"

Adina squeezed his hand. "I do."

"Her first day at school," Chaim went on, "she came home so excited and told us everything she learned." He choked back tears. "And how my Zivah loved to learn. And to read. She was so smart, my Zivah was." He cleared his throat. "Her first date. Her first heartbreak. Her first job. Her first pet. All these things I remember. When it came time for her to go in the military, she didn't complain like the others. She proudly served her country. She had compassion. And intelligence. And personality. She was my joy, my comfort, my life." Tears began to roll down his cheeks. He looked at Adina. "Didn't she grow up to be a fine young woman?"

"Yes, she did." Adina reached over and rubbed Chaim's back, consoling him.

"I just wanted you to know that about my Zivah," Chaim said. "I wanted you to know she was a very special person."

Adina took Chaim's hand. "We must go now, Chaim. To the airport. The plane is waiting." She looked at Conor. "One of Zivah's friends, Kenneth Madison, has offered to fly us home with our daughter."

"Mr. Gavish," Conor began, "I promise you I will do everything in my power to—"

Chaim held up his hand, stopping Conor in midsentence.

"Do not promise anything to me. Promise only to yourself."

Conor escorted Chaim and Adina to the door. As he watched them walk slowly away, he tried to grasp how they must be feeling. The devastation of it, the hollowness. The encounter had filled him with a little of their grief. It was hard enough for him to remain detached without confronting the reality of those the deceased had left behind. Other cops he knew had no problem with compartmentalizing, avoiding any feelings about the victim. Why couldn't he? *Because I'm not really a cop. I'm a musician.* The mental state required to write a song or sing onstage meant digging deep, dredging up emotions. Which was the antithesis of a homicide investigation. Probably a different area of the brain was required, he reasoned, suddenly realizing that he spent his life jumping from one region of his psyche to the other and back again. *No wonder I'm fucked-up.*

Conor returned to find Rosita sitting at her desk. She was dabbing her eyes with a tissue. He was surprised that his tough-talking partner had been so deeply affected by the visit from Zivah's parents.

"Stop acting like a girl," Conor said.

Rosita sniffled. "You're right. I'm sorry." She crumpled the tissue and tossed it in the wastebasket. "Don't worry. It's my first time. I'll get used to it."

Conor didn't have the heart to tell her she never would.

Chapter Thirty-six

Conor stared across the room. "That's all I need right now."

She followed his eyes. "Who is it?"

"Clifford Stevens. He works for the developer of the building. I met him Monday night at the loft."

Stevens was wearing an expensive suit. No tie. Open shirt collar. A pair of smooth leather driving moccasins. He rushed over to Conor. "Detective, I'm glad I caught you."

"How are you, Mr. Stevens?"

"Not good. I was just speaking with the officers downstairs trying to find out what's going on with the investigation and I must tell you, they were extremely rude."

"I'm sorry, Mr. Stevens, but they aren't allowed to release information about an ongoing case."

Stevens tapped his foot. "Well, what *is* happening?"

"We're working on it."

"What does that mean?"

"It means we're working on it."

Stevens rubbed his forehead in obvious distress. "This needs to be resolved right away."

"I'm with you on that one."

"You have people looking into it, right? I mean, it's not just *you*, is it?"

Rosita stifled a laugh.

"No," Conor said. "It's not just me. We have people."

"I hope this is over soon." Stevens placed his left hand on his forehead. "We've already had one deal fall through. And I'm quite certain it's because—"

"That's too bad," Conor interrupted.

"You have any idea when you might release the apartment?" Stevens asked.

"It won't be long," Conor said flatly.

"We've got three units we want to show." Stevens checked his watch. "In fact, I've got an appointment in half an hour." He held his arms wide. "How can I show a place with police tape all over the building?" He produced a business card, handed it to Conor. "I'd appreciate it if you keep me apprised of the progress."

Conor took the card. "No problem."

"Thank you."

Stevens spun around and walked away.

Rosita laughed. "Oh, my God, what an idiot!"

Conor watched Stevens disappear around a corner. "Would you want to live in a building where somebody was murdered?"

"Hell, no."

"Why not?"

She wrinkled her nose. "Ghosts."

He looked at her. "You believe in ghosts?"

"Not really. But why tempt fate and live someplace where a ghost might be walking around?"

"Ghosts could be walking around anywhere."

"No," she countered. "Usually it's where they were killed."

"Thanks. I'm glad you cleared that up."

Conor decided he might as well release the apartment, assuming the DA and Crime Scene Unit concurred, which they did.

"The place is all yours," Brian said when Conor called him. "And if you find any loose diamonds under the couch, they're yours too."

Conor next phoned Madison and informed him that the loft had been released.

"Thank you, Detective," Madison said, relief in his voice.

Conor hung up the phone and looked at Rosita, who was yawning.

"Go home," he said. "You're making *me* tired."

She yawned again. "Yeah, maybe I will." She glanced at the wall clock. "I've been here twelve hours." She stifled another yawn. "Have fun on your hot date with Tasha Sen."

"It's not a date," he countered.

"Right."

"You think it's a date?"

"Okay. If it's not a date, what is it?"

"An interview," Conor insisted.

"For what position? Missionary?"

"I told you to come with me. If it was a date, would I have asked you to come?"

"Depends on how kinky you are."

He couldn't help himself. "So . . . have you ever . . ."

"Don't even go there, Bard."

"Okay. We won't go there."

She began straightening things on her desk. "What time you want to start tomorrow?"

"Normal time. Eight."

"All right. I just hope I can sleep past three in the morning."

"Take something," Conor suggested.

"Like what? You mean a sleeping pill?"

"Yeah."

"I hate those things. Rather have a shot of whiskey."

"Come on," Conor said. "I'll drop you at home."

They started walking toward the exit.

"The way I see it," Conor began, "we've got two possibilities."

"Number one, some lowlife from the tenement."

"Right. And then there are the people who might have targeted the diamond."

"Who would have benefited most from getting the diamond back?" Rosita wondered aloud.

"That's the seventy-million-dollar question," Conor observed.

Conor pulled to the curb on East 110th Street and looked at Rosita. "Don't come in before eight."

"Yes, sir."

"Seriously. I'm waiting for the sarge to have the overtime conversation with us."

"Even though this is a homicide?"

"Used to be different. You worked round the clock, racked up a big check. These days, the way the economy is, the city's watching every penny."

"Tell you what," Rosita said as she climbed out of the car, "I get there before eight, it's on me."

Conor drove west along 110th, across the north end of Central Park, and cruised down Columbus Avenue. His cell phone rang. He flipped it open. "Bard."

"Conor, Ross Marks. I've got some information for you."

"Great."

"I don't think you realize what you've gotten yourself into."

"What do you mean?"

"Hendrik Kruger is a cold-blooded killer."

Chapter Thirty-seven

Ross Marks greeted Conor in the lobby of the FBI field office on Tenth Avenue. Forty-seven years old, Marks was tall, six-four, with closely cropped dark brown hair.

"Conor, my boy, good to see you."

They embraced.

"Same here . . . I *think*."

"Don't kill the messenger," Marks said.

Marks led Conor through security.

"You have a new partner yet?" Marks asked.

"Yeah. Her name's Rosita Rubio."

"A woman? How's that working out?"

"So far so good."

They entered the elevator.

"Before we get into Kruger," Marks began, "let's talk about the other guy."

"Wouter Marwala?"

"He's on everybody's list," Marks observed. "And I mean *everybody*. Turns out we've got a unit at the Bureau tracking him and we're not alone. DEA is all over him. O'Brien at ATF told me Marwala's suspected of running guns. Immigration and Customs. Interpol. CIA.

MI5. Name a country, they've got law enforcement on Marwala's case."

"South Africa," Conor said.

"*Especially* South Africa."

"What about Kruger?"

"My contact at the consulate was very familiar with Mr. Kruger and his exploits as a member of the Scorpion unit."

The elevator stopped. They walked out into the hall.

"Kruger has been under investigation on several occasions for, shall we say, operating outside the parameters of South African law." Marks motioned Conor into his office. "On two of those occasions, a suspect was shot and killed."

Marks sat behind his desk. Conor sat across from him. "Rumor is," Marks continued, "Kruger mowed them down in cold blood. But the only witnesses to the shootings were other members of the Scorpion unit."

"Not very talkative."

"Hardly. Now, I don't want to sound like I'm issuing an indictment of the Scorpions—for my money it was one of the most effective police forces in the world—but there's no getting around the fact that Kruger doesn't like rules. And that the two suspects who were killed had, over time, become an obsession to Kruger."

"Just like Marwala is now." Something occurred to Conor. "If Kruger is so bad, how did he land at the South African Police Service?"

"Good question. Apparently he still wields power. Either that, or they were afraid to fire the guy. Better to put him where they can keep an eye on him."

"You said there was an agent at the Bureau assigned to Marwala. He have anything on Kruger?"

"Only as it pertains to Marwala. Apparently Kruger is in New York to pursue a valuable item belonging to Marwala."

"Do you know what the item is?"

Marks looked off. "I'm not at liberty to say."

"Can we speculate?"

"Sure," Marks replied. "Go ahead."

"Let's suppose this object is . . . oh, I don't know, something worth a lot of money, something rare." Conor paused. "How about a red diamond?"

Marks rubbed the back of his head. "Okay."

"What does Kruger want with this red diamond?"

Marks placed his elbows on the desk. "If I were to speculate, I'd say Kruger wants to use the red diamond as bait. To draw Marwala out into the open. Set some kind of trap."

"Yeah, but Kruger told me about the diamond. So if he stole it, why would he mention it to me in the first place?"

"Maybe Kruger knew you'd eventually find out about it," Marks speculated. "If you discovered it was missing at some point, Kruger would be a likely suspect. But once again, we're assuming Kruger has the red diamond."

Conor rubbed his eyes. "That's one hell of a scenario—Kruger the killer."

"You never considered that?"

"Sure. But only as a remote possibility. I mean, from the minute I saw him I felt he was capable of murder . . ."

"Now you know for sure," Marks said.

"So by telling me the red diamond existed, he made himself an ally instead of a suspect."

"Why else would Kruger mention the red diamond except to send you down the wrong path?"

"All this is very interesting," Conor allowed. "But my job is to solve a homicide, not track down a red diamond."

Marks drummed his fingers on his desk. "Looks like you can't do one without the other."

Chapter Thirty-eight

Conor drove up Tenth Avenue deep in thought. There was only one thing to do now: speak with Kruger, try to get inside his head.

"I was about to call you," Kruger said when Conor reached him on the phone. "There is something we need to discuss. Why don't we meet at that restaurant down the street from Xai Xai."

"You mean Braai?"

"Yes. Braai. I have a yearning for some South African wine."

It was just six o'clock and Braai was empty. Unlike the other restaurants in the area, Braai didn't cater to the pretheater tourist crowd, rather the regulars who filed in after eight. Conor was greeted by the manager, Tarita, a young woman in her thirties who had moved to New York from Canada and, like Tanya, the owner of both Xai Xai and Braai, was of Indian descent.

"You're early tonight, Conor."

"I'm meeting someone for a drink."

Conor thought about ordering a martini but opted for an espresso instead.

"An espresso?" Tarita was surprised. "You on the wagon?"

"No," Conor replied. "I've got a long night ahead of me, that's all."

"Don't you always?"

As Tarita drifted away, Conor wondered how to question Kruger. Be direct? Dance around the issue?

"I hope I didn't keep you waiting too long."

Conor looked up to see Kruger entering the bar.

"No, I just got here."

As Kruger sat across from Conor, Tarita reappeared. "Can I get you something to drink?"

"Do you have a good cabernet from the Stellenbosch region?" Kruger asked.

Tarita nodded. "Yes, we have a very nice cabernet from Thelema Mountain Vineyards."

"A bottle of that, please."

Tarita walked toward the bar. Kruger stared at Conor hard. "In my business, the people I deal with, you learn to read the eyes. Not the body language—someone can learn to adopt a certain posture—the eyes. Knowing what the eyes say can mean the difference between life and death. And you know what your eyes tell me, Conor?"

Kruger's demeanor was bordering on the sinister, revealing the menacing side of him Conor now knew existed. "No. What?" Conor was growing increasingly uncomfortable under Kruger's probing gaze.

"They tell me you had me checked out," Kruger said. "That certain people said some very bad things about me. That I was unstable. Am I right?"

Conor saw no point in denying it. "Yes."

Kruger exhaled through his nose. "Disinformation. My government is very good at it. So is yours. The CIA is a master at disinformation. The contact your FBI friend spoke with at the consulate is a member of the ANC, the African National Congress, which, as we know, was never a fan of the Scorpions."

Conor bristled. How did Kruger know he met with the FBI?

"You *did* speak with the FBI, didn't you?"

"You had me under surveillance?"

Kruger smiled. "I am simply making an educated guess."

But Conor knew better. That was no guess. *Jesus. He has the gall to put a tail on an NYPD detective.*

A waiter delivered the espresso and the red wine. Kruger took a sip, his motion slow and deliberate. "Actually, I was thinking of flying back to Johannesburg tonight."

"First class, I hope."

"No. The best I can get out of this government is business class. But it doesn't matter. I wouldn't be flying commercial."

"Private jet?"

"Nothing so comfortable. South African government transport. Nine o'clock. Leaving out of Teterboro Airport in New Jersey. Rather convenient if one is carrying a red diamond once in the possession of a murdered Israeli woman and would prefer to avoid airport security."

Kruger was toying with him now. In fact, Kruger was using a technique Conor himself employed when interrogating a suspect. Rattle the interviewee, unnerve him with oblique statements, half truths.

"I could make a call," Conor said, playing along. "Get a warrant."

"To search me? My luggage? That would be foolish."

"Not if you have the diamond."

"Perhaps I don't." Kruger patted the pockets of his jacket as if he were looking for the diamond. The gesture was clearly meant to make Conor feel foolish. "In that case, the best course of action would be to return to South Africa."

"Without the diamond? Why?"

"Quite simple. If I am here too long, Marwala will speculate that I do not have the red diamond. If I left now, he'd believe I do." Kruger sighed heavily. "But after giving the situation more thought, I realized that returning to South Africa would not deceive Marwala." He stared into his glass of wine. "You think I flew to New York to steal the diamond? Lure Marwala out into the open?"

"I have no idea. I just want the truth, Hendrik."

"Truth has many meanings."

"Not in my book."

"All right. Let's say I did steal the diamond. Then I would certainly have killed Zivah Gavish. Witnesses can be troublesome down the road. Dead men tell no tales. Isn't that the expression? Well, neither do dead women."

"Is that a confession?"

"No. A scenario. One I'm sure you have already considered. But the mystery is, *why* would I steal the diamond?"

"I don't know. Why don't you tell me?"

"Because I knew that when Marwala learned his priceless red diamond, his most ambitious plan to enrich himself, had been stolen, he'd do anything to get it back. And I knew I could use the diamond to entice Marwala into the trap I have so carefully laid out. But the truth is"—Kruger locked eyes with Conor—"you said you wanted the truth, did you not?"

"Yes," Conor replied simply.

"The truth is, Conor, I do not have the diamond. So I came up with another plan."

"And that is?"

"Marwala has a low-level bureaucrat on his payroll, working at the South African embassy in Johannesburg. We will be arresting him soon. But in the meantime, he is extremely useful. Marwala's mole was allowed to see an e-mail I sent to headquarters in which I notified my superiors that NYPD had recovered the diamond." Kruger lifted his glass, swirled the wine around in a crimson whirlpool. "And now Marwala is on his way to New York. He arrives tomorrow."

Chapter Thirty-nine

Conor's face registered disgust. "So you're using me, using the department."

"I understand your reaction," Kruger said. "And I perhaps should have spoken to you before I sent the e-mail. But I was struck with the idea at three in the morning and I didn't want to wake you."

"How considerate."

"Don't you see? Marwala has taken the bait."

"So Marwala is coming to New York? So what? He's just another tourist."

"I can deliver him to you," Kruger said. "Tomorrow night."

"And what am I supposed to do with him?"

"Arrest him, of course."

"On what grounds?"

"That's up to you," Kruger replied.

"Look, Hendrik—"

"I need to link Marwala to that red diamond." Kruger's eyes narrowed. "Then I'll have him."

"Hendrik . . ."

"It's *your* collar, Conor. Would it not be beneficial to your career to arrest an international criminal?"

"Why come to me? What have I done to deserve such generosity?" Conor crossed his arms. "That's a quote from Don Corleone in *The Godfather*. But a very good question. Why don't you just arrest Marwala yourself?"

"I agree," Kruger replied. "That would be easier. But there are jurisdictional issues, political considerations. That's why it is far better this way. And don't worry, Conor, once he's in custody, we'll take it from there."

"This is America, Hendrik. We don't just go around arresting people for no reason."

"You suspect that Arun Punjabi cut the diamond. Just tie Punjabi to the illegal transaction and tie Marwala to Punjabi. There's your reason."

"How do you know what I suspect?"

"You've been to Punjabi's office."

"So you *are* following me."

"You're getting paranoid, Conor. I told you before, we still don't know who cut the rough stone. So we have the Diamond District staked out, that's all."

"That's *all*?" Conor laughed. "Can you guys operate in the United States like that?"

Kruger picked up the bottle of wine and filled his glass. "I don't know. Can we?"

Conor felt alternately outraged and intrigued as he strode up Eighth Avenue to meet Tasha Sen. Sure, arresting Marwala would be a big step toward becoming Detective First Grade—and it might lead somewhere in the homicide investigation—but in reality, this was all about Kruger's obsession with his elusive archenemy. Even though there wasn't enough evidence to take Marwala into custody, Kruger was suggesting that Conor ignore such minor details. Which was proof enough that Kruger had no boundaries. What was Kruger really capable of? Was anything he said the truth or was it all some enormous lie? *Kruger is dangerous. Do not play his game.* But then again, where was the homicide investigation anyway?

Basically nowhere. Silberman's bandaged wrist and fingerprints on the jewelry box. Punjabi "forgetting" to mention he had met Zivah for dinner on Sunday. The crackheads next door in the tenement. The deliverymen, one of whom certainly could have been tempted by the opulence of Zivah's loft and ease of access. A lot of suspects. No clear motive. No definitive evidence.

Conor decided he'd give Kruger's scheme some thought before deciding what to do. In the meantime, perhaps Tasha Sen could help sort out the diamond business aspect of the case. But that really wasn't the reason he was going to dinner with her, was it? She was sexy and exotic. *That* was the point. Still, she *was* in the diamond business.

His cell phone rang. It was Richard.

"I've got fantastic news," Richard said. "Alan Woodcliff stopped by the store just now."

"And?"

"He listened to the CD. Loved it. Thinks you have a unique voice."

"Really?"

"Of course I *am* giving him a great deal on tires. What *could* he say? Anyway, he told me to give you his number. He wants you to call him."

Conor took down the number. What should he say to Alan Woodcliff? How should he begin the conversation? Although he hated to admit it, he was reluctant to make the phone call. *This is ridiculous,* he thought. *Hell, I'm just calling a kid. So what if he's made it in the music business? He's still just a kid. A lucky kid. I'm a cop. I'm twice his age. Fuck, let me just call him and quit thinking about it.*

He dialed the number. A woman answered.

"Speak."

"It's Conor Bard. Is Alan Woodcliff there?"

"*Who* is this?"

"Conor Bard. Richard Shorter told me—"

"Who?"

Conor took a deep breath. "Richard Shorter. Mr. Woodcliff was just in his tire store."

Conor could hear muffled voices. She obviously had put her hand over the mouthpiece. There was a long pause, then "Hey! Conor. Alan Woodcliff. Sorry, man. That was Anna, my cell phone girl. She's very protective."

Conor wasn't sure how to respond. *Cell phone girl? Who has a cell phone girl?*

"Listened to your CD," Woodcliff continued. "I really dug it."

"Thanks."

"We should talk. Soon. What are you doing tomorrow night?"

"I'm free."

"Good. I'm in the studio mixing my new album. Session starts at six. Why don't you come by around eight, eight thirty? Whenever you can get there."

This could be it, Conor thought. *This could be the break I've been waiting for. Good thing I got past the cell phone girl.*

Chapter Forty

Conor stopped in front of Joe G's. *Why am I always eating Italian?* he wondered. *I'm Scotch-Irish. Shouldn't I be dining on corned beef and cabbage, the Irish staple, or haggis, the Scottish national dish—a medley of lungs, heart, and liver prepared inside a sheep's stomach?* He shuddered. *Better a little pasta.* The truth was, he loved everything Italian—the cuisine, the music, the people. Joe G, the owner of the ristorante, was always good for a night of stories, Italian style. The food was good and Joe G's was only two blocks from the precinct. The dining room, down a flight of stairs in the basement of a small boutique hotel called Da Vinci, also owned by Joe G, provided Conor with a perfect retreat in the middle of a case, or, given its dim lighting and European ambiance, a perfect place for a romantic encounter.

"You just missed Kevin and Sal," Joe G said.

Good, Conor thought. Kevin and Sal were detectives from the precinct. Had they seen him with Tasha, they would have delighted in doing everything they could to sabotage the evening. All in good fun, of course—Conor had done it himself many times when one of the detectives brought in a date—but tonight he was happy not to have the distraction.

Tasha, looking sexy as hell in a pink blouse that offered a muted view of her black bra, arrived.

"*Mama mia!*" Joe G whispered in Conor's ear. "Good thing Sal isn't here. He'd be all over that."

After introducing her to Joe G, Conor led Tasha to a table in the back. He ordered his usual martini, as well as a bottle of Valpolicella.

"All I've been able to think about is poor Zivah." Tasha sighed. "She had everything to live for and some . . . some . . . whoever, just takes it all away."

"Anything you can think of, anybody who might have wanted to do this to her?"

"If you brought me here for information about Zivah, you're going to be disappointed. I really didn't know her very well. As I told you, we had a couple of business transactions in the last year and that's it."

"Let's change the subject. Why don't we talk about you?"

"Perfect."

"I know you're in the diamond business. But what is it you do exactly?"

"I represent a diamond-cutting firm in Mumbai. The vast majority of stones are cut and polished in India."

"So somebody sends you a what? A big rock?"

Tasha laughed. "A rough stone."

"Okay. I pull this rough stone out of a mine in South Africa. Now what? I FedEx the stone to you in Mumbai?"

She laughed again. "It's not quite that simple. There's something called the Kimberley Process. Actually, it's the Kimberley Process Certification Scheme—KPCS. India, and most other countries around the world, will not allow a rough stone to be imported unless the exporter can certify that the stone is from a region free of conflict."

"To stop blood diamonds from supporting wars and terrorism."

"Yes."

"So when you get this rough stone, then what?"

"It's marked, then cleaved, then sawed."

"Sawed? Like with a hacksaw?"

"In this case the saw is a small disk made of either copper or phosphor bronze."

He was surprised. "Phosphor bronze? I know about phosphor bronze."

"Really?"

"It's made from copper, tin, and phosphorus."

She gave Conor a quizzical look, obviously wondering why a cop would have any idea about a metal used in a diamond-cutting disk. "How do you know what phosphor bronze is made of?"

"There are a couple of companies that manufacture saxophones out of phosphor bronze instead of brass," he explained. "They're reddish orange in color and the tonal quality is deeper, darker." He reached over and touched her hand. "So we have something in common. Phosphor bronze."

"That's a start." She nodded, leaving her hand under his as she continued. "Anyway, the disk is sharp, hard, and very, very thin. Paper thin. A roller is used to coat the edge of the disk with diamond dust. Only diamond can cut diamond. Then, after sawing, a diamond goes through bruting—which is rounding—faceting, and finally polishing."

"Is there any way you could get me one of those phosphor bronze disks?" he asked.

She tilted her head. "Why do you want one?"

"A friend of mine who's a sax player has a phosphor bronze sax," Conor lied. "I'm meeting him tomorrow afternoon and I'd love to show it to him."

"I've got a few in the office. I'll messenger one over to you in the morning."

"Thanks."

"What else do you want to know about diamonds?" she asked.

"Okay, let's say I've smuggled a rough stone out of South Africa to India to be cut."

She held up her hand. "Wait. There's a problem. The cutter wants to know how it got there. He needs documents."

"But I don't have any. So what do I do?"

She pretended to be writing on the tablecloth with her finger. "You could forge the documents. Or you could find somebody to cut it without documents."

"Like who?"

"Like someone who wants to make a payday off the books." She held up her hand and rubbed her fingers together. "The money is irresistible. I know. I've been asked."

"Did you . . . ?"

"Never. Our little company is totally legit. Getting caught doing something like that could put us out of business."

"What about the man you mentioned before? Arun Punjabi?"

"Arun? Definitely not Arun. His family has been cutting diamonds for centuries. Buyers will even pay more if a stone comes from Bombay Sawing. He wouldn't risk all that no matter how much money was on the table."

Despite Tasha's proclamation of Punjabi's status in the industry, the bidi-smoking diamond cutter was still high on Conor's list of suspects. Punjabi had met Zivah Gavish on Sunday night for dinner. What did they talk about? Was a rare red diamond enough to entice Punjabi into jeopardizing his family name? After all, everybody has a price. If Zivah Gavish was the dealer, was Punjabi the seller? If so, did something go wrong? Did Zivah Gavish threaten to expose him? Is that why he used a diamond-cutting disk to slit her lovely throat?

Chapter Forty-one

"**M**y theoretical diamond," Conor said, resuming the conversation, "has now been cut and polished. So I come to India, pick up my diamond, put it in my pocket, and fly back to America."

"No. There are taxes and duties to pay. And paperwork."

"But what if I want to avoid all that paperwork and expense? What if I want to take it out of the country?"

"Without a Kimberly certification or any other documentation?"

"Right."

"Well, in that case, you're back to smuggling."

"I hide it in my luggage?"

"Too dangerous," she said. "Particularly with all the security since nine eleven. If someone finds the diamond, you're out a lot of money and you're in serious trouble with the authorities."

"Then how?"

She touched her necklace, which looked like a string of brightly colored pebbles. "You wear it."

"Wear it?"

"Have the stone mounted in a necklace, a ring, a pin, whatever."

"Hide it in plain sight?"

She nodded. "For example, you have a diamond, rather large, so you buy six or seven crystals of cubic zirconia cut the same way. Make them look like buttons on a jacket. Who's going to think that one of the buttons is a diamond worth a fortune?"

"Sounds like you're a veteran at these things," he teased.

She struck a pose. "You never know."

"Can we keep going?"

"Sure. This is fun, actually."

"So now I have this cut and polished diamond in the U.S. No paperwork. How do I sell it?"

"If you've gone to all this trouble, you probably have a buyer in place. Someone who doesn't care about documentation."

"What if it's really valuable? I mean really, really valuable. What if it's a red diamond?"

He watched her reaction carefully.

"Red?" She seemed unprepared to hear the color red associated with a diamond. "You never see a red diamond."

"Never?"

"Not exactly *never*. But let me put it this way. Six hundred million diamonds come out of South Africa every year. Maybe fifty or sixty are red. That's one in ten million."

"That's better odds than Mega Millions," he countered. "A hundred ninety-five million to one. And people *do* hit the lottery."

She looked at him suspiciously. "Why are you asking me all these questions about diamonds?"

"Zivah was a diamond dealer, so—"

"You think she was killed by someone in the diamond industry?"

"I don't know. That's what I'm trying to find out."

They ordered dinner and spent the remainder of the evening trading personal stories back and forth. By the end of the night, conversation had morphed into alcohol-fueled flirting.

"Were you planning to kiss me good night?" she asked seductively as they left Joe G's and strolled down Eighth Avenue.

"No." He feigned sincerity. "I was going to wait until our second date."

"Well, I was thinking about kissing *you* good night."

He took her hand. "It's not a bad idea."

"You think?"

They stopped on the corner of Forty-eighth and Eighth. She eased her arms around his waist. They kissed. A taste of passion but not too much.

"Thank you," she said. "That was nice."

They started walking again, stopping in front of the Ritz Plaza. *I'm in,* Conor thought.

"I had a great time," she said, now keeping her distance. "I'd like to see you again."

"Absolutely."

She gave him a little wave, then walked into the building. Conor shrugged. *Guess I'm not in.*

Chapter Forty-two

It was only a little after eleven and Conor was torn between stopping off for a nightcap or just going home. He opted for the comforts of home, poured half a glass of vodka, picked up his guitar, and sat on the couch. The dinner with Tasha had promised further delights. The call from Alan Woodcliff had revived hope in a music career. Endorphins flowing, he plucked at the guitar strings, limbering his fingers. Soon he might be playing guitar in front of a microphone in a studio *with* a recording contract. He savored the thought, strumming mindlessly. A Billy Joel song emerged from all the random chords. Conor began singing.

"I'll meet you any time you want, in our Italian restaurant . . ."

Conor was accustomed to events triggering songs in his head. It happened so frequently that he often thought his life had its own soundtrack—an appropriate tune for every scene. He guessed that the evening with Tasha at Joe G's had coaxed Billy Joel's "Scenes from an Italian Restaurant" to the forefront of his consciousness but suddenly realized that wasn't it at all. The Italian restaurant that was the source of his spontaneous rendition was Uccelli. The place where Arun Punjabi met Zivah Gavish for dinner. He placed the guitar on the couch and headed out the door.

*   *   *

Uccelli was an upscale Italian restaurant on East Fifty-fourth Street that found its way into gossip columns almost every day. Conor remembered a rave review of the place pointed out that it often took six months to secure a reservation. So either Punjabi or Zivah must have been a regular customer even to get in, he reasoned, which meant the staff would have recognized one or both of them and might have some useful information about their dinner.

Uccelli was located on the first floor of a brownstone. Even the outside of the place was daunting. Heavy wooden door, polished brass fittings, a uniformed doorman.

"Do you have a reservation?" the doorman asked.

Conor produced his gold shield. "I'd like to speak with the manager."

"That would be Danny."

"Is he here?"

The doorman pulled open the door without responding. Conor went inside.

Being an expensive joint, which these days was synonymous with foreign patrons and euros, the place was still going strong at eleven thirty, catering to the late-night habits of its international clientele.

A maître d' stepped up to Conor. "May I help you?"

"I'm looking for Danny."

The maître d' regarded Conor suspiciously. "Does he know you?"

"No." Conor produced his shield. "But I'd like to speak with him."

The maître d' picked up a phone on the podium and dialed. "Danny. There's a detective here to see you." He looked at Conor. "He'll meet you in the bar."

Conor didn't mind. Might as well have a drink while he waited.

The bar was actually part of the dining room and tables near the bar were cherished by the regulars. At least that was what the review said. Conor guessed it was because they would have more visibility. In other words, the patrons would be seen. Why spend all that money if no one knew you were there?

CRYSTAL DEATH

"What can I get you?" the bartender asked as Conor slid onto a stool.

The bartender was young, Conor guessed not more than twenty-three, and was dressed entirely in black—black pants, black T-shirt.

"Ketel One martini straight up with a twist. No vermouth."

"Very dry," the bartender said, his response as arid as the martini would be.

Conor turned to see a man around thirty approaching. Sharp suit. Sharp shirt. Sharp tie. Sharp shoes. Sharp haircut. *This is a very sharp guy*, Conor mused.

"How can I help you?" the man asked.

"You're Danny?"

"Yes."

Conor stood. "I'm Detective Conor Bard."

"What can I do for you?"

Danny's delivery riled Conor. Maybe Conor had had too much to drink—which sometimes tended to lower his tolerance for anything even vaguely annoying—but everything about the place was bothering him all of a sudden.

"Do you know a man named Arun Punjabi or a woman named Zivah Gavish?" Conor asked.

"Perhaps."

"Do you or don't you?" Conor was really getting pissed off.

"Yes. I know Mr. Punjabi."

"I have information that he was here last Sunday night."

"He could have been. I don't remember."

Conor squared off with Danny. "Look. Danny. I'm not a gossip columnist. I'm a cop. And I'm investigating a murder."

Danny looked at the bartender. "Antonio. Do you recall if Mr. Punjabi dined with us last Sunday?"

"Yes. He was here." Antonio pointed to a table near the bar. "Mr. Punjabi sat at table four."

"Well, there you go, Detective," Danny said condescendingly. "He was here on Sunday night. Does that help you?"

169

Conor came to the conclusion that speaking with Danny further would be a waste of time. "Yes. Thank you."

Antonio slid a martini across the bar.

"That's on me," Danny told Antonio. He nodded at Conor. "Enjoy."

"Thanks."

Conor was happy to see Danny walk away. The person he really wanted to speak with was Antonio. Over the years, Conor had noticed that most bartenders possessed the unique ability to observe and retain. They were always vigilant, always watching, always listening, always remembering.

Conor took a sip of his martini, then looked at Antonio. "You mind if I ask you a couple questions?"

Antonio gave him a look: *It depends.*

"They're simple questions," Conor assured him.

Antonio nodded. *Go ahead.*

"Mr. Punjabi is a regular customer?"

"He's in two, three times a week."

"Must have one hell of an expense account."

"He's very generous," Antonio noted deliberately.

"Mr. Punjabi. He was with a woman? Dark hair? Very pretty?"

"Yes. She was Israeli."

Exactly what I'm talking about, Conor thought. *Bartenders don't miss anything.* "Were they having a nice dinner?"

"They were celebrating some business deal." Antonio picked up a lemon and a knife, began cutting sections of the peel. "Must've been a hell of a payday. They ordered a 1995 Krug Clos Ambonnay."

"What's that? A champagne?"

Antonio laughed. "A champagne? Liquid gold if you ask me. It's on our list at ten thousand five hundred."

Conor wasn't sure he heard correctly. "Excuse me?"

"That's right," Antonio confirmed. "Ten grand a pop."

Chapter Forty-three

Conor walked from Uccelli back to Forty-eighth Street, all the while trying to fathom how a bottle of champagne could cost ten grand. Or, more to the point, why anyone would pay it. *Guess Punjabi was expecting a windfall.* It now seemed clear that Punjabi was the seller of the missing red diamond, which he also cut and polished. But did Punjabi kill Zivah Gavish? And if he did, why?

It was late. Too late to start advancing an endless array of theories about Punjabi's motives. Conor had accomplished something important by going to Uccelli: he had all but connected Punjabi to the red diamond. That was enough for tonight.

Conor entered his apartment and poured a vodka. *This doesn't cost ten grand but it gets the job done.* He picked up his guitar, strummed a few random chords, and thought about the dinner with Tasha. She was going to be great in the sack. He could just feel it. Beautiful. From India. All of a sudden he found himself playing "Interlude," a song by a female vocalist he admired, India.Arie. *Why the period between the first and last name?* He had always wondered why. Someday he would ask her. He began singing the lyrics.

"John Coltrane . . . Miles Davis . . . Dizzy Gillespie . . . This is a song for you . . ."

The lyrics essentially were composed of the names of dead singers set to music. Jimi Hendrix, Karen Carpenter, Billie Holiday, Ella Fitzgerald, Bessie Smith, Minnie Riperton, Tammi Terrell, Sarah Vaughan.

"Your memory still lives on in me . . . ," he sang.

He hit the final chord and let the strings vibrate until they were silent. *Your memory still lives on in me.*

Immortality. What more could an artist want other than to be remembered forever?

He closed his eyes.

After finally getting a solid night's sleep, Conor arrived at the precinct rejuvenated. Rosita was already there.

"What's that?" Conor asked, pointing at a flowerpot on her desk.

"A plant."

He looked at the vase containing one flower that she had brought in the day before. "A flower's not enough?"

"A flower is temporary." She stroked the leaves of the small plant. "A plant is forever."

"That would be a good slogan for the gardening business."

She scooped up a stack of paper, stood, and walked over to him. "Zivah Gavish's credit card statements came in." She handed him the documents.

"She liked to spend money," he noted as he flipped through the pages.

"So how was your date?" she asked.

He placed the credit card statements on his desk. "It wasn't a date. It was an interview."

"Sorry," she said sarcastically. "How was your interview?"

He filled her in about his conversation with Tasha and his visit to Uccelli.

Rosita whistled. "Ten thousand dollars!"

"Don't forget the five hundred. Ten thousand *five hundred*."

"Punjabi just nailed himself."

"As far as the red diamond, I think so."

"Not bad for a night's work," Rosita said.

"Wait. There's more." He related Kruger's suggestion that they collar Marwala.

"Wow," she said. "All this international intrigue. I feel like a Bond girl."

"What happened to 'one of the guys'?"

"Just for that split second," she said.

He started walking away. "Come on. I need to run this Kruger thing by the lieutenant."

Conor, Rosita, and Amanda gathered in Rooney's office to discuss Kruger's proposition.

Rooney scratched the back of his hand. "Why not? If it's our collar. Just make sure you have something that will stick."

That, of course, was the problem. At the moment, Conor really didn't have anything on Marwala.

"And we have a shot at this guy Punjabi too," Rooney said. "Right?"

"Right," Conor acknowledged.

Conor had a feeling Rooney would react that way. The commanding officer was responsible for arrest numbers in the same way a CEO at a major corporation was responsible for the balance sheet. A big arrest like this would make Rooney's month.

Conor wasn't sure if he was imagining it but it appeared as if Rooney's eyes were watering.

"A red diamond," Rooney said wistfully. "Ten-grand bottle of bubbly. My God!"

"Yes, it was quite a good champagne." Punjabi nervously slipped a pack of bidis from his jacket pocket, started to shake one out of the pack, then stopped, placed them back in his pocket.

"What's the matter?" Conor asked. "No smoking in the building?"

"Sometimes I forget." Punjabi was nervous now. "See, I've had this office for twenty years. Back when I moved in, you could smoke. But now you Americans have made smoking a mortal sin."

"So, Mr. Punjabi," Rosita interjected, "business must be good. Ordering a bottle of the best champagne in the house. Ten thousand dollars?"

Punjabi assumed a defensive posture. "Krug Clos Ambonnay is a rare sparkling wine made entirely from Pinot Noir grown within a one-and-a-half-acre vineyard in the village of Ambonnay. Yearly production is only three thousand bottles. Uccelli is one of the few restaurants in the world with a cellar where one can find Krug Clos Ambonnay."

"The champagne, the dinner, must have been a pretty big check." Conor nodded slightly. "Way over my MasterCard limit."

"I have a black American Express card, Detective. There is no limit." Punjabi adopted a haughty demeanor. "I make a great deal of money and, as a result, I enjoy the finer things in life."

Punjabi stood and walked around his desk. "I must say, it is rather disconcerting that you are investigating my every move."

"It's just police procedure," Conor countered, trying to sound nonchalant. "You told us you had dinner at Uccelli so we had to confirm that." He stood. "Thanks for your time."

Rosita gave Conor a confused look. *Why are we leaving?* Conor responded with a glance. *Just follow my lead.*

Punjabi, happy they were leaving, escorted them across the room. "If there's anything I can do to help, anything at all . . ."

They stopped near the door. Conor pointed to the other room. "Mind if I take a look?" Conor started walking. Rosita and Punjabi followed.

Conor picked up a bronze cutting disk, touched the edge. "It's very sharp."

"Yes it is," Punjabi acknowledged, clearly anxious to get them out of the cutting room.

Conor placed the disk on the table. "I'm thinking about buying my girlfriend a ring. But *not* an engagement ring. I have a problem with commitment."

Punjabi, now beginning to relax, shared a moment of male bonding with Conor. "So many beautiful women out there."

"You got that right." He stepped closer to Punjabi. "So, anyway, I wanted to get her something special."

"I could recommend someone," Punjabi offered. "I do business with many of the jewelers on the street. I can get you a very good deal." He was now much more at ease. "What did you have in mind?"

Conor waited, like a boxer ready to deliver an overhand right that had been set up by a jab. "You know anything about colored diamonds?"

Punjabi swallowed. "Colored diamonds?" His voice was up an octave.

"Diamonds come in colors, right?"

Punjabi cleared his throat. "Yes."

"I'm really not ready to buy anything right now," Conor said. "But when I am, I'll get that recommendation from you, okay?"

Punjabi nodded, avoiding eye contact. "Of course."

Chapter Forty-four

Conor and Rosita walked across Forty-seventh Street. He grabbed her hand.

"Why don't we stop in here, honey?"

Rosita pulled her hand away. "What?"

"Punjabi just left his office," Conor whispered. He opened the door to a jewelry store.

"Oh," she said, getting it, taking his hand again.

They entered the store.

A clerk approached. "May I help you?"

Rosita smiled sweetly. "We're looking for a bracelet."

As the clerk led Rosita to a counter, Conor kept an eye on the street. Punjabi rushed past the window. *Where is he going?* Conor positioned himself so he could see farther down the block. Punjabi stopped in front of Silberman's store, checked to make sure no one was watching him, then ducked inside.

Conor stepped over and put his arm around Rosita's shoulders. "You find something you like, honey?"

She held her wrist out so Conor could see it. "Yes, dear."

She was wearing a sparkling diamond-and-gold bracelet.

"What do you think, darling?" Rosita asked Conor.

"It looks nice." He looked at the clerk. "How much is it?"

The clerk checked the small metallic tag, which contained a coded price. "Three thousand."

"Three thousand?" Conor recoiled in horror. He looked at Rosita. "Honey, we can't afford that much."

"Oh, *really*." Rosita placed her hands on her hips. "You just bought yourself a motorcycle that cost ten times what this bracelet costs."

"That's different."

"Different? Yeah, it's different all right. Any time I want something, it's different."

The clerk stepped in. "I can give it to you for—"

"What about that nice dress I bought you last week?" Conor challenged her.

She made a face. "You mean the see-through hooker outfit? You bought that for *yourself*, not me."

Rosita slipped off the bracelet and slapped it into Conor's palm. "Take this and ram it up your—"

"I'm sure there are pieces within your budget," the clerk quickly interjected. "If you'll just step over—"

Rosita glared at Conor, then stormed out of the store.

Conor handed the bracelet to the clerk. "Sorry."

"If you really want to make her happy—"

"No," Conor replied. "I really don't. Matter of fact, I was thinking of dumping her anyway. Before my wife finds out."

Conor headed for the door. The clerk, holding the bracelet in the air, trailed him.

"Perhaps your *wife* would like this," the clerk suggested, a sales-pitch melody in his voice.

"Don't think so," Conor said. "She's a Southern Baptist."

The clerk was puzzled. *What does that mean?*

Conor pushed through the door. Rosita was waiting nearby.

"Punjabi went into Silberman's," Conor said.

They entered an office building and stood just inside the lobby, taking up a position where Silberman's storefront was visible.

"Silberman must be involved somehow," Rosita observed.

"Looks that way."

A couple of minutes later, Punjabi came rushing out of Silberman Jewelry and hurried back toward his office.

Conor and Rosita crossed Forty-seventh and stopped in front of Silberman's store. Silberman spotted them through the window. He listed to the right as if he was about to faint, then buzzed them in.

"Mr. Silberman," Conor said as he entered. "I hope we're not disturbing you."

"No." He trembled slightly.

"We just stopped by to do a follow-up." Conor looked at Silberman's wrist. "How's that sprained wrist coming along?"

Silberman licked his lips. "My wrist?"

"Yes," Rosita chimed in. "The one you hurt when you tripped on the street."

Silberman involuntarily grabbed his still-bandaged wrist. "It's . . . it's better."

"Good to hear that," Conor said. "You have a minute? This won't take long."

"Okay." Silberman appeared unsure what to do, what to say.

"You know someone named Arun Punjabi?" Rosita asked.

Silberman's eyes darted around the room. "I buy stones from him sometimes."

Conor took out a pen and notebook. "Buys stones from him sometimes," he muttered as he jotted down that bit of information. "Have you purchased any stones recently?"

Silberman swallowed. "Recently?"

"Yes. Like in the past two weeks."

Rosita slowly strolled along the counter, examining the jewelry.

Silberman rubbed his forehead. "Let's see. No. Not in the last two weeks."

Conor scribbled in his pad. "Okay, Mr. Silberman. Thanks for your time." He looked at Rosita. "You ready, Detective Rubio?"

She looked up at Silberman. "How much is that ring?"

He hurried over to her. "Which one?"

She pointed under the glass at a small solitaire diamond. Silberman opened the back of the case and removed it. His hands were shaking so much, he dropped it on the countertop. He made an effort to hide his embarrassment by rubbing the two offending fingertips together—as if there was something oily on them—then carefully picked up the ring again. He checked the small coded price tag. "It's twenty-two hundred."

She took the ring from Silberman, rotated it in her hands.

"I can give you a nice discount," Silberman added with an acquired sincerity.

She looked at Conor. "Are we allowed to take a discount?"

"Depends," Conor said.

"On what?" she asked.

"Whether or not somebody's involved in a crime we're investigating."

Silberman was really suffering now.

Rosita handed the ring back to Silberman then scanned the display case. She pointed to another ring. "That one looks nice."

Silberman removed the ring and checked the price. "I can give you this ring for nine hundred." He handed it to her.

Rosita held it in front of her face and pointed to the red stone set elegantly atop six silver prongs. "Is that a red diamond?"

Silberman laughed. "Red diamond? Heavens no. That's a ruby." He laughed again. "If that were a red diamond, I'm afraid it would be well out of your price range."

Chapter Forty-five

Conor and Rosita left the store.

"He doesn't know about the red diamond," Conor observed. "The way he reacted. He laughed, seemed to relax. Not like Punjabi's reaction."

"What about his wrist?"

"Could have happened just like he said."

They climbed into the car. She was driving.

"Okay," Rosita began, "even if Silberman didn't know about the red diamond and sprained his wrist when he tripped and fell, it still doesn't explain why Punjabi rushed over to Silberman's store."

"My guess is that Silberman played some role in the transaction but wasn't kept entirely in the loop by Punjabi."

"So how do you want to handle this?" she asked.

"We'll bring them in. Let them see each other at the precinct, keep them separated. Maybe somebody will fold."

"And we'll be able to collar Punjabi for smuggling?"

"Exactly. And if we're lucky, for murder too."

* * *

As Conor and Rosita entered the precinct, Amanda motioned them into her office.

"You've got visitors," Amanda said. "Three guys in white robes. I put them in the conference room."

Conor and Rosita left Amanda's office and headed down the hall.

"Aziz?" Rosita asked.

"Either that or the Ku Klux Klan," Conor said.

"Hope it's Aziz."

Conor and Rosita entered to find Aziz and his two bodyguards seated around the table.

"Mr. Aziz," Conor said as he entered. "How are you?"

Aziz stood. "I am fine, Detective. Thank you."

"So what can I do for you?" Conor asked.

"I am returning to Abu Dhabi," Aziz said. "So I would like to ask that you please inform my attorney, Mr. Kramer, if the diamond is recovered."

"Well, Mr. Aziz, if there are no legal issues—"

"I understand," Aziz cut in. "I am only asking that you notify Mr. Kramer if it is appropriate."

A nod of Aziz's head caused the two bodyguards to rise in unison, coming to life like puppets at the pull of a string.

"You should visit sometime," Aziz offered with a smile. "The accommodations at the palace are quite comfortable."

Conor motioned toward Rosita. "We'll need two rooms."

"Of course," Aziz said, smiling for the first time.

"So we strike Aziz from the list," Conor said as he settled in behind his desk. "Even if he *was* involved in the murder, which I doubt, it doesn't much matter. Extraditing a billionaire from Abu Dhabi? As the goombahs say: fuggedaboutit." He looked down and spotted a manila envelope that had been placed on top of a stack of papers. He opened it and found a note from Tasha.

Dear Conor. Had a great time last night. Here's your phosphor disk. Hope to see you soon.

He removed the disk from the envelope and held it up so Rosita could see it. "What do you think, Rubio? Our murder weapon?"

"Death by diamond-cutting disk?" Brian carefully examined the small bronze object. "Son of a bitch."

"You never saw one before?" Rosita asked.

"No," Brian replied. "Never."

"Could a disk like that be the murder weapon?" Conor wondered aloud.

"Maybe." Brian opened a countertop refrigerator and took out a tomato.

Conor laughed. "You having lunch?"

Brian placed the tomato on the counter and proceeded to cut into it with the bronze disk. He carefully examined the incision. "Look at that cut. Hairline."

"So it's possible?" Conor pressed.

"Very possible." Brian held up the disk. "I want to take another look at the photos of the victim's neck. Compare the cut to this disk. Can I hang on to this?"

"Sure."

Brian used the disk to cut the tomato in half. "*Now* I'm having lunch."

Conor tossed Rosita the keys. "You drive."

"You're a real gentleman."

"Is there a lady around here?" He looked in all directions. "I don't see a woman. All I see is one of the guys."

"You should have bought me that bracelet back at the jewelry store. *Then* you'd see a woman."

They climbed in the car. Conor frowned. "What if—"

"The fine powder on Zivah Gavish's neck was diamond dust."

Conor gave Rosita a bemused look. "We haven't been together long enough for you to start finishing my sentences."

Conor took out his cell phone and called Selzer.

Selzer was incredulous. "You think it could be *what*?"

"Diamond dust," Conor repeated. "Ask the lab to check it out."

On the way back to the precinct, Kingston called.

"They've got a lot of video at the Crowne Plaza," he said. "It's going to take a while to match faces. And you're going to have to go over there. They don't want to release the tapes. Talk to their head of security. Guy named Wilkes."

"Yeah, I know Wilkes." Conor had been summoned by Wilkes on several occasions to discreetly handle investigations into various crimes. "What about the tenement?"

"Nothing yet. But a preliminary check of the deliverymen turned up something interesting. Green Life Nursery in the flower district? That's where your victim bought the plants on her terrace. One of the deliverymen has a rap sheet. Assault with a deadly weapon. Burglary. Attempted rape. Just got out of prison."

"Name?"

"Bruno Morrison. I'll text you his info."

"Thanks."

Conor snapped the phone shut and looked at Rosita. "One of the men who delivered the trees on Zivah Gavish's terrace is a very bad boy."

Chapter Forty-six

Conor and Rosita parked on Seventh Avenue then walked across Twenty-eighth Street. The sidewalk of the entire block was covered with large plants and potted trees. When they stopped in front of Green Life Nursery, a burly man wearing a dirt-covered T-shirt stepped up to them. "Can I help you?"

"We're looking for Bruno Morrison," Conor responded.

"Who shall I say is calling?" the man asked mockingly.

Rosita pulled out her shield. "One of his admirers."

"What's he done?" the man asked.

"We ask the questions," Rosita replied. "Where is he?"

The man hesitated, then: "He's out on a run. Should be back anytime."

Conor and Rosita started for the door. Conor stopped, turned, and looked at the man. "Don't call him and tell him we're here. Because if he doesn't show up, I'm taking *you* in."

"For what?" the man demanded.

"Interfering with an investigation."

The man held his arms in the air. "No calls."

They didn't have to wait long. As they walked out onto Sixth Avenue, a delivery truck pulled to the curb. Bruno Morrison and another man climbed out. Bruno was a huge man with the wide flat paws and sneering scowl of a grizzly bear. Conor recognized him from the video.

"Bruno Morrison?" Conor said as he approached him.

"Yeah?" Bruno replied.

Conor slid his shield out of his jacket. "Detective Conor Bard. NYPD."

"What the fuck do you want?" Bruno growled.

"Something that doesn't need a lot of light," Rosita said. "My apartment doesn't get much sun."

Conor nodded toward Rosita. "My partner. Detective Rubio. Loves plants. Doesn't like rude people."

"That's too bad," Bruno sneered.

"Plus," Conor continued, "she's a black belt."

"Well, to me she's just a black broad." He laughed at his own joke.

"That was very funny, Bruno," Rosita offered.

"You delivered a tree last Wednesday," Conor said.

"That's very possible," Bruno responded, "since that's what I do for a living."

"To a building on Forty-fourth Street and the river," Rosita added.

"You know how many trees I deliver? What? I'm supposed to remember that one?"

"Actually," Conor said, "you delivered three trees. And I think you'd remember the apartment. A penthouse loft. High ceilings. Big terrace."

Bruno grabbed the sides of his pants, which were sliding off his hips, and hoisted them back into place. "Yeah, I remember. Nice-looking girl living there. Tipped me a hundred bucks. How's she doing?"

"She's dead," Rosita said.

"Don't come around my job and accuse me of shit like that." Bruno's voice rose into a bellow. "It was hard enough finding work when I got out of the joint."

Rosita got in Bruno's face. "We're not accusing you of anything,

Bruno. We just want to know where you were last Monday night between five thirty and nine."

"I don't have to answer you," Bruno snarled.

Rosita removed a pair of cuffs from her belt.

Bruno took a step back. "What kind of crap you trying to pull? You have no reasonable cause."

Rosita looked at Conor. "A smart aleck."

Bruno took another step away from Rosita. "I was home. All right?"

"Where's home?" Rosita asked.

"Brooklyn."

"Anybody with you?" she pressed.

"No."

Conor held his arms open wide. "Sorry to hear that, Bruno."

"Why? Because I have a record? So now every time something happens you're gonna come around and hassle me?"

"Hey, Bruno," Conor said. "You don't know how hard it is to solve crimes. We've got to pin it on somebody."

"Did you kill that woman?" Rosita asked, really in his face this time.

"Fuck you."

Rosita frowned and looked at Conor. "I'm new at this. Is that a yes or a no?"

"I think that was a yes," Conor replied.

"You want to arrest me? I don't give a fuck." Bruno held out his hands, ready for the cuffs. "Just do it. But I didn't kill nobody. And if you come up with some forensic bullshit like my prints are in the place, well duh! I was there delivering a fucking tree."

Chapter Forty-seven

Rosita climbed behind the wheel. "He really didn't give a damn about us. What does that mean? Guilty? Innocent?"

"It means nothing. That's the way he deals with cops."

"So we add him to the list?"

"Definitely." Conor exhaled, frustrated. "You know what, Rubio? We've got two completely opposite theories here. One, it was all about the diamond. And two, it was just a run-of-the-mill burglary. We need to focus on one or the other."

"Which one?" Rosita asked.

"I keep going back to the fact that the only thing missing was the red diamond. Sure, some ordinary perp could have happened to grab the most valuable thing in the place, but what are the odds?"

As Conor and Rosita entered the precinct, Amanda waved them into her office.

"You guys planning to buy a country house?" Amanda asked as they entered. "With all the overtime you're putting in, the number crunchers down at City Hall are going to scream like a pen full of stuck pigs."

"You know how it is, Sarge," Conor said. "First few days of a homicide investigation."

"Yeah, I know how it is. Unfortunately, the city is broke. Biggest deficit in history."

Conor bristled. "They want crimes solved or not?"

"All I'm saying is, unless it's absolutely necessary, keep the overtime to a minimum."

Amanda's phone rang. "Rooney's looking for you," she said as she reached for the receiver.

Conor and Rosita walked toward Rooney's office.

"There you go, Rubio. Our overtime is breaking the budget. I told you the sarge was going to say something sooner or later."

"What about *her*? She's here all the time."

"Doesn't matter. She's sleeping with the comptroller."

"Are you serious?"

"I wouldn't put it past her."

Conor and Rosita entered Rooney's office. He looked up from his desk. "Detective Rubio. Could I have a minute alone with Detective Bard? If you don't mind."

"Sure." She gave Conor a quick glance, then left the room.

Rooney motioned to a chair. "Have a seat."

Conor sat down. Rooney got up, walked over and closed the door, then returned to his desk.

"What do you think of Rubio?" Rooney asked as he returned to his desk and sat down.

Conor took a moment to decipher what Rooney was really asking. "Rubio? She's great."

"I know she's great, Bard. She looks good. And she's smart. That's not what I meant. What do you think of Rubio as a homicide detective?"

Now I get it, Conor thought. "I think she's doing fine. She's been a big help in the investigation."

"The chief of detectives called me this morning. There's a lot of heat. I just thought you might want somebody more experienced to work with you on this one."

"Rubio's really doing a great job, Lu. You bring somebody else in now, I've got to get them up to speed."

"All right. Just checking. Because I don't want to have to take you off the case."

Was that a threat? Was that supposed to motivate him? Or was Rooney laying pipe for replacing Rubio?

Rooney stood, signaling the meeting was over. "Just let me know if you want somebody else, all right?"

Conor left Rooney's office feeling as if he had just been hit with a sucker punch. *It's not Rubio's fault the case hasn't been solved.* Hell, it had only been three days. He wondered if Ralph ever had a meeting like that, back when he first became Ralph's partner, if Ralph had ever been asked, "You want to replace Bard?" Ralph would have said, "Go fuck yourself."

"Am I in trouble?" Rosita looked up at Conor, concerned.

"No, no. Nothing like that. He just wanted to know how we were coming along with the case."

Rosita pressed her tongue against the inside of her cheek. "Come on, Bard, you're not a very good liar. He's worried that I don't have the chops to do the job."

"Yeah. Something like that."

It was the first time Conor saw even a hint of fear in Rosita's eyes.

"Hey," she said, clearly wounded. "I'll take myself off the case. I'll go see Sergeant Pitts and ask her to reassign me. You get somebody with more experience."

"No, Rubio, you're stuck with me. We're going to solve this case together. That's what I told Rooney. All right?"

Rosita didn't respond.

"I know I'm hard to partner with, Rubio, and you're looking for any excuse to get away from me. What are you, a *girl*?"

She smiled appreciatively. "Thanks, Bard."

"Let's go."

"Where?"

"To the Crowne Plaza. Let's see what time the party really got started."

Chapter Forty-eight

Glenn Wilkes, chief of security for the Crowne Plaza, was accommodating. The hotel was constructed on a plot of real estate right in the middle of the precinct and cops frequented the bar after a long shift.

Conor, Rosita, and Wilkes filed into a room called the command center. A technician racked the videos and wound them to the right spot—between 5:45 and 6:15, the window of time in which Kruger, Silberman, and Punjabi said they arrived at the dinner.

Kruger appeared first, arriving at 5:56—or seventeen fifty-six as he put it. *Rather precise*, Conor thought. Given the fact that the video from Zivah's apartment showed her reentering the lobby at 5:36—the last time it could be confirmed she was alive—Kruger's arrival at the Crowne Plaza twenty minutes later boded well for his alibi but did not necessarily place him in the clear. Sure, twenty minutes wasn't much time to kill Zivah Gavish and make it to the Crowne Plaza but it *was* possible. And if there was one thing Conor had learned over the years it was that drawing the line at likely was not good enough. Was it *possible*? That was the acid test.

Punjabi entered the Crowne Plaza next. He had described his arrival as "just before six." Actually, it was 6:12 when Punjabi entered—thirty-six minutes after Zivah Gavish's last appearance on video—making his recollection suspect and his alibi now shaky at best.

Next up was Silberman at 6:19—which wasn't really "just after six" as Silberman had indicated. Forty-three minutes. Plenty of time.

So no one had an absolutely airtight alibi. There was ample time for any of them—even Kruger with a narrow window of twenty minutes—to have killed Zivah and gotten to the Crowne Plaza. Especially Kruger. Unlike everyone else, he was a professional. He would have planned the whole thing like any operation—with precision.

It was five thirty by the time they finished with the video and left the hotel by the side entrance on Forty-eighth Street.

"Let's grab something to eat," Rosita said. "I'm starved."

"You're always starved. What? You pregnant?"

"Now *that* would be an immaculate conception."

"No love life? Is that what you're saying, Rubio?" He looked at her. *Hell, she could have any man she wanted.*

"Just broke up with a guy."

"How long ago?"

"A year," she replied.

"That's not what I call *just* breaking up."

"The year went fast."

"Nobody in a year?"

"Nope. Just haven't been in the mood."

Damn, he thought. *A year.* He'd never been without sex for a year. Like any man, he was an opportunist—when the right situation presented itself, he was there. On the other hand, a woman *created* opportunities then decided if she wanted to follow through. George Bush had once called himself The Decider. *Sorry, George. Women are the deciders.*

They stopped at Brazil Grill, on the corner of Forty-eighth and Eighth Avenue. It was one of Conor's haunts, not just because of its proximity to the precinct, or its sturdy South American fare, but also because they had live music on the weekends. He liked to hang out at the bar, have a martini, and take in an hour or so of bossa nova. The more music Conor absorbed, the more diverse the styles, the more adventurous he became when he wrote songs.

Conor and Rosita sat at the bar. He ordered his usual—Ketel One martini, twist, no vermouth. Technically, it wasn't a martini without the vermouth or at least a hint of Lillet—it was straight vodka shaken and poured into a chilled martini glass—but that's the way he liked it. Rosita opted for a caipirinha, a cocktail made with cachaça, a Brazilian spirit distilled from sugarcane juice, similar to rum. She perused the menu.

"Don't eat too much," he said. "There's going to be plenty of food at the memorial."

"This memorial service should be interesting," she remarked as she placed the menu on the bar. "Especially if Silberman *and* Punjabi are on the guest list."

Thank God for cameras, Conor thought as he sipped his martini. The video from the lobby of the loft and the video from the Crowne Plaza framed the case with a temporal border. Unfortunately, nothing that came out of either video was definitive enough to draw specific conclusions. Yet the footage from the Crowne Plaza *did* indicate that none of the suspects could be ruled out. Which is the way it often was with evidence—you couldn't prove it happened but, conversely, you couldn't prove that it didn't happen. And sometimes that was the only thing that kept an investigation moving forward. Because until you proved it hadn't happened, there was always the possibility that it had.

Chapter Forty-nine

A surly bouncer clutching a clipboard and standing next to a velvet rope stopped Conor and Rosita at the front door of Le Lounge, a trendy spot on Avenue C in the East Village.

"You on the guest list?"

"Yes. Name's Bard."

The bouncer scanned the clipboard. "Sorry. No Bard."

"We're guests of Kenneth Madison," Conor insisted.

"You're not on the list," the bouncer said, devoid of emotion.

Rosita whipped out her shield. "How about Rubio? You got a Rubio on the list?"

The bouncer gave the badge a quick glance. "Yeah, there's a Rubio." He raised the velvet rope.

"I'm with *her*," Conor said as he followed Rosita through the door.

"These places ought to use retired cops for security," Conor groused, "instead of bozos like that."

"Stop complaining," she replied. "I got you in."

They entered a large room with dim lighting. The walls were adorned with vintage French advertising posters. Rap music vibrated out of the speakers.

Rosita half laughed. "*This* is a memorial service?"

The place was packed. As Conor scanned the crowd, he spotted Silberman and Punjabi huddled together. Silberman looked over and saw Conor and Rosita watching him, said something to Punjabi, then moved quickly away.

"They don't want to be seen together," she remarked.

"What does that tell you?"

"We're in the right place."

"Detective Bard! Detective Rubio!" Madison hurried over to them. "Glad you could make it." He motioned toward the bar. "Can I get you a drink?"

"Sure," Conor replied. "Ketel One martini. Twist. No vermouth."

Madison looked at Rosita. "And you?"

"I'll have a Bud Light."

Madison motioned to the bartender. "And give me another scotch. Neat." He glanced toward the front door. "You know, it's funny. I keep expecting Zivah to come walking in. That all this was nothing but a nightmare."

Conor turned and glanced toward the door as well. *That's the thing about terrible tragedies,* Conor thought. *They don't seem real. And neither do great things that happen in your life. Only the mundane feels real.*

The round of drinks arrived. Madison held up his glass. "To Zivah."

"To Zivah," Conor and Rosita said in unison as they raised their glasses.

Madison downed the scotch like a shot, placed the glass on the bar. "If you'll excuse me, I have a few guests I need to say hello to. Enjoy yourselves."

Madison waded into the crowd and, like a heat-seeking missile locking onto a target, zeroed in on a group of attractive young women. He appeared to have them captivated within seconds.

"What can I tell you?" Conor asked. "He likes women."

Rosita smiled. "And you don't?"

She nodded across the room. Conor followed her eyes and saw Tasha Sen making her way toward him.

"Hi, Conor."

Tasha looked particularly radiant in her little black cocktail dress. No, not radiant. Ravishing.

"Hello, Tasha."

They stood facing each other for an awkward moment.

"Would you like something to drink?" Conor asked.

"No, thank you." She glanced at her watch. "I've got a dinner at seven." She looked at Rosita. "Hello, Detective Rubio."

"Hi, Tasha," Rosita replied flatly.

Tasha turned back toward Conor. "I had a wonderful time last night. Let's do it again."

"I'll call you," Conor promised.

"That would be a good idea." Tasha tossed him a provocative glance then headed toward the exit.

"I think you better interview her one more time," Rosita suggested.

Conor detected her sarcasm but chose to ignore it. "You're right, Rubio. I'll do that the next chance I get."

She elbowed him. He grabbed his side. "Take it easy, Rubio. That hurt."

"It was supposed to," she said as she walked away.

Chapter Fifty

Conor watched as Rosita strolled across the room and was immediately set upon by a slick-looking young guy. *A sexy partner? Why not?*

For the next twenty minutes, Conor struck up conversations with several men and women. Not one of them had even met Zivah and only two had ever heard of her.

"This is a *memorial*?" a shocked young man blurted out when Conor mentioned the purpose of the event. "I thought it was just one of Kenny's parties." He put down his drink. "Wow! That's a buzz kill!"

Conor made it a point to seek out Punjabi.

"Too bad you can't smoke in clubs anymore," Conor said. "Probably be nice to have a bidi right now."

Conor then worked his way over to Silberman, who was attempting to hide behind a cluster of people.

"How's the wrist?" Conor asked.

Having rattled his two suspects to distraction, Conor focused his attention on a young brunette woman dressed to impress, a glass of champagne in her hand. Her name was Kristin.

"I'm a friend of Kenny's," Kristin said. "We used to date. Nothing really serious." She looked at Madison, who was now regaling two willowy blondes. "Kenny's a survivor. Even in *this* economy he does well."

"Looks like he does as well in the bedroom as he does in the boardroom."

Kristin laughed. "Kenny? He's a player. Everybody knows that." Kristin took a sip of champagne. "But I had a great time while it lasted. The best restaurants. A week in Bali." She held up her wrist, adorned with a diamond bracelet. "He bought me this last Christmas."

"Did you know Zivah?" Conor asked.

"No. Never met her. But Kenny says she was a wonderful person." She eyed Conor. "So what do you do?"

"I'm a cop."

Kristin reacted as if Conor had said, *I make eighty thousand a year. Sometimes more with overtime.*

She smiled and excused herself. Conor stood there feeling like a Little Leaguer in Yankee Stadium.

As it turned out, most of the people in attendance were Madison's friends. Those who were there because of Zivah spoke well of her but had had nothing more than a casual relationship. Conor began to feel sorry for Zivah. It appeared that she hadn't made any close friends in New York. She was dating an unabashed playboy. And now her short life was over.

Except for an opportunity to shake up Punjabi and Silberman, the party was a bust as far as the investigation went. Conor caught Rosita's eye and motioned for her to meet him at the door.

"You get anything?" he asked as they rendezvoused.

"Yeah. Two marriage proposals and a dozen business cards." Rosita checked her watch. "It's almost seven. I think I'm going to head home."

"Why don't you come with me?"

"You heard what the sergeant said about overtime."

"This isn't work. I'm stopping by a recording studio to see Alan Woodcliff."

"Alan Woodcliff? You mean *the* Alan Woodcliff?"

"Yeah."

"How do you know *him*?" she asked.

"I don't. Richard, my piano player, runs a tire store in Jersey. Alan Woodcliff came in the other day. Anyway, Richard gave him a copy of my CD and now he wants to meet me."

"Good thing Alan Woodcliff needed tires," Rosita observed.

Conor laughed. "That's what *I* said." He couldn't help himself—he was starting to dream again. *Maybe my music career has finally picked up a little traction.*

Conor and Rosita drove downtown to the recording studio on Lafayette and East Ninth. They entered and were greeted by a busty young woman at the reception desk who was munching on a carrot.

"He expecting you?" she asked.

"Yes," Conor replied.

She pointed down the hall.

Conor and Rosita found their way to a lounge area where Alan Woodcliff, flanked by two women in tight jeans, was sitting on a huge black leather couch. He was wearing a T-shirt commemorating his recent world tour.

"Mr. Woodcliff?" Conor asked as he approached.

Woodcliff looked up. "Yes?"

"I'm Conor Bard."

Woodcliff gave Conor a confused look, then emerged from his mental fog. "Hey, man. How you doing?" He stood, extended his hand. "Nice to meet you. And please, it's Alan."

"Alan. My partner, Rosita Rubio."

Woodcliff looked at Rosita. "You're a cop?" he asked, unable to hide his surprise.

"Yeah. Want to see my badge?"

Woodcliff held his arms in the air. "Want to strip-search me?"

The women laughed. Woodcliff laughed. Conor and Rosita didn't.

Woodcliff's smile faded. "Guess you've heard that before."

"No," Rosita said sarcastically. "First time."

Conor wondered if he had made a mistake bringing Rosita to the session. Even though he had known her only a couple of days, it was clear she had a tendency to say exactly what was on her mind. Which might be a problem since she obviously wasn't impressed with Alan Woodcliff.

Woodcliff motioned toward the two women, a blonde and a brunette, and introduced them. The blonde was Anna—Woodcliff had previously described her as his "cell phone girl"—and the brunette was Jody.

"Your CD is really nice." Woodcliff put his arm around Anna's waist. "Right, Anna?" He looked at Conor. "I played it for her."

"I love your voice," Anna said demurely.

"Thanks." Conor was relieved that the cell phone girl approved.

"Let's go inside," Woodcliff said. He pointed to the coffee table. "Grab some sushi."

Conor looked down and saw all manner of sushi and sashimi spread out next to a couple of bottles of sake and white wine. *How times have changed,* Conor thought. *Where are the burgers and beer and booze?* That used to be standard fare for musicians. Still was for him. Staring at the raw fish and chardonnay made him feel oddly out of place.

"Thanks," Conor said. "But we just came from a cocktail party. Been hitting the hors d'oeuvres."

They entered a control room where two more women were lounging on a fluffy velvet couch. Apparently they were farther down the pecking order because Woodcliff didn't even bother to introduce them. Arm candy, that's all.

A young man who looked about seventeen was sitting at a console. He sported a close-cropped haircut and was wearing a blue dress shirt neatly tucked into ripped jeans.

"This is Toby," Woodcliff explained. "The engineer."

Engineer? Conor would have pegged him as a geek. And, in a way, that's exactly what he was. In front of Toby was a computer keyboard, a stack of hard drives, and an array of monitors displaying virtual controls. As he surveyed the digital setup, Conor recalled the first time he had ever been in a recording studio. He was eighteen at the time, eons ago, and went to visit a friend who had gotten a summer job as a gopher at a studio on Fifty-seventh Street. And what a place it was. Monstrous twenty-four-track tape machines, their noisy cooling fans whirring like helicopter rotors, wires snaking everywhere, amplifiers with tubes glowing and emitting a warmth that he could still feel. It was then that Conor decided he wanted to be a recording artist. A rock star. And now, here he was, forty-three years old, standing in the middle of a quiet room. No humming fan blades, no glass-enclosed filaments generating thermal waves, no spaghetti collection of cables. So how old was his dream? Twenty-five years when measured conventionally. But when viewed on a music business timeline, it was ancient, having seen the transition from whiskey to wine, analog tape to digital technology. Was it too late to keep dreaming?

What's wrong with me? Conor asked himself. *I'm in a recording studio with Alan Woodcliff. He likes my music. He's going to help me. Relax. Go with the flow.*

Chapter Fifty-one

Toby tapped a few keys on the computer keyboard. An up-tempo tune vibrated from a huge pair of speakers hanging from the ceiling. Conor was impressed with both the driving rhythm and the solid rock lyrics.

Woodcliff said he needed a few minutes to set up the next song and suggested that Conor and Rosita have a drink in the kitchen, where there was a full bar. As they left the studio, Conor snuck a glance at one of the ornaments on the couch.

"They're half your age," Rosita whispered in his ear.

"Then maybe I should take them both," Conor whispered back.

They entered the kitchen and sat on two bar stools facing a well-stocked bar.

"He's a little prick," Rosita observed.

"Come on, Rubio. Lighten up. He's a rock star. What do you expect?"

She yawned. "I'm heading home. One more night and I'll finally be on a day schedule."

"What am I supposed to tell Woodcliff?"

"Tell him I'm tired." She looked toward the studio door. "You want *me* to tell him?"

"No. That's all right."

"Mañana," she said as she walked away.

Conor returned to the studio.

"What happened to your sidekick?" Woodcliff asked.

"She was tired. Just coming off nights."

Woodcliff wasn't happy about someone walking out on him. "Guess she didn't dig the music."

"No, really. She loved it. It's just that she hasn't had much sleep the last couple of days."

Conor took a seat next to Woodcliff and listened to the next song, which was a power ballad. Woodcliff played the song over and over, adjusting levels and EQ. He grew increasingly frustrated whenever he reached the bridge, which thundered into the final chorus. Jody yawned, presumably bored, and sashayed out of the control room. Anna stretched out on the couch, nodding off. The ornaments had left somewhere along the line. Finally, Woodcliff appeared to have a solution to whatever was bothering him.

"Stop it right there," Woodcliff shouted at Toby.

Toby tapped the computer keyboard. Silence returned.

"It needs another guitar in the bridge," Woodcliff said. "Something with a nice rhythm and blues flavor." He looked at Toby. "How long will it take you to set up for that?"

"Give me ten, fifteen minutes," Toby replied. "Which guitar you want to play?"

"What do I have here?" Woodcliff asked.

"You've got the Les Paul, the Strat, the—"

"Les Paul," Woodcliff said. He looked at Conor. "You want to play it?"

"Me?" Conor couldn't believe it.

"Sure. That lick you played on one of your songs. What was it called? Oh, yeah, 'Don't Know How to Save You.' That kind of feel would be perfect here."

Conor hesitated.

"I'll pay you scale," Woodcliff pressed. "That's what? Three hundred?"

"No, I can't . . ."

"It's not my money. It's Sony's money."

Sony's money? He was about to be paid by a record company for the first time. "Okay. Why not?"

Woodcliff stood. "Come on, let's get a drink."

They walked into the kitchen. Woodcliff poured himself a gin. Conor had a vodka.

"So here's what I'm thinking," Woodcliff began. "I'll call my guy at Sony Records and get him to give a listen. If he likes it, I'll take you into the studio, produce a couple of tracks—that's what I really want to do in the future, produce other talent."

Conor wanted to pump his fist in the air and scream *Yes!* "That would be great," he said, trying hard not to sound overly enthusiastic. Or desperate. That would be worse.

"You better get ready," Woodcliff said. "This could all happen fast."

"No problem. I'll start rehearsing with Richard and—"

"Who's Richard?"

"Richard. My piano player. From the tire store."

Woodcliff placed his hand on Conor's shoulder. "Conor, Conor, Conor. We're talking Sony Records here. You don't want some guy from a tire store playing piano on your record."

"He played piano on the CD. I mean—"

"Yeah, yeah. I know. But that CD is a diamond in the rough. It showcases your talent but it's not ready for prime time, know what I mean? I want to put you with a group of real studio musicians. The guys *I* use. There's nobody better."

Conor stared off. What now? He couldn't just kick Richard to the curb after all these years.

"Listen, Alan," Conor began, "I really think—"

The door opened. Toby stuck his head out. "Let's do it."

Chapter Fifty-two

Conor settled in front of the microphone, guitar on his lap. Suddenly the music track filled his headphones. He prepared himself for the bridge and then, when it arrived, he played the hell out of a bluesy guitar solo.

The music stopped.

"That's great!" Woodcliff sounded pleased. "Let's try that one more time."

Again Conor played his heart out. And again. And again. Seven takes. Until finally . . .

"That's it!" Woodcliff shouted through the headphones. "You nailed it."

Conor propped the guitar against the amp, slipped off his headphones, and walked back into the control room. Woodcliff stood and gave him a hug. "That's just what it needed."

"Thanks," Conor said. "I really appreciate this."

"It's all part of my plan," Woodcliff explained. "A few weeks from now, millions of people are going to hear your guitar lick on that song. Plus, when I call my Sony guy tomorrow, I'll tell him you're on my new CD. See, those guys don't know what's good or bad. Anyway, he'll already like your stuff before he even hears it."

*   *   *

Conor left at ten thirty. He walked for blocks, filled with a mixture of excitement and apprehension. Excited to have played on an Alan Woodcliff record. Excited to think he might be signing with Sony Records. Apprehensive about the Richard situation.

Conor needed a course of action. He decided he wouldn't press the issue yet. Too early in the game. He'd go to the meeting at Sony and see what happened. If the unthinkable really occurred, if Sony offered him a recording contract, he'd retain a lawyer, negotiate the deal. Certainly there wouldn't be anything written into the language about who played on the record, nothing that would prevent Richard from being one of the musicians. Then, when it came time to go into the studio, Conor would insist that Richard play piano. That's right, *insist*. What would Alan Woodcliff do? Kill the whole thing?

But what if Alan Woodcliff refused? What then? That would be it, wouldn't it? No way Conor was going to betray a lifelong friendship. Richard would play piano on his first commercial CD or there wouldn't be one.

As he walked along, his cell phone rang. He checked the caller ID. It was Richard. Conor let the phone ring a second time. What should he say? That Alan Woodcliff wants to replace him? The phone rang a third time. No, Conor decided. He wouldn't say anything. He had Richard's back. So why even bring it up?

"Hey, Richard."

"How'd it go with Alan Woodcliff?"

"It went great. I played on one of the tracks."

"Are you serious?"

"Yeah."

"That's awesome."

"And he's setting up a meeting at Sony Records."

"You realize what this means?" Richard exclaimed. "This means we're on our way." He laughed. "Good thing he needed tires."

"Listen, man," Conor said. "I'm beat. Let's talk tomorrow."

"Talk? We're going to celebrate!"

*   *   *

Conor needed a nightcap, something to even him out. But where? He decided to stop by the Cutting Room, one of the last remaining true music venues in Manhattan. The Cutting Room was actually two places in one—a bar in the front and a cabaret in the back, replete with a stage and a killer sound system. He had played there a couple of times, sitting in at the Monday-night jam, when musicians from all over the city straggled in and offered an impromptu concert. But a real gig at the Cutting Room was something he had never been able to pull off, given the long list of well-known artists who often played there. Maybe now, after what had happened with Alan Woodcliff, he would be able to take the step up from the Rhythm Bar.

Steve, the owner of the Cutting Room, greeted Conor warmly. "Hey, Conor, what's happening?"

Conor told Steve about the session with Alan Woodcliff and the upcoming meeting with Sony.

"Incredible," Steve said. "Congratulations."

"Congratulations may be premature," Conor countered. "Let's see what happens at Sony first."

"Whatever happens, you're on an Alan Woodcliff record. That's cool."

Conor couldn't argue with that. "Yeah. I guess it is cool."

"When you going to play here?" Steve wanted to know. "Better schedule you before your Sony CD comes out. I'll never be able to get you after that."

Conor laughed. "I'm available. Anytime."

Conor went to the bar and ordered a martini. He savored the clear, icy vodka, took his time drinking it. Steve's reaction was a confirmation that something extraordinary had happened. Just the mention of Alan Woodcliff was enough to get him booked at the Cutting Room. Signing a deal with Sony would change everything.

Here comes the sun, Conor thought. The melody of the Beatles song played in his head.

Seems like years since it's been here . . .
Here comes the sun . . .

Conor entered his small one-bedroom apartment to discover that nothing had changed. Yet. But he couldn't help thinking that a future was taking shape, that there was a new possibility looming in front of him, so there was no chance he was going to sleep. He picked up his acoustic guitar. It felt different in his hands. Lighter. Smoother. He fingered the steel strings, which were strands of silk tonight, strummed slowly. The chords resonated like never before. A rich, textured sound vibrated from the spruce top. Was this the same guitar he had played all these years?

He started singing the song Woodcliff had mentioned, "I Don't Know How to Save You Anymore."

Your love is like the sea, ever changing, ever tossing me around
And the storms you put me through, made me weak, left me seeking
   out high ground
And I just want to catch the wave that's heading into shore
And I just want to save you, babe, but I don't know how to save you
   anymore

He had written that about Heather. What a disastrous relationship. She had betrayed him and now she was truly history. At least he got a song out of it.

It occurred to him that he was playing *his* song, not a cover, not somebody else's music and lyrics. In places like the Rhythm Bar he played only the hits. Once in a while he would slip in one of his own compositions. But he could always feel the energy in the room drop. Bar crowds want familiar tunes. They want to sing along. *One of these days some guy will be performing* my *songs in a bar and people will be singing along.*

Conor ran through a repertoire of material that would be good for the Sony CD. "I Forgot to Be Afraid," a ballad. "For Love and Whiskey," a country-flavored midtempo tune. He began to allow himself to believe it was all real, visualizing the recording session, onstage at Madison Square Garden, touring the country. His daydreaming was cut short by the ringing of his cell phone.

"Bard."

"Conor. It's Hendrik. Did you think over our proposition?"

Chapter Fifty-three

The rude and effective slap sent Conor spiraling back to reality. He was not a rock star. He was a cop.

"Sorry to call so late," Kruger said. "But they've kept me in meetings all day and then scheduled a dinner with the ambassador."

Conor arranged to meet Kruger at the Aspen Social Club, a bar located in the chic boutique Stay Hotel on Forty-seventh Street between Sixth and Seventh. As at every bar he frequented, Conor knew someone who worked there. In this case, Cristy the manager, a young woman who was an aspiring writer. *At least she's not an actress*, he had thought when he first met her. In New York there are no waiters or waitresses. Just actors.

"What can I get you?" Cristy asked.

"The usual. I'm not feeling too adventurous tonight."

Conor took a seat at one of the small, low tables against the wall. He was halfway through his martini when Kruger arrived and handed him an envelope.

"What's this?" Conor wanted to know.

"The trail of the diamond. E-mails. Phone records. Documents linking Arun Punjabi to Marwala. Punjabi to Zivah Gavish."

Conor opened the envelope, slid out several sheets of paper, and perused a couple of the documents. "You've heard of six degrees of separation, haven't you, Hendrik? You can connect anybody to anybody."

"Yes, but what I've given you, I think it's enough for you to arrest Marwala for attempting to receive illegal contraband. The consulate lawyers will keep him behind bars until we can extradite him to South Africa."

Conor slid the documents back into the envelope.

"May I ask how it is that these documents happened to surface now? Quite a stroke of luck, don't you think, Hendrik?"

"Luck? Nothing to do with luck. What you have in your hand is the result of tireless research performed by my Scorpion"—Kruger caught himself—"by my SAPS colleagues."

Conor thought about what Kruger wanted him to do. Throw a few trumped-up charges at Marwala using evidence that was likely created out of whole cloth by Kruger's South African cohorts, make the arrest, then walk away and let SAPS finish the job.

"So Marwala, this man you've so far not been able to bring down, is just going to walk up to me and get himself arrested? Sorry, Hendrik. He doesn't sound that stupid."

"He's not. He'll produce some paperwork, forged, of course, claiming it's an heirloom, mined before all the diamond trade laws were passed, before the Kimberley Process went into effect."

"If you say so."

"This red diamond, this little colored piece of crystallized carbon, is the crowning jewel, so to speak, in Marwala's lifetime of smuggling. He's not just going to walk away."

"Okay," Conor said. "How do I find Marwala?"

"Quite simple. In fact, you provided me with the location the night we met. Xai Xai."

"South African restaurant, South African smuggler. Makes sense, Hendrik. But how are you going to get him there?"

"Marwala's palate is extremely limited," Kruger replied. "Ostrich tartare is his favorite dish. He is so fond of it that he raises ostrich on his compound. Every morning one of the birds is slaughtered, dragged into the kitchen, then chopped up and served raw."

Conor made a face. "Raw ostrich?"

"It's quite good. You should try it sometime."

"Sorry, I like my birds well-done."

Kruger smiled then continued. "I noticed that Xai Xai features ostrich tartare on its menu. So we arranged for one of our agents to be Marwala's seatmate on the long flight from Johannesburg. Our agent will make certain Marwala is well aware that a plate of ostrich tartare can be had at Xai Xai. I doubt Marwala will be able to resist the temptation."

Conor took a sip of martini. "Sounds like you have a pretty thorough dossier on Marwala."

"In fact, we know a great deal about him. His taste in wine, food, even his sexual proclivities. Our prostitutes have given us a full report. Would you like to know what Marwala finds stimulating?"

"No, thanks," Conor replied quickly.

Conor stopped at the precinct and flipped through the contents of the envelope Kruger had given him—a collection of dubious evidence loosely linking Wouter Marwala, Arun Punjabi, and Zivah Gavish. Still, if presented in the right way, it could work. He decided he'd send copies down to Ralph in the DA's office, get his opinion.

Armed with a small digital voice recorder, Conor walked the three blocks to Xai Xai. Even though it was almost one in the morning, the place was packed. When he entered the bar, he spotted Jack Bailey at a table with a beautiful young woman. Bailey was with ICE, Immigration and Customs Enforcement, and Conor had worked with him on a couple of cases in the past. He was fifty-two, had reddish-blond hair, was quite a drinker, and liked to have a good time. And from the looks of his date, maybe he was about to. But then Conor was struck with the notion that it was no accident that Bailey was sitting in Xai Xai on this particular night. *Kruger. That son of a bitch. He's playing both sides of the fence.*

Conor approached the table. "Looks like South African food has gotten popular with federal agents."

"Even civil servants need variety," Bailey said. He motioned toward the woman. "Conor Bard, meet Agent Ann Elliot."

Conor nodded. "Nice to meet you." *Looks like Bailey isn't getting lucky tonight after all.*

"Likewise," Ann said warmly.

"Want to join us?" Bailey asked.

"Sure."

Ann Elliot was quite engaging and would've been a possibility except for Conor's self-imposed ban on dating federal agents. One gun in the bedroom was enough.

Conor looked at Bailey. "So what's the deal?"

"Just thought we'd have a little ostrich," Bailey replied.

"Come on, Jack," Conor countered. "You're not an ostrich kind of guy. Why are you here?"

"Okay," Bailey admitted, "I'm here on a case. That's all I can tell you. Why are *you* here?"

Conor didn't need Bailey to explain further. It was clear exactly what was going on. Kruger had a backup plan—he had brought in ICE. Conor decided to have a little fun.

"Why am I here?" Conor pointed out the window. "I live three blocks away. This is one of the places in my hood." He went out of his way to sound unconvincing.

"Good try," Bailey said. "Why are you *really* here?"

"I'm working a case too," Conor admitted. "Just like you." He paused for effect. "A South African guy."

Bailey frowned. "What's his name?"

"Marwala. Wouter Marwala. You heard of him?"

"Yeah." Bailey cleared his throat. "I heard of him."

"He's not coming in tonight though."

"How do you know?"

"Got a guy following him," Conor lied. "Marwala's in Brooklyn. Holding court at another South African restaurant called Madiba."

Bailey looked at Ann then pushed a half-full bottle of wine across the table to Conor. "Here's our parting gift."

"Thanks."

Conor watched them leave. *NYPD one, Feds zero.* He picked up the bottle of wine and moved to the bar, where he ordered droëwors, South African cured dry sausages.

A waiter walked past Conor and greeted someone entering the front door.

"Would you like a table?" the waiter asked.

"The bar will be fine," came the reply. The voice was deep, commanding.

Conor twisted around on the bar stool and found himself staring into a pair of ice blue eyes set deeply within a coal black face.

Marwala stepped up to the bar, followed by his two cohorts, presumably bodyguards.

"Good evening, Mr. Marwala." Conor motioned to the bottle on the bar. "May I offer you a glass of wine?"

"Do we know each other?" Marwala asked.

"No," Conor replied.

"But you know my name."

"Yes."

"You have me at a disadvantage," Marwala said. "May I ask your name?"

"Conor Bard. *Detective* Conor Bard. And I'm here to arrest you."

Chapter Fifty-four

Marwala, appearing unruffled by Conor's proclamation, picked up the bottle and examined the label. Conor seized the opportunity to reach in his pocket and turn on the digital recorder. He wasn't sure how much the microphone would pick up from inside his jacket, but it was worth a try.

Marwala placed the bottle back on the bar. "You have expensive tastes, Detective."

"Oh, not me. The Feds left this. They have a much bigger expense account than NYPD." He looked at the bartender. "Two wineglasses, please."

The bartender produced two glasses, poured some wine in each. Conor handed one to Marwala.

"Gesondheid," Conor offered.

Marwala slid onto a stool. *"Gesondheid."* He took a sip then waved off his bodyguards. "So, Detective, may I ask why you intend to arrest me?"

"For smuggling a rare red diamond into the country."

Marwala smiled. "Are you referring to the diamond that was taken from the home of Zivah Gavish?"

"Exactly."

"That diamond is an heirloom," Marwala explained. "A very dear friend of mine has had that diamond in his family for nearly a century. Ms. Gavish was engaged to test the market, see what it might fetch."

Just as Kruger had predicted, Conor thought. Marwala was claiming heirloom status.

"I am here to retrieve my property," Marwala said. "What must I do?"

"What makes you think I have the diamond?" Conor asked.

"I have sources."

Not for long, Conor thought. "Assuming we do have it, the diamond would be entered in evidence. Even if I wanted to, I couldn't just walk in, sign it out, and turn it over to you."

"There must be a way to return property to its rightful owner."

"Yes," Conor said. "But in order to do that, a release must be obtained from Zivah's estate since it was stolen from her apartment. In America we say possession is nine points of the law."

"The other point. Can we do something about that?"

Marwala had denied ownership, claiming to be working for an unnamed owner in South Africa. Plausible deniability—something he had used to extricate himself in his previous two arrests in South Africa.

"I'm not sure what I can do," Conor said carefully. "A claim of ownership for the diamond has already been filed."

"Who might that be?"

"A collector named Sulaiman Aziz."

"Do not worry about Mr. Aziz," Marwala said dismissively. "Can you help me sort all this out?"

"Mr. Marwala, determining ownership of the diamond is a legal matter."

Marwala took a sip of wine, probed Conor's eyes.

"Do you know a good American lawyer?" Marwala asked. "I'm prepared to pay one million American dollars for the diamond's return."

Conor studied Marwala. A bribe? But then again, not really. He was offering to pay a lawyer, not a cop. Of course, if a cop took him up on it . . .

"That's a lot of money," Conor noted.

"Indeed it is. But well worth it if you can help me bypass all the red tape and arrange for the diamond to be returned to me so I can convey it to its rightful owner."

Conor took a sip of wine, savored the rich taste for a moment before swallowing. "You say you have documents that prove the ownership of the diamond?"

"Of course. I certainly wouldn't want to do anything illegal."

Conor realized that even if Marwala came to the precinct with forged documents, it still might not be enough to justify an arrest. After all, Marwala could hide behind plausible deniability again. On the other hand, if Conor could get Punjabi to admit he received the rough diamond from Marwala, that would seal the deal. But how to convince Punjabi to admit that he played a role in an international diamond-smuggling operation?

"I do happen to know a very good lawyer," Conor said. "Let me speak with him. In the meantime, why don't you give me a number where I can reach you?"

"Very good."

Marwala jotted down a number on a napkin and handed it to Conor.

"If one million is not enough," Marwala said without flinching, "please let me know."

Conor nodded, hoping the recorder was picking up Marwala's voice.

Marwala placed his elbow on the bar, leaned closer to Conor. "Do you still want to arrest me, Detective?"

Conor smiled conspiratorially. "I don't think so."

Chapter Fifty-five

Conor walked down Ninth Avenue thinking about his conversation with Marwala. He pulled out the digital recorder and navigated to the beginning of the recording. Surprisingly, Marwala's deep voice was clearly audible. There was no question that Marwala had offered a bribe but had couched it in a way that was open to interpretation by insisting it was for legal fees. Conor half laughed. *A bribe?* A couple grand is a bribe. A million is a life. So how to handle the situation? He flipped open his cell phone and called Kruger.

"You awake?" Conor asked.

"I'm always awake," Kruger replied.

"Marwala offered me a million dollars for the return of the diamond."

"A million?" Kruger sounded pleased. "So you arrested him?"

"No."

Conor's response was met with silence.

"Look. Hendrik. I'm building a case. That's the way we do it here."

"Of course."

"And remember, I *am* working a homicide, not a smuggling investigation."

"They're connected, Conor. And you know it. Besides, I have done you a favor. If Marwala had arranged for Zivah Gavish to be killed, he wouldn't be in New York. I have eliminated a suspect for you."

"You wouldn't happen to know why Immigration and Customs agent Jack Bailey was at Xai Xai tonight, would you?"

"A lot of agencies are after Marwala," Kruger said, his voice betraying nothing. "All I'm doing is trying to help you get the lion's head before anyone else does."

The lion's head. This was just one big safari to Kruger.

Conor walked into his apartment, picked up his guitar, then immediately put it down again. The creative surge he had felt earlier was gone. He climbed into bed but sleep eluded him. Tossing and turning, he finally gave up at five thirty, staggered into the shower, then walked into the precinct at seven.

Rosita was there, bottle of Windex in her hand, carefully cleaning the glass of a small silver frame, which held the picture of a young girl no more than five years old.

"Who's that?" Conor asked.

She slid the frame so it was facing him. "Maria. My sister Candida's daughter."

Conor stared at the picture.

Rosita put her hands on her hips. "You don't like it."

"No, no. I do."

"But?"

"It's just that I'm not used to seeing things on that desk. I mean, there's a flower in a vase and a plant in a little pot. And now a silver frame."

"So?"

"So it looks great."

She glanced at his desk, devoid of any form of decoration. "You ought to put something on *your* desk."

"I like my desk the way it is."

"Okay. It's *your* desk."

Conor walked to the coffee machine, poured a cup. "I met Wouter Marwala last night."

"You did?" She was surprised.

"Yes. At Xai Xai, this South African wine bar around the corner." He walked back to his desk, eased into the chair. "I ought to take you there sometime." He took a sip of coffee. "You like raw ostrich?"

"I'll stick with well-done steak. So, what did Marwala say?"

"He offered me a million dollars."

She walked to his desk. "A million dollars?"

"All I have to do is make sure he gets his little red diamond back." He reached in his pocket and took out the digital recorder. "I recorded the whole conversation."

"Don't you need a warrant for that?"

"There wasn't time."

"Let me hear it," she said.

He handed her the recorder. Marwala's voice resonated out of the small speaker, finally concluding with "If one million is not enough, please let me know."

Rosita snapped off the recorder. "Since we're partners, we split the million, right?"

"I'll give you a hundred grand."

"Half," she insisted. "Or I'll turn you in."

"You'd rat me out?"

"For half a mil? In a heartbeat."

He stood. "Let's go talk to Rooney. See how he wants to handle this."

"Okay. But don't cut him in."

"All right. Then don't tell him about the recording."

"You want me to lie about the fact that you conducted an illegal eavesdropping operation?"

"No. I just want you to keep quiet about it."

"No problem," she said. "But that means it's a sixty-forty split on the million."

"Who's sixty?"

She curled her fingers in front of her mouth, blew on her fingernails. "Who do you think?"

Chapter Fifty-six

Conor, Rosita, and Amanda convened in Rooney's office. Rooney perused the documents spread out across his desk.

"So Kruger gave you all this?" Rooney asked.

"Yes," Conor confirmed. "I'd like to get everything to Ralph Kurtz. See what they think down in the DA's office."

"Marwala would be a nice collar." Rooney slid the documents across the desk to Conor.

"Yes, he would," Amanda agreed. "But I have a couple of concerns."

Rooney looked at her. "Go ahead."

"Well," Amanda began, "we're talking about a sting of sorts, aren't we?"

"More or less," Conor allowed.

"That's a slippery slope," Amanda said. "Unless it's done right, we could find ourselves being accused of entrapment."

"Where's the entrapment?" Conor countered. "There's no entrapment. He offered a bribe and—"

"That's exactly what I mean," Amanda interrupted. "He didn't offer you a bribe. He offered to pay a lawyer."

"Whether it's a bribe or legal fees," Rooney interjected, "it's a moot point until we have solid evidence the diamond has been smuggled into the country."

Conor held up the documents Kruger had given him. "But—"

"Are those facts? Or is it just a manufactured paper trail that fits Kruger's agenda?" Rooney waved at the stack of documents. "Would I like to collar an international smuggler like Marwala? Damn right." He looked up at Conor. "On the other hand, I don't want this office to be an auxiliary of the South African Police Service." He tapped his desk with his forefinger. "Bring me facts," he said, asserting his authority as commanding officer, "not Kruger's version of the facts, then we'll talk about it."

Conor stood. Rosita followed suit.

"Don't forget," Rooney added, "we're investigating a homicide. And I've already told you how much pressure I'm getting on this one. So, unless you're sure Marwala had something to do with the murder of Zivah Gavish, don't get sidetracked. Is that clear?"

"Very," Conor replied.

Conor and Rosita walked slowly toward their desks.

"Does this mean we don't get the million dollars?" she asked.

"Not a penny of it."

She sighed. "And I was going to buy a really nice pair of shoes."

They slid behind their respective desks.

Conor stared off. "A collar like Marwala? Could get me promoted to First Grade."

He had been Detective Second Grade for years, stuck at that pay scale. First Grade meant more money, more prestige.

"And I could retire with a First Grade pension," he added.

"You thinking of retiring?" She pouted. "And leaving me here alone?"

"No, Rubio. I'd hire you as background singer."

"I can't sing."

"Take lessons."

Conor picked up the phone and called Ralph, apprising him of the situation.

"What did he say?" Rosita asked when Conor hung up the phone.

"Said it doesn't sound too promising unless we can get somebody to talk. Like Silberman or Punjabi."

"Didn't you say you wanted to bring them in?"

"Yeah."

"On what pretense?" she asked.

"The red diamond. The cat's out of the bag on that one."

Conor called Punjabi and convinced him to stop by the precinct. Silberman, on the other hand, received the VIP treatment.

"We've got a real problem here," Conor said as he and Rosita swept into Silberman's jewelry store.

"What problem?" Silberman was quaking.

"Can't talk about it here," Rosita said. "We need you to come with us."

"I'm just a one-man shop," Silberman protested. "There's nobody here to—"

"Guess you need to close up for a while," she said quickly.

"Won't take long," Conor added. "Arun Punjabi is already on his way to the precinct. Wants to make some kind of statement." He leaned in on Silberman. "You have any idea what that might be?"

"No." Silberman trembled.

Rosita turned on her charm and adopted a sympathetic tone. "Mr. Silberman. If you have anything you want to say, it would be better for you to tell us now, before Mr. Punjabi makes his statement."

Silberman started to respond.

"Hold that thought, Mr. Silberman," Conor said. "Let's go over to the precinct where we can make it official."

Chapter Fifty-seven

Timing is everything, Conor thought as they led the quaking Silberman into the precinct just as Punjabi arrived. The two suspects allowed themselves a quick glance at each other before looking away.

"Detective Rubio," Conor said, "why don't you escort Mr. Silberman to an interrogation room? I'll take care of Mr. Punjabi."

Rosita led Silberman down a hall. Conor walked up to Punjabi.

"Thank you for coming in, Mr. Punjabi."

"If I can be of any help—"

"Do you know Mr. Silberman?" Conor asked.

Punjabi didn't respond immediately. "We have done business together," he finally said.

"You have any idea why he wants to make some kind of statement to police?"

"None," Punjabi said, shifting his feet.

"If you'll come with me, please, Mr. Punjabi."

Conor led Punjabi to an interrogation room.

"Can I get you a coffee? Some water?"

Punjabi fidgeted slightly. "No. I'm fine. How much time—"

"Please have a seat, Mr. Punjabi."

"Detective, I have appointments and—"

"Let me just see what Mr. Silberman wants to tell us. Then I'll come right back."

Punjabi swallowed hard. "Okay."

Conor left Punjabi and walked to the interrogation room where Rosita was sitting with Silberman. Conor poked his head inside. "Detective Rubio?"

Rosita looked at Silberman. "Excuse me."

Silberman, panic written all over his face, nodded.

Rosita walked out of the room and followed Conor into the observation area.

"He's petrified," Rosita said.

"Good. When we walk back in, let's act like we know something. Maybe you can pretend to be sad. Like, poor guy. He's about to be sold down the river by his business associate."

"Don't worry, Bard. I know what I'm doing. If I hadn't become a cop my next choice was actress."

"Really?"

"Yeah. I played a flower once in grammar school."

"What? A rose?"

"Don't call me Rose. I hate that."

"I didn't call you Rose, I asked if you *played* a rose."

"No. A tulip."

They entered to find Silberman on the verge of hyperventilating.

"Mr. Silberman," Conor said as he sat across from him. "We're about to speak with Mr. Punjabi. He's very anxious to give us a statement."

Rosita regarded Silberman sympathetically. "You recall, Mr. Silberman, that I strongly advised you to tell us what you knew before Mr. Punjabi had an opportunity to give his side of the story. Well, this is your last chance."

"I have nothing to say," Silberman replied, managing a bit of defiance, "because I have done nothing wrong."

Conor stood, paced back and forth. "Okay, Mr. Silberman, let me tell you what we know. We know that a diamond entered this country

CHARLES KIPPS

illegally within the last week." He removed the photo of the red diamond and held it so Silberman could see it. "*This* diamond."

Silberman looked stricken.

Rosita leaned across the table. "Recognize the diamond, Mr. Silberman?"

"No." Silberman rubbed his forehead in anguish. "Oh, my God! I was the one."

"The one who did what?" Rosita pressed.

"The one who caused the death of Zivah Gavish," Silberman blurted out, tears welling up in his eyes.

Chapter Fifty-eight

Conor and Rosita exchanged a glance.

"What do you mean by that, Mr. Silberman?" Rosita asked.

"The diamond. She must have been killed over that diamond." He buried his head in his hands.

Rosita reached over, touched his shoulder. "Mr. Silberman?"

Silberman, now crying, looked up at her. "If I hadn't . . ." He sobbed.

"If you hadn't what?" Rosita asked gently.

Silberman took a deep breath. "Arun called me three weeks ago. He had just cut a rare piece and was looking for a buyer. Not just any buyer. Someone who would be willing to purchase the piece without documentation. Someone extremely wealthy. I told him, no, I didn't know anyone like that. Because I understood what Arun meant. The diamond was obtained illegally and I didn't want any part of it. But he called again. And he offered me fifty thousand dollars to find a buyer."

"That's a great deal of money," Rosita observed.

"Business has been slow," Silberman admitted. "I needed the cash. With the economy so bad . . ."

"I understand," Rosita said, meaning it. "For a small-business owner like yourself, I'm sure it's extremely difficult."

Conor delighted in watching Rosita use her femininity and a convincing display of compassion to make Silberman feel at ease. Male detectives were able to show empathy and even offer camaraderie, which could be quite effective, but there was a subtle difference when female detectives interviewed males. Even the most hardened criminals were no match for their "sister" or "mother" sitting across from them.

"And I've lost my lease," Silberman continued, "because half the street is being torn down to build the tower."

Conor winced, not in solidarity with Silberman's predicament but because another piece of old New York was fading into history. Buildings that had housed sidewalk-level diamond dealers for decades had been torn down to make way for a forty-one-story high-rise in the middle of the block. The New York Diamond Tower, as it was known, would alter the personality of the Diamond District. Sparkling gems that once beckoned pedestrians would now be hidden high above Forty-seventh Street, no longer offering up their tiny shafts of dazzling light to the collective glow of the city.

"I have no idea what the rents will be." Silberman sighed. "I don't even know if I can afford a small office." He rubbed his eyes, shook his head. "But I *still* told Arun no."

Rosita nodded sympathetically. "So what made you change your mind?"

"Arun called back and doubled the offer. A hundred thousand. And all I had to do was make an introduction."

"A hundred thousand?" Conor shrugged. "Doesn't sound like much when you consider it's a red diamond we're talking about."

Silberman grew agitated. "I didn't know it was red until you showed me the picture. Red? My God! They're priceless."

"A hundred thousand to move a red diamond without documentation?" Conor laughed derisively. "It looks like Arun Punjabi was playing you for a fool."

Rosita resumed the questioning. "When Mr. Punjabi came to your store, what did he say?"

"He said there could be a problem with police and I was not to mention anything about setting him up with Zivah."

"You arranged for Mr. Punjabi and Ms. Gavish to meet?" Rosita asked.

"Even after Arun offered me a hundred thousand dollars, I wasn't sure if I wanted to get mixed up in something like that. But then Zivah stopped by the store. While we were talking she got a phone call. When she hung up she told me the person on the phone was a client. She said she had visited his home in Abu Dhabi and that he loved rare diamonds and didn't care where he got them." Silberman paused. "I thought, *This is providence*. Like God was handing me the answer to all my troubles."

"If you were to get a hundred thousand," Rosita began, "how much did you think the diamond was worth?"

"For finding a buyer," Silberman replied, "a fee of five percent is customary."

"Five percent?" Conor took a seat across from Silberman again. "So you thought the diamond was worth around two million."

"Yes," Silberman answered. "But the diamond in the picture could sell for anything, especially to a rich Arab. Even seventy million would not be too much."

Conor nodded. "Five percent of seventy million comes to three and a half million."

Silberman looked at Rosita, his eyes pleading. "You don't know the people in the diamond business. They can be without conscience when it comes to trading diamonds. A red diamond? Arun never told me it was a red diamond. I would have never gotten involved at any price. People kill for baubles. For a red diamond they would murder their brother." Tears rolled down his cheeks. "If it wasn't for me, Zivah would still be alive."

"So you believe Zivah was killed because of the diamond?" Rosita asked.

"Well, of course she was!" Silberman exclaimed. "Why else would someone do that to her?"

Rosita touched Silberman's shoulder again. "Do you know how the diamond got into the U.S.?"

"Arun brought it in somehow," Silberman replied. "I don't know how."

"Are you familiar with someone named Wouter Marwala?" Conor asked.

"I've heard of him. Everyone in the trade has heard of him. He's not someone you want to deal with." Silberman cowered. "What does he have to do with this?"

"He may be the origin of the diamond," Conor replied.

Silberman gasped. "Oh, no."

After another half hour of questioning, it became clear that arranging a meeting between Zivah Gavish and Punjabi was Silberman's only involvement. Conor and Rosita stepped outside the interrogation room to confer.

"You know what I find odd?" Conor asked.

"What?"

"Why didn't Arun Punjabi come to the precinct after Zivah was killed? Wasn't he concerned about the red diamond? According to Kramer, the transaction hadn't been concluded. No diamond, no big payday for Punjabi."

"Maybe he was afraid to go to the police because the diamond was illegal," she speculated.

"Or maybe this is really simple. Arun Punjabi already had the diamond because he killed Zivah Gavish."

"With a diamond-cutting disk no less." She laughed. "Beautiful."

They walked back into the interrogation room.

"We're not going to charge you with anything at this time," Rosita assured Silberman, "but you do understand you committed a crime."

"Yes."

"I think you should hire a lawyer," Conor suggested.

"I know."

"I'm sure you can work out something with the DA in exchange for your testimony," Rosita added.

Silberman appeared relieved, unburdened. He signed a written statement and was allowed to leave.

Chapter Fifty-nine

Conor and Rosita entered the other interrogation room, avoiding eye contact with Punjabi, hoping to make him as uncomfortable as possible.

"Sorry to keep you waiting," Conor said.

Punjabi bolted to his feet. "Detective, I really must get back to the office. If you'll just tell me—"

"Do you know why Mr. Silberman would implicate you in a diamond-smuggling operation?" Conor asked.

Punjabi drew in a sharp breath, as if he'd been hit in the stomach. "I have absolutely no idea."

Conor wasn't sure how he wanted to proceed. He could arrest Punjabi based on Silberman's statement but Punjabi would likely be given bail so what would that accomplish? It might be better to let Punjabi sweat out a pending arrest, keep him looking over his shoulder. If the pressure got too great, he might crack and offer up at least some sort of explanation regarding Marwala and the red diamond.

"So you know nothing about this diamond?" Conor asked, holding up the photo of the red gem.

"Nothing whatsoever," Punjabi said after a quick glance at the photo.

"Okay, Mr. Punjabi. If you'd just sign a statement to that effect."

Punjabi clenched his fists. "I'd like to retain an attorney before I sign any statement."

"That might be a good idea," Rosita said.

"Am I free to go?" Punjabi asked.

"Yeah," Conor replied. "Just have your attorney give us a call."

Punjabi hurried out of the room.

Conor looked at Rosita. "You noticed that, right?"

"What? That he wasn't surprised that you were holding up a picture of a red diamond?"

"Exactly. You see, Rubio, sometimes it isn't what someone *does* that gives them away, it's what they *don't* do."

They walked toward their desks.

"You know what would be helpful?" Conor asked.

"What?"

"If I had more information about the mechanics of diamond smuggling."

Rosita mockingly held her forefinger up to her cheek. "And where might you gain such helpful knowledge?"

He grinned, caught.

She checked her watch, stood. "It's four o'clock. Don't want to push the overtime my first week at Midtown and get on the wrong side of Sergeant Pitts. You go see the lovely Tasha Sen. I'm going home."

"It's all business," he insisted.

"Right." She started walking away. "Call me if something comes up." She stopped, looked at Conor. "No, let me rephrase that. Something's definitely going to come up."

"I hope so."

"Call me if anything happens with the case."

"Which case? The pillowcase?"

She tried not to laugh. "And to think I had these high hopes for you. That you weren't like other men."

"I'm not."

"That's what they all say."

She turned and continued out of the room. Conor pulled out his cell phone. Tasha was free for dinner. He decided a French restaurant was in order this time and suggested Tout Va Bien on Fifty-first Street between Eighth and Ninth.

"I love French," she said. "That sounds great."

"I'll pick you up at—"

"Let's meet there," Tasha said quickly.

"Okay." He hung up and wondered why she always wanted to meet at the restaurant. *Does she have a boyfriend?*

Now that there was no doubt that Punjabi the cutter was connected to Marwala the smuggler, Conor felt it was appropriate to keep the illegal diamond aspect of the case alive. Although Ralph didn't know it yet, Conor was planning to have Ralph pose as the high-priced lawyer who collected Marwala's million-dollar payment for the diamond's return. *Might as well get the ball rolling.* Conor dialed Marwala's cell phone.

The call went directly to voice mail. Conor waited for the standard automated greeting. "Mr. Marwala. Detective Bard. Could you please call me when you have a chance?" He left both his cell number and the precinct number. *Strange*, Conor thought. *So much at stake and he doesn't pick up.*

Conor began filling out the DD5 forms chronicling his interviews with Silberman and Punjabi.

"Hey, Conor."

Conor looked up, saw Danny Hahn, the union rep, approaching.

"Danny. What's happening?"

Hahn dropped into a chair next to Conor's desk.

"I just got out of a meeting with IAB," Hahn said. "You've got a little problem."

Chapter Sixty

Conor was usually happy to see Hahn—they were friends—but not under these circumstances.

"Why the hell is IAB trying to jam me up over a fucking bar? Don't they have enough to do with real corruption?"

"Don't worry," Hahn reassured him. "I've got a plan."

"I sure as hell hope so."

"The way the rule is written, you can't be *employed* by a licensed establishment. But it's my opinion, and the opinion of the union counsel, that there's nothing to stop you from performing there. As long as you're not paid."

"Well, I'm not getting rich playing there, I'll tell you that. But I am being paid."

"How much?"

"After paying the band, I usually wind up with about a hundred, a hundred fifty."

"Okay. Here's our response. You perform at the Rhythm Bar in hopes of being discovered by some recording company guy who might walk in the joint one night. That's why you're doing it without being paid. Whatever money the bar pays, it all goes to the band. Not you. Understand?"

"Got it," Conor said.

"So now all you've got to do is talk to the owner of the bar. Make sure if IAB comes around, he tells them you don't make any money."

After Hahn left, Conor grew annoyed. He hated playing games like the one Hahn suggested but some of the rules and regulations in the department were archaic and illogical, which gave cops little choice, especially in situations like this one. After all, he wasn't really doing anything wrong, just playing a gig. Anyway, maybe none of this would matter if all went well with Alan Woodcliff and Sony Records. Maybe this time next year he wouldn't be a cop.

Conor went home, showered again, then changed into a pair of gray slacks and one of his favorite sports coats. He swung by the Rhythm Bar to tell John about the IAB investigation. The place was doing a nice business—it always attracted an after-work crowd on Friday nights.

"Okay," John said. "We don't pay you a nickel. That what I'm supposed to say?"

"That's it," Conor replied.

"No problem."

Conor decided to have a quick martini. When he stepped up to the bar, he noticed Ingrid sitting there.

"Hi, Conor."

"Ingrid, how are you?"

"Good. Really good."

"Can I get you a drink?"

Ingrid held up a nearly full glass of wine. "No. I'm fine, thanks."

Conor motioned to Susie, the bartender, who was already making his martini. "Put Ingrid's wine on my tab."

Susie drained the shaken vodka into a martini glass, slid it across the bar to Conor.

Conor raised his glass. "Cheers."

"Cheers," Ingrid echoed.

He looked at her. She had a serene aura about her, one that softly whispered, *I'm not crazy. I won't mess with your head.*

"When are you going to play here again?" she asked.

"I don't know. I'm in the middle of a case. Maybe a couple weeks or so, I'll be back."

"I'll look forward to that."

Conor thought about getting Ingrid's number but changed his mind. *She's a musician. She can't be normal. It's all an illusion.* He finished his martini, left the bar, and walked toward Tout Va Bien. His cell phone rang. "Bard."

"Hey, Conor, it's Alan Woodcliff."

"Hey, Alan."

"I mixed your guitar part in. Sounds great. Brought it way up. Featured it."

Featured it? Conor felt a rush. His guitar solo would be soaring above the track on an Alan Woodcliff recording.

"And I spoke with Sony," Woodcliff continued. "We've got a meeting set up Tuesday afternoon. Three o'clock."

"That's great," Conor said. "Thanks."

"Like I told you, we're going to get you signed to a deal."

Conor hung up and found himself walking at a fast pace, so fast he was beginning to perspire. He swallowed, took a breath, slowed down. Could all this really be happening? A meeting scheduled at Sony. A sexy date on her way to meet him. *Life's good,* he thought. *Life's very good.*

Chapter Sixty-one

Conor entered Tout Va Bien and pulled up a bar stool. He thought about having a second martini—not an unusual occurrence—but decided to pace himself and opted for a glass of cabernet instead.

Tasha arrived, elegantly attired in a full-length, midnight blue, sari-inspired dress. Conor stood, greeted her with a kiss on each cheek, then led her to a table against the wall and ordered another cabernet. After a few minutes of general conversation, he asked her, "When we were talking about smuggling, you said you could just wear a diamond into the country. What about other ways to get a diamond past Customs?"

"Foolish me," she replied, her face flashing disenchantment. "I thought I was going out on a date, not meeting a detective for an interview."

Conor smiled sheepishly. "This *is* a date. I was just wondering."

"Okay, hiding a diamond in your luggage is too risky, especially these days. Somebody I know got caught with about fifty diamonds hidden in a tube of toothpaste. But you're talking about one diamond, right? You're not talking about a large number of gems."

"One or two."

"You've traveled abroad?"

237

"A few times," Conor replied.

"Okay. When you passed through Customs, did anybody examine your watch? Or your belt buckle? Your watch could have been an expensive stolen timepiece. Your belt buckle could have been made out of pure platinum. No problem. Just walk right through. Like I said before, wear it."

"So basically . . ."

"If you're smuggling one at a time, flaunt it." She squinted her eyes slightly, as if something had dawned on her. "You asked me last time about a red diamond. Does a red diamond have something to do with Zivah's murder?"

"No," he lied. "I asked you about red diamonds because I was curious."

"Did I satisfy your curiosity?"

"Yes."

She moistened her lips seductively. "Good. Now let's satisfy something else."

Conor pretended not to know what she meant. "Like what?"

"Like our appetite," she said, her eyes locked on his.

"Which appetite?" Conor teased.

She picked up a menu. "First things first."

But Conor's thoughts weren't focused on food. At least not French food. What he had in mind was an Indian dish, which now seemed assured.

The dinner conversation was full of double entendres—an incredibly effective method of verbal foreplay.

"Would you like dessert?" he asked.

"Absolutely," she replied. "Let's get out of here."

Conor and Tasha exited Tout Va Bien and ambled down Eighth Avenue toward Forty-eighth Street.

"Let's go to your place," she said.

"It's a mess."

"What? You didn't make the bed?"

They walked hand in hand to the brownstone, neither of them speaking. They stopped at the front door of the building. He took

238

out his keys, ready to open the door. But before he could, his cell phone rang. He pulled it from his pocket, checked the caller ID. It was Amanda's cell phone.

"Don't answer it," she pleaded.

He hesitated. It rang again. "It's the sergeant. I have to see what she wants."

Tasha, clearly ready for action, didn't hide the fact that she was annoyed at the interruption.

He flipped open his phone. "Hey, Sarge. What's up?"

"The homicide squad called," Amanda said. "They just grabbed a guy trying to sneak into the tenement. And I think it's the guy you're looking for."

"What do you mean?"

"He's got a strip of white hair across the top of his head."

Chapter Sixty-two

Conor snapped the phone shut and looked at Tasha. The expression on his face said it all.

"I told you not to answer it," Tasha said sweetly.

"I'm sorry. This could be the break in the case I've been waiting for."

"I understand. No need to walk me home. It's only a half a block."

"No, I want to—"

She stopped him, put her arms around his waist. "Go. Do what you have to do." She kissed him on the lips. "Next time."

"Name's Theodore Foley," Amanda said as Conor rushed into the precinct. "Usual rap sheet. Drug possession. Aggressive panhandling, that sort of thing."

Conor started toward the interrogation room.

"Make sure you Mirandize this guy," Amanda insisted as she strode next to him.

"Absolutely, Sarge. This is America. We give criminals every opportunity to avoid prosecution."

She grabbed his arm. "I know you, Bard. I've seen suspects have to drag Miranda out of you."

"Don't worry."

"I *do* worry. You hear about that case in Florida? They left out one word when they read some guy his rights—*one word*—and now some lawyer's trying to get the confession thrown out." She started for the door. "I'm going in there with you."

They entered the interrogation room and took a seat across from Foley. The stench emanating from him was sickening—a combination of body odor, feces, urine, alcohol, and the pungent remnants of marijuana smoke. Jeans tied around his waist with a rope, shirt tattered and filthy, a coat reeking of mildew. He looked to be around forty-five, although it was impossible to tell for sure. His eyes were glassy and vacant. A scruffy beard covered his face. And, just as Madison had described, a strip of white hair across the top of his head. He really did look, and smell, like a skunk.

"Mr. Foley," Amanda began, fighting her gag reflex, "I'm Sergeant Pitts. And this is Detective Bard."

They took a seat across from Foley.

"We'd like to talk to you," Amanda said. "Okay?"

Foley nodded.

"But first we need to advise you of your rights," she added. "Okay?"

Foley nodded again.

Amanda launched into the reading of the rights with fervor. Not the version printed on small laminated cards carried by officers, but what was known as the "detailed Miranda warning."

"You have the right to remain silent and refuse to answer questions. Do you understand?"

Foley nodded a third time.

"You need to say yes if you understand. Okay?"

Foley nodded again.

"Mr. Foley . . ."

"Yes," he said.

"Very good." She continued. "Anything you do say may be used against you in a court of law. Do you understand?"

"Yes."

"You have the right to consult an attorney before speaking to the police and to have an attorney present during questioning now or in the future. Do you understand?"

"Yes."

"If you cannot afford an attorney, one will be appointed for you before any questioning if you wish. Do you understand?"

"Yes."

Conor grimaced, shot a glance at Amanda: *How many chances you going to give this guy to lawyer up?*

Amanda gave Conor a scolding expression, then faced Foley again. "If you decide to answer questions now without an attorney present you will still have the right to stop answering at any time until you talk to an attorney. Do you understand?"

"Yes."

"Knowing and understanding your rights as I have explained them to you, are you willing to answer questions without an attorney present?"

Foley hesitated.

"Mr. Foley?"

"Yes."

Amanda stood. "Detective Bard will be conducting the interview, Mr. Foley. Thank you for your cooperation."

"Sarge. Can you let Rubio know what's going on?"

"I'll call her right now," Amanda said. She spun around and almost ran out of the room. Conor heard her dry heave as she shut the door.

"Mr. Foley. How are you this evening?"

"Okay."

"Would you like some coffee? A water? Something to eat?"

Foley nodded.

"All three?"

Foley nodded again.

"Be right back," Conor said. He walked out of the interrogation room. Amanda was standing in the observation area.

"What do you think?" Amanda wanted to know.

"I think it's a miracle he didn't lawyer up after all the chances you gave him."

Conor went into the kitchen, poured a coffee, grabbed a bottle of water from the refrigerator, found a package of cheese crackers in a basket on the counter, then returned to the interrogation room and gave them to Foley, who ripped the paper off the crackers like a wild animal.

"Thanks," Foley mumbled as he stuffed his mouth.

"Do you know why we want to talk to you?" Conor asked.

"Because I was in that old building and I'm not supposed to be."

"That's right."

"I won't go in there anymore." Foley was nervous. "I promise."

"There's a building next to the old building. You know what I'm talking about?"

"Yes."

"Have you ever been in that other building?"

"No."

"No?" Conor shrugged. "Well, you can get in that building from the roof of the old building."

"I know."

"But you never climbed up on the terrace?"

"No."

"Do you know what happened in that apartment, Mr. Foley?"

Foley nodded. "A woman was killed."

"How do you know that?"

"I read it in the paper."

"Were you in the old building on Monday night?"

"I don't know what night it was."

For the next half hour, Conor continued to question Foley, often repeating the questions to make sure the answers were consistent.

"So how do you know a woman was killed?" Conor asked.

"I already told you, I read it in the paper."

"Yes, you did tell me that," Conor acknowledged. "And you told me you were there on Monday night, right?"

"No, no, no, no!" Foley shook his head back and forth. "I said I didn't know what day it was."

The door to the interrogation room opened. Rosita entered and immediately coughed in an attempt to keep from gagging.

"Mr. Foley," Conor said, "this is my partner, Detective Rubio."

"Hello, Detective Rubio." Foley blinked and stared at her breasts.

"I was just asking Mr. Foley about the night of the murder," Conor said. "He was in the abandoned building next to the loft Monday night."

"I don't know what night I was there," Foley protested.

Rosita looked at Conor. "Did you ask him if he climbed onto the terrace?"

"Yes," Conor replied. "He says he didn't."

She looked at Foley. "You didn't?"

Foley shook his head. "No."

She turned toward Conor. "You climbed up there, right?"

"Yes," Conor said.

Foley was surprised. "You did?"

"I dropped down to the roof then climbed back onto the terrace," Conor acknowledged.

"I'm sure that was very difficult," Rosita observed. "You have to be strong to do it." She motioned dismissively at Foley. "Look at him. No way he climbed onto the terrace. He's too weak. Not strong enough."

"I'm strong enough," Foley shot back. "It's easy to climb up there."

"So you *did* climb onto the terrace?" Rosita asked.

Foley fidgeted. "I shouldn't have said that."

"Did you climb up onto the terrace that night?" Conor pressed.

"What if I did?" Foley asked defiantly.

Conor leaned in on Foley. "If you did, it would be better to tell us now. Because we're going to find out. Fingerprints. Fibers from your coat. These days forensics can do anything."

Foley jumped to his feet. "You have my fingerprints?"

Conor stood, stepped close to Foley. "Do you think we have your fingerprints?"

Foley clenched his fists, sat down again, rocked back and forth in the chair. "You do. You have my fingerprints. I know you do. I know you do."

"Why would we have your fingerprints, Mr. Foley?" Conor asked, hovering over him.

Foley started to cry. "Because I killed that girl."

Chapter Sixty-three

A confession? Conor had been readying himself for a long, drawn out game of cat and mouse.

"Mr. Foley, how did you—"

"She was so beautiful," Foley said wistfully. "She used to give me money."

"Mr. Foley," Conor tried again, "how did you kill the woman?"

Foley bent over, placed his head on the table. "I want to sleep now. Can I sleep?"

"Mr. Foley," Rosita began, "you need to tell us how you killed her and then you can sleep."

Foley didn't respond.

Rosita touched Foley's shoulder. "Mr. Foley?"

Foley sat up. "I want a lawyer. You have to get me a lawyer! That's what that other woman cop told me. I could have a lawyer."

Conor drew in a breath. "Of course you can have a lawyer present, Mr. Foley. But if you want to, you can waive—"

Foley put his head on the table again. "I want a lawyer."

The door to the interrogation room opened. Amanda leaned inside. "Detective . . ."

Conor and Rosita exited the interrogation room, happy to breathe clean air again.

"The guy just confessed," Amanda said. "Let's don't make any procedural mistakes here. Give him his phone call then take him to Central Booking."

Central Booking was a nightmare of a place at 100 Centre Street. You could spend hours there walking someone through the system.

"And no questions on the way downtown," Amanda insisted. "You understand?"

"Yes," Rosita said.

"I know *you* understand." Amanda shot a glance at Conor. "*He's* the one I'm worried about."

Conor and Rosita placed Foley under arrest and searched him thoroughly, but there was absolutely nothing in his pockets. Foley had no one to call so they led him to the holding cell to await transfer to Central Booking, where an attorney would be appointed.

Could it be that simple? Zivah Gavish killed by some lowlife? Many times the truth really was that simple. A drug dealer, a pimp, a homeless person with a mental problem, an addict. There wasn't always a well-heeled, high-profile killer to arrest and parade in front of the cameras.

"Congratulations, Rubio," Conor offered as they walked back to their desks. "Your first homicide and it's cracked in under a week." He looked at her with admiration. "Telling him he wasn't strong enough to climb onto the terrace was very good."

"The male ego? It's almost too easy to wound you guys sometimes."

They stopped at the coffee machine.

"I *was* hoping for a News at Eleven kind of bust," she said as she poured a coffee. "You know, like Punjabi. That would've been a big finish." She struck a pose then began reciting. "'This is the way the world ends / Not with a bang but a whimper.'" She looked at him. "T. S. Eliot. 'The Hollow Men.'"

Conor laughed. "Ralph used to quote Thoreau. Now you're quoting T. S. Eliot."

"A quote can be perfect to sum something up."

"I feel that way about lyrics." He poured a coffee for himself. "So why did Foley only steal the red diamond? A guy like him would've gone for the cash, not the diamonds."

"Maybe he scooped up a handful of diamonds. I mean, we don't know how many other diamonds might be missing, right? Then when he went for the cash, he heard a noise, got spooked. Ran out the door with a fistful of diamonds. One of them happened to be red."

It was a plausible explanation, one that would have to suffice for now. Foley had lawyered up, meaning no more questions. Even worse, he was homeless, with no known address that could be searched. So where was the red diamond?

Chapter Sixty-four

Central Booking was quieter than usual. It took only two hours to get the now incommunicado Foley charged and arraigned, which included the appointment of an attorney—a man named William Coleman, who had a large belly, deep sunken eyes, and a hangdog expression. An ambulance chaser if there ever was one.

"I got myself a real winner of a case this time," Coleman intoned with a mixture of sarcasm and disgust.

Conor looked at him. *Nice way to mount a defense.* Not that Conor thought Foley deserved one, having allegedly killed a woman in cold blood, but Foley was supposed to be afforded an attorney who would at least make an effort. That clearly wasn't Coleman.

"We'd like to question him as soon as possible," Conor said.

Coleman sighed. "Yeah, yeah. I'll head over to the DA's office on Monday, try to cut some kind of deal. Maybe plead innocent by reason of insanity. You saw him, right? He's a mess. Better just cop a plea."

Rosita was annoyed. "You're really going to the wall for your client, huh?"

Now it was Coleman who was annoyed. "And what would you expect me to do?"

"I don't know," Rosita replied. "But the way you're handling this, I've seen it a million times in the Bronx. Just plead it out and that's it."

"I don't want to waste taxpayers' money," Coleman countered evenly. "Or my time." He looked at Conor. "Good-bye, Detective."

Coleman walked away.

"I saw a lot of black suspects get railroaded into pleas," Rosita said with an edge.

"Foley's white," Conor pointed out. "So that evens things out a little."

His attempt at levity fell flat. He knew what she meant. It was all about the dollar. If you had money, you were more equal in the eyes of the law. Or at least your expensive attorney was.

Out on Centre Street, a familiar figure rushed up to them. Lew Michaels from the *New York Post*.

"I heard you just made an arrest in the murder of Zivah Gavish." Lew was out of breath. "Give me the details. I've got ten minutes to make the morning edition."

Conor shook his head. "Jesus, Lew. You hang around down here all night hoping for a story? You've got to get a life."

"Hey, Detective, you got your job, I got mine. They both suck." He looked at Rosita. "Who are you?"

"Detective Rosita Rubio."

Lew held up a small tape recorder. "Can you tell me—"

"Get that thing out of my face," Rosita demanded. "Or I'll ram it up—"

"Put it away, Lew," Conor insisted.

Lew clicked off the recorder, slid it into his pocket. "Come on, guys, give me something."

"What you heard is true," Conor began. "We have made an arrest in the Zivah Gavish homicide. Name's Theodore Foley. A homeless guy."

"What else?" Michaels asked.

"Sorry," Conor replied. "That's all I've got for you."

"Thanks. That's better than nothing." Lew looked at Rosita. "Which is what he usually gives me."

Michaels jogged off into the night. Conor and Rosita walked along Centre Street.

"I should call Madison," Conor said.

"Now?"

"It's going to hit the papers tomorrow. Better if I tell him."

Madison answered on the fourth ring, his voice full of sleep.

"Kenneth. Detective Bard."

"Detective." Madison cleared his throat. "What happened?"

"We made an arrest."

"Thank God! Who was it?"

"I really can't go into detail. I just wanted to let you know."

"Well, just let me be a witness when they fry the son of a bitch."

"You'll have to wait awhile for that. It takes the state a long time to kill people."

Conor snapped the phone shut and looked at Rosita. "Take the day off tomorrow. Coleman's not going to do anything until Monday anyway."

They stopped at the car. Conor opened the passenger-side door. "Climb in. I'll drop you home."

"I can take the train."

"Not at this hour."

"I've got a gun."

"Get in the car," Conor demanded.

Both of them were so drained they didn't speak much on the way uptown. He watched her until she was safely inside the lobby of her building then steered the car toward Midtown. The window was rolled down, allowing a flow of cool air to dance across his unshaven face. *Zivah Gavish killed by a derelict. What a waste.*

Chapter Sixty-five

Conor entered his apartment and instinctively headed for the kitchen to pour a nightcap. He stopped. *Nightcap?* Hell, it was five in the morning. He walked into the bedroom, undressed, then collapsed on the bed. He slept until twelve thirty, when his ringing cell phone woke him. It was Richard.

"John at the Rhythm Bar just called," Richard began. "Said he had a cancellation tonight. Could we fill in. I told him the band could make it. How about you?"

Back on the stage. Just what he needed. "Yeah. Why not?"

Conor rolled out of bed and began to dress. It occurred to Conor that Marwala hadn't responded to the message he had left the day before. Which seemed odd. He dialed Marwala's cell phone and again got voice mail. Then he called Kruger.

"Hendrik," Conor said. "I've left a couple of messages for Marwala but I haven't heard back from him."

There was no immediate response. "You know what I have a penchant for?" Kruger finally said. "An American hot dog. Sauerkraut. Onions. Mustard. Meet me at the entrance to Central Park. Fifty-ninth Street. Say, ten minutes."

"Listen, Hendrik, I don't have time to—"

But Kruger had already hung up.

Conor walked the eleven blocks to Columbus Circle and found Kruger standing near a stone wall just inside the park.

"I'm sure you don't appreciate this wonder of culinary perfection," Kruger said, taking a bite of hot dog, "because you live here. You can have one of these anytime you want. But in Johannesburg—"

"Hendrik, what's going on?"

Kruger took another bite of hot dog. "ICE took Marwala into custody yesterday."

Conor drew in a breath. "Nice, Hendrik. Really nice."

"You must understand. I felt your hesitation. I really had no choice."

"Well, you got your lion's head, Hendrik. Go hang it on the wall." Conor started walking away.

"Wait," Kruger called out.

Conor stopped, turned.

Kruger slipped a copy of the *New York Post* from under his arm and held the front page so Conor could see it. The headline blared: *Deadbeat Diced Diamond Dealer: Cops Bust Homeless Man.*

"Let me guess," Conor said. "You want to know if I recovered the diamond."

"Did you?"

"You see the headline? The suspect was homeless."

"So?"

"So where am I going to search?"

"I need that diamond," Kruger said. "Marwala may be in custody but the South African courts still must be convinced of his guilt. I can't let Marwala slip through my fingers. Not this time."

"You give my collar to the Feds and now you want me to help you?" Conor shook his head. "Sorry, Hendrik."

As Conor walked back down Eighth Avenue, his cell phone rang. It was Ralph.

"I just saw the *Post*," Ralph said. "Congratulations."

"Yeah, I guess so."

"What's the matter, kid? You make a collar on a homicide, you should be popping the champagne."

"I don't know, Ralph. Some vagrant leaves cash on the floor and in a stroke of incredible luck just happens to make off with the most priceless item in the loft?"

"Sometimes it is what it is," Ralph said. "Remember that case at the real estate office? Woman shot as she was locking up for the night. We had a million theories. You were thinking it was the husband, I was thinking it was her boss. Turned out to be some vagrant. Nothing but a crime of opportunity."

"But you told me you thought the red diamond was the target. Diamond District death. Isn't that what you said?"

"Maybe I was wrong," Ralph said.

"I thought you were never wrong."

"Well, kid, sometimes I *am* wrong. I know that's devastating for you to hear but—"

"I'm crushed. I always believed in you."

"Yeah? Well, there's no Santa Claus either so get over it."

"By the way, I'm playing at the Rhythm Bar tonight. You want to come?"

"Tonight? No, can't tonight. My neighbor's birthday party. She makes the best lasagna I ever had. Sends some over to me every week. If I don't show up, she might cut me off."

Conor laughed. "I wouldn't want to come between you and a plate of lasagna."

Chapter Sixty-six

Conor called Tasha and asked her to meet him at the Rhythm Bar at eight thirty.

"We going to make it to breakfast this time?" Tasha asked seductively.

"Brunch," Conor countered. "We won't be getting up early enough for breakfast."

Next, Conor called Rosita.

"What are you doing tonight, Rubio?"

"The same thing I always do on Saturday night. Nothing."

"I'm going to be at the Rhythm Bar. I'd like you to come. As my guest."

"Gee, Bard. That sounds great."

"You can bring a date if you want."

"Do I have to?"

He laughed. "No. Just bring yourself."

Conor told Rosita about Marwala's arrest by ICE agent Jack Bailey.

"We got played," Rosita observed.

"You got that right," Conor replied.

*   *   *

Conor spent the rest of the day opening mail and catching up on small chores.

At seven, Conor showered then walked to the Rhythm Bar.

"Hey, Susie, give me a coffee."

"Too early for a martini?" she quipped.

"Chill the glass. I'll have one of those right before I go on."

He noticed Ingrid sitting at the bar. She was dressed in a pair of jeans and a flower-print top. No makeup. Or at least none that he could discern. Didn't matter. She was a natural beauty.

"Hi, Ingrid."

"Hi, Conor." She glanced toward the stage. "I thought the Trembles were playing tonight. I was happy to find out you'll be onstage."

"The Trembles are a good band," Conor countered.

"Yes. But I'd rather see you."

He studied her for a long moment. "You want to play something tonight?"

Her face flushed. "What do you mean?"

"Come on. Where's your . . ." His voice trailed off. *What the fuck does she play? Violin or viola?*

"My violin?"

"Yes. Where's your violin?"

"It's at home."

"Where do you live?"

"On Forty-fifth between Ninth and Tenth."

"That's not far. Go get your violin."

"Really?"

"Really. But hurry up. We're going on in half an hour."

Ingrid left. Conor walked backstage.

"I saw you talking to Ingrid," Richard said.

"Yeah, she seems cool," Conor replied.

"I asked her out a couple times. She shot me down."

"So she has good taste," Conor joked. "I asked Ingrid to play a couple songs with us."

"Are you kidding? She plays with the Philharmonic. And you asked her to play cover songs in this dump?"

"I don't know if you've noticed, but the place is picking up these days."

"I know. But it's still not the Philharmonic."

"So she'll slum it tonight," Conor said. "The crowd'll probably dig it."

"I heard her perform at Lincoln Center. Rossini's Sonata a Quattro Number Six. She was incredible."

Richard was a real musician. Conor, on the other hand, knew how to play the guitar well enough. But beyond the realm of popular music, Conor was lost. Philharmonic? Lincoln Center? It wasn't Conor's thing. And it didn't need to be. Virtually every pop and rock and rhythm and blues hit was utterly simple. Four or five chords at the most.

"I'm telling you," Richard continued, "that girl's got talent. I don't recall your past girlfriends having any talent." Richard slapped his forehead with his palm. "Sorry. I forgot. They *did* have one talent."

Conor grinned. "It's the only talent I need."

"That's your problem," Richard observed. "You still think you're an eighteen-year-old jock. You're not."

Conor considered what Richard was saying. He had a point. How many more women could he go through before settling down? Ingrid presented a real possibility. After the show he'd get her number, call her. Who knows? *But she's a musician.*

Conor opened the guitar case and removed his Fender Stratocaster. He recalled the session with Alan Woodcliff and the conversation with Woodcliff about using studio musicians.

Richard looked at Conor. "Is everything okay?"

"What do you mean?"

"We've known each other a long time and I can tell there's something on your mind."

Better not to get into it right before a show, Conor thought. "No, nothing. I'm just a little ragged around the edges, that's all. Been a rough week."

257

Conor went to the bar to have his ritualistic preshow martini. He had almost finished it when Rosita arrived.

"Hey, Rubio."

"I'm excited, Bard. My partner the superstar."

"Not yet."

He pointed to the center of the room. "I've got you at my table. Tasha Sen is coming too so you'll have company."

Rosita didn't seem pleased with the seating arrangement. "You know what? I'm more of a bar person than a table person. If it's all the same to you, I'd rather hang out here. At the bar."

"Okay. If that's what you want."

He motioned to Susie the bartender. "She's my guest."

Conor eased off the stool and glanced toward the door. "Look who's here."

Lew Michaels charged toward them, a man on a mission. "Conor!"

"What's up, Lew?"

"I need the story," Michaels pleaded.

"You already have it," Conor remarked. "I saw the *Post* this morning. Front page. Not bad, Lew."

"That was nothing but a teaser." He looked at Conor, eyes pleading. "Come on, Conor, my editor's all over me. All I need is a couple of facts. Off the record. Not for attribution. However you want to play it."

"How'd you know I was here?" Conor asked.

"I didn't. But I know you hang out here, play here sometimes, so—"

"Stalking me, Lew?" Conor asked.

"Yes. I admit it. I was stalking you. That's how desperate I am for this story."

As Conor contemplated what to tell Michaels, if anything at all, Rosita motioned for Michaels to come closer. "Come here, Lew."

Michaels took a step toward her. "Yeah?"

"You say you need some facts, right?"

"Please. Anything you can give me."

"*Give* you?" She shook her head. "Nothing's free, Lew."

"What does that mean?" Michaels asked cautiously.

Conor looked at Rosita. *Where's she going with this?*

Rosita twisted all the way around so that she was face-to-face with Michaels. "What that means is, we need something too."

Michaels's eyes pleaded with Conor for help. Conor gave his head a slight shake. *You're on your own.*

"What do you need?" Michaels asked her cautiously.

She glanced toward the stage. "Detective Bard is about to perform."

Michaels frowned. "Yeah . . ."

"It would be nice if there was a review of Detective Bard's performance in the *Post.*"

Michaels shook his head. "Music's not my beat."

"Then I guess you're not getting anything from us," she countered.

"That's blackmail," Michaels protested.

"Blackmail?" Rosita's voice rose as she placed emphasis on the word *black.* "What are you, some kind of racist?"

"Look, I can't promise anything, but I *could* call Dempsey, our music guy."

"Up to you," Rosita said calmly.

Michaels snapped open his cell phone. "Dempsey," he shouted into the receiver. "You've got to come meet me at the Rhythm Bar. There's this cop, fantastic singer, and I think you should give him a listen."

Michaels drifted away.

Conor smiled at Rosita. "You should be my publicist."

"Remember that when you start making money." She patted him on the back. "Because next time you're getting a bill."

Chapter Sixty-seven

onor headed backstage and went over the repertoire with Richard and the new bass player, an Italian kid named Vinny.

"You want a plucking sound or slap?"

"A Motown bass," Conor replied.

"Got it," Vinny said.

Twenty minutes later they took to the stage to tune up. Conor spotted Tasha walking in. Tight jeans. High heels. A silk blouse showing lots of cleavage. He propped his guitar against the amp and jumped from the stage.

He greeted her with a kiss on both her cheeks then led her to a table in the center of the room. As he pulled out a chair, he saw Ingrid, carrying her violin case, watching him. She quickly turned away.

"Who's that?" Tasha asked, trying not to sound jealous.

"Her? Oh, she's a violinist I know. She's going to play a couple tunes with us tonight."

"She's pretty."

Conor knew enough not to enthusiastically agree. "Yeah. Kind of." He looked at Tasha. "Excuse me. It's showtime."

Conor walked over to Ingrid. "I'll bring you up after a couple songs, okay?"

"Okay."

"We've got some sheet music. Nothing for a violin, but—"

"That's all right. I'll be okay."

"What's your last name?"

"Romano."

"Right."

Conor climbed onto the stage. The band warmed up with an instrumental version of "Stand by Me" then Conor stepped to the microphone and launched into the Spinners' classic "One of a Kind (Love Affair)."

"One of a kind love affair is"—Conor lasered a look at Tasha—"the kind of love that you read about in a fairy tale . . ."

When the song finished, Conor leaned into the microphone. "I've got a special guest here tonight." He glanced over at Ingrid, who was standing just to the left of the stage. She lowered her eyes. "Her name is Ingrid Romano and she's a violinist with the New York Philharmonic. But tonight, she's agreed to come down from the mountain and play at the Rhythm Bar."

A curious but not overwhelming response emanated from the tables and provoked an utterly embarrassed expression from Ingrid as she made her way to the stage.

"I've decided I want to lay back and listen to her play," Conor continued, "so I'm going to ask Richard Shorter to sing a song."

As Richard started the intro to the Willie Nelson classic "To All the Girls I've Loved Before," the crowd erupted. Obviously they knew Richard's rendition well.

"To all the girls I've loved before . . ."

Even Conor was enthralled. Despite all the times he heard Richard sounding uncannily like Willie Nelson, it was always a surprise. If you closed your eyes, you could imagine Willie himself onstage.

"Who traveled in and out my door . . ."

Richard and Ingrid made eye contact. She stepped up to a microphone, placed the violin against her neck, raised the bow, and eased into the melody. The music soared now, totally transcending the venue.

Conor was mesmerized by the display of talent in front of him. So much so, he could hardly concentrate on playing the guitar part. And he had totally forgotten about Tasha. When he finally turned and met Tasha's eyes, they were burning like two torches. Conor couldn't tell if she was appreciating Ingrid's talents or pissed off by them. Maybe a little of both.

Ingrid ended her solo with a flourish, generating a wave of applause. When Richard finally hit the last chord, Conor stepped up to the mike and looked at Ingrid. "That was incredible. Can you hang out for a couple more songs?"

Before she could respond, a collective chant rose from the room: "*More! More! More!*"

Conor smiled broadly. "I guess you don't have a choice."

The band launched into the Percy Sledge song "When a Man Loves a Woman."

"When a man loves a woman, he can't keep his mind on nothing else . . ."

Conor wondered where to look. At Tasha? Or Ingrid? At fire? Or salvation?

"He'll trade the world for the good thing he's found . . ."

He directed his attention at Tasha, thinking she was a safer bet. Nothing too serious. Nothing too permanent. Nothing too taxing on the emotions.

Ingrid floated in with another violin solo so penetrating, Conor felt goose bumps. *Better steer way clear of her,* he thought. *She's not playing fair.*

For the rest of the set, he sang at least a few lines of each song directly to Tasha.

Bill Withers's "Ain't No Sunshine."

"Hey, I ought to leave the young thing alone . . . But ain't no sunshine when she's gone . . ."

The Four Tops' "Baby I Need Your Loving."

"Another day, another night . . . I long to hold you tight . . ."

The Miracles' "You've Really Got a Hold on Me."

"Baby, I don't want you, but I need you . . . Don't wanna kiss you, but I need you . . ."

Conor and Tasha locked eyes. He had stumbled upon a new form of romantic prelude—lyrical foreplay.

Chapter Sixty-eight

After the show, Conor brought Rosita, Tasha, and Ingrid backstage and introduced them to the band. He ushered Rosita to a corner of the room.

"So, Rubio? What did you think?"

"You were great, Bard. I've got to try and remember I'm your partner and not a groupie."

"You can be my groupie if you want."

"Never mind. The moment's passed."

They both looked across the room in tandem. Tasha posing like a centerfold. Ingrid demurely shrinking in a corner.

Rosita stared at the ceiling.

"What?" he asked.

"We'll talk about it later."

If Conor knew one thing about women, it was not to press when they said, "We'll talk about it later."

"Choices," Rosita said. "That's what makes life interesting."

"What is that supposed to mean?"

"I said: We'll talk about it later."

"Look, Rubio, I know I'm fucked-up . . ."

"You're preaching to the choir." She glanced toward Tasha. "I think you're going to get lucky tonight."

"You think so?"

"Trust me on that, Bard." She waved. "See you in the morning."

Conor walked over to Ingrid. "You were wonderful."

"Thanks for giving me the opportunity to play with you guys."

"Are you kidding? Anytime you want."

She blushed. "I better go. I've got a student at nine in the morning."

"Student?"

"I teach violin."

They stood there in awkward silence.

"Okay," Conor finally said. "See you soon."

"I hope so."

Ingrid left. Conor made his way over to Tasha.

"Are you ready?"

She slid her arm around his waist. "Never been so ready."

"Forty-eighth and Eighth," Conor said as they climbed in a taxi.

And then they were kissing. So passionately that the ride uptown seemed to last only seconds and they were caught off guard when the driver brought the cab to a halt and bellowed: "You said Forty-eighth Street, right?"

Conor paid the fare. They climbed out of the cab.

"Your place," Tasha whispered.

He didn't argue.

They entered the apartment and almost tripped over each other getting to the bedroom. An hour later, he was lying beside her, totally spent. "That was incredible."

She laughed. "Don't sound so surprised. After all, we invented the Kama Sutra."

*   *   *

They woke late, went to brunch.

"Tell me more about yourself," Conor said.

"Haven't you ever heard the expression 'Familiarity breeds contempt'?" She took his hand. "Let's don't get too personal."

Don't get too personal? He couldn't imagine being more personal than they had just been. But he knew what she meant. Their connection was purely physical. Why ruin it by getting to know each other?

Tasha went home for a couple of hours then returned at six. They made love then headed to dinner at SW 44, an Italian restaurant at the corner of Forty-fourth Street and Ninth Avenue.

After dinner, Conor and Tasha returned to his apartment and to bed.

After making love again, Tasha kissed him gently. "I better head home." She got out of bed and started to dress. Conor swung his legs on the floor.

"Stay there," she insisted. "It's only a block."

He stood. "No, really. I want to walk you home."

She eased over to him, kissed him. "No."

"Why not?"

She picked up her blouse and slid her arms into it. "I don't want the doorman to get the wrong idea."

"You're a big girl. You can have men over."

She fastened a button. "I'm a big *married* girl."

Conor wasn't sure he heard her correctly. A *what? Married?*

"It's a long story." She pulled on her jeans. "It's not a real marriage. Our parents arranged it."

Arranged marriage? Isn't that a thing of the past? He wanted to ask her if their little rendezvous was the type of thing she did often. But then again, what was the point in asking? The answer wouldn't have mattered either way.

She finished dressing, kissed him again. "I'll be back in three weeks."

"That's too long."

"Okay. Maybe tomorrow night. But we'll have to make it a quickie. I've got to pack for the trip."

After she left, Conor crawled back into bed, letting the weekend of passion replay through his mind. *What about karma? Isn't it bad karma to sleep with another man's wife?* That was a question for an Indian guru. Too heavy for a Scotch-Irish guy to contemplate.

Conor was just beginning to drift off when his cell phone rang. The number on the caller ID was familiar. It was Jimmy, his confidential informant in Washington Heights.

"Hey, Jimmy. What's up?"

"That guy, Detective. That guy in the mug shot! I just saw him."

Conor was unimpressed. "That's what you told me the other day."

"I didn't get a good look at him before," Jimmy whined. "But when I saw him tonight—"

"Jimmy. It's one o'clock in the morning. If I come all the way up there—"

"It's him! I *swear*! He just went in the Grotto."

"What's that?"

"A hotel. Amsterdam and a Hundred and Sixty-sixth."

Conor's heart began to pound. *Maybe I've finally got the son of a bitch.*

Chapter Sixty-nine

Conor wondered if he should call the Washington Heights precinct for backup. But what if it was just another one of Jimmy's false alarms? Still, it would be good to have somebody there when he entered the hotel. He checked his watch. One fifteen. *Maybe Rubio's still up.*

"No," Rosita said when she answered the phone. "I'm not sleeping. I had to wake up to answer the phone."

"Sorry, Rubio, but I'm on my way to Washington Heights."

"Why? You know a good bar up there or what?"

"Remember Jimmy? The CI? He told me he saw Hicks."

"Isn't that what he said before?"

"Yeah," Conor acknowledged. "But he sounded sure this time. Said Hicks was at some dive hotel."

Rosita didn't need any more prodding. "I'll be waiting in front of the building."

Conor jogged to the precinct, grabbed a set of keys, climbed into the car, then hit the lights and sirens, making it to 110th Street in twelve minutes.

Rosita slid into the passenger seat. "Nice of you to call me."

"How could I let my new partner miss out on our second collar of the week?"

"You *hope* it's a collar. And not a scam. Jimmy didn't look like the most reliable guy in the world."

"Let's see what happens. We're meeting Jimmy around the corner from the hotel. Then we'll hit the place."

"Look, Bard. I know how bad you want this guy. So maybe it's a little personal. But personal is perilous."

"Personal is perilous?"

"That's what my commanding officer at the Academy used to say. And he's right. I don't want you going in there trigger-happy. Know what I mean?"

Maybe she's psychic. For more than a year Conor had had an image in his mind of finding Hicks and blowing him away.

"Don't worry," he assured her.

"I always worry. Even when we would go to pick up some low-level pimp, I would worry. You never know how these guys are going to react." She looked at him. "You want to call for backup from the Heights guys?"

"I thought of that. But I don't want to be embarrassed if this is one of Jimmy's money grabs."

"Better embarrassed than dead. What if this guy Hicks is armed?"

"He's a sexual predator. Never used a gun in any of his attacks. I doubt he started holstering a weapon now." At least Conor hoped that wasn't the case.

They rode in silence for a few blocks.

"You know, Bard. You really are a good singer. You ought to pursue that."

"What do you think I've been doing for the last twenty years?"

"Well, your time will come. It has to. You've got the talent. All you need is a break."

"You just saying that because we're partners?"

"No, I'm saying that *despite* the fact we're partners. I really think you've got what it takes to make it." She looked at him. "Maybe I should get your autograph now?"

"Might not be a bad idea. When I'm out touring, I won't have time for autographs."

"I thought you wanted to be a groupie."

"Whatever. I just want to tour the world." She looked at him, clearly had something to say.

"What?" he asked.

"It's none of my business."

"Since when is anything not a woman's business?"

"Number one," she said sharply, "I'm not a woman. At least not to you. I'm your partner. We need to watch each other's back. How many times I have to tell you that? And two, forgive me for saying this, but you don't know jack about women."

"I never claimed to. But may I ask what brought this on?"

"Last night."

"What about last night?"

"That girl Ingrid? The violin player? You hurt her feelings."

"Wait a minute. I had a date with Tasha. I invited Ingrid up onstage to play. Tell me, what the fuck did I do wrong?"

"Come on, Bard. You know what I'm talking about. You could have been more sensitive to the situation. Ingrid really likes you."

"Hey, I like her too. But last night I was with Tasha."

"Let's drop it," she said. "We've got a potentially dangerous perp to take down. I wouldn't want you being uptight."

Conor pushed down hard on the gas pedal. "Too late for that."

270

Chapter Seventy

Conor parked the car on 165th Street, just off Amsterdam Avenue. Jimmy was on the corner.

"So this hotel . . ." Conor looked north, up Amsterdam Avenue. "Where is it exactly?"

"Between One Sixty-six and One Sixty-seven."

Conor removed his wallet, flipped it open so Jimmy could see Hicks's mug shot. "Are you sure this is the guy you saw?"

Jimmy was hopping from one foot to the other. "Yeah! Yeah! That's him."

Conor looked at Rosita. "All right. Let's stop at the desk. Get confirmation that Hicks is inside."

They started toward the hotel. Jimmy walked beside them.

"Detective. I could use a little cash. How about twenty? No, make it thirty. I got a coupla things I got to take care of."

Conor reached in his pocket, removed a roll of cash. "Here's a twenty, Jimmy. This guy turns out to be John Hicks, I'll give you another hundred."

"It's the guy. It's really the guy. I swear." Jimmy held out his hand. "So you can give me the hundred now, okay?"

"No, that's not okay." Conor pointed at Jimmy. "Stay here."

Conor and Rosita walked a block up Amsterdam Avenue to the seedy Grotto Hotel. They swept into the lobby to find the reception desk securely situated behind a set of steel bars, making it appear that the elderly clerk was sitting in a holding cell.

"Can I help you?" the clerk asked, yawning.

Conor flashed his badge, then the mug shot of Hicks. "Have you seen this man?"

The elderly clerk grinned. "I don't see too well these days."

Rosita reached through the bars and grabbed the clerk by his shirt collar, pulling him out of his chair, smashing his face against the bars. "What room, fuckhead?"

Conor smiled. *Not bad.*

"Room two oh one," the clerk answered quickly.

Rosita released her grip. The clerk fell heavily back into his chair.

Conor and Rosita climbed the stairs to the second floor.

"How you want to handle this?" she whispered.

"We'll announce ourselves. If he doesn't answer, we'll break down the door."

They moved quietly down the hall, stopping in front of room 201. Conor banged on the door. "Open up! Police!" No response. He banged again, this time harder, his voice louder. "Police! Open the door!" No response. He kicked the door. It didn't budge. He stepped back then barreled into the door. All he managed to do was aggravate his chewed-up shoulder.

"Move away," Rosita screamed. And with one violent motion, she swung her leg up and into the door. It shattered like balsa wood.

They rushed in, guns drawn.

"Clear!" she yelled as he checked the bathroom.

"Clear," he screamed as he opened a closet door.

No John Hicks. Conor gritted his teeth. "Fuck!"

But then a noise, a slight rustling. Rosita pointed at an open window, curtains blowing in the breeze. "The fire escape!"

Conor climbed through the window onto the fire escape; Rosita was close behind. They clambered down the metal stairs into an alley. There was no direct lighting but the glow of the city gave him enough visibility to see something moving. He made eye contact with Rosita, pointed underneath some cardboard boxes. Conor knelt down. "Come out! Hands where I can see them!"

No response. Conor pointed the gun at the boxes. "Now!"

Slowly, a shell of a man edged into the dim light. It was, in fact, John Hicks.

"All the way out!" Conor screamed.

Hicks crawled from under the boxes. He positioned himself on one knee.

"Hands behind your head!" Conor ordered.

Hicks raised his arms. "Hey, man. What's this all about?"

"I *said*, hands behind your head!"

Hicks stood, locked his fingers behind his head. "You got the wrong guy."

Conor pointed the gun at Hicks's heart. His finger tightened on the trigger.

Rosita edged toward Conor. "Hey, Bard. Hold on, now."

But Conor didn't respond. He steadied his aim. "You sick son of a bitch!"

"Bard," Rosita said, panic creeping in. "Let me cuff him."

"Rubio! Walk out of the alley!" Conor shouted.

Hicks was beginning to realize what was going on. "Hey, lady. Don't leave me here with him!"

"Bard, listen—"

"Walk out of the alley! Now!"

Hicks, now seemingly certain of his fate, dropped to the ground and curled into a fetal position. He began whimpering. Conor took a step closer, leveled the gun right at Hicks's head. "You lowlife fucking bastard! This is for all the women—"

"Drop the gun!"

"Freeze!"

Two uniformed officers, weapons drawn, had Conor in their sights.

Chapter Seventy-one

"**W**e're on the job!" Rosita shouted, bending down and placing her gun on the ground then raising her hands in the air.

"Drop the gun!" one of the officers roared at Conor.

But Conor kept a steady aim on Hicks.

"Put the gun down," the other officer screamed.

"This man is a fugitive," Conor shouted back. "He may be armed."

"Put the gun down," the officer shouted again. "Now!"

Conor slowly lowered his gun, dropped it on the ground. He pointed at Hicks. "Take that man into custody!"

The other uniformed officer swung his gun toward Hicks. "On your knees! Hands behind your head!"

Hicks eased onto his knees.

The officer kept his gun pointed at Hicks while the other officer holstered his gun and cuffed him.

Conor glared at Hicks. "You bastard. Now you're going to get what you fucking deserve!"

Hicks looked at one of the officers. "I ain't done nothin'."

"He's wanted for rape and murder," Conor said. "Call Fred Schroeder at Cold Case."

Rosita looked at one of the officers. "Detective Rubio. Midtown North. That's my partner, Detective Bard."

Conor cocked his head down toward his inside jacket pocket. "My ID."

The other officer reached in Conor's jacket, removed a badge and ID. "You should have displayed this."

"Yeah," Conor said. "I know."

A team from the cold case squad arrived and took custody of Hicks. As they led him away, Hicks sneered at Conor. Conor lunged at him. Jimmy appeared out of nowhere, grabbed Conor around the waist, pulled him away.

"Hey, man," Jimmy said. "Take it easy. What are you doing?"

Conor looked down at the diminutive Jimmy. *What* am *I doing?* Conor dug into his pocket and pulled out a handful of cash. He started to count out a hundred then just slapped the entire stash into Jimmy's hand.

Jimmy stared at the money in disbelief. "Thanks, man."

Conor drifted toward the car, his eyes probing somewhere a million miles away.

Jimmy looked at Rosita. "You better take care of him."

"Yeah. I know."

Jimmy hurried into the night with his newly acquired fortune. Rosita caught up with Conor.

"You okay?"

Conor nodded. They climbed in the car. Rosita drove.

"Jesus, Bard," she said. "You were going to blow him away."

Conor thought about that for a minute. "Yeah. I probably would have if the unis hadn't shown up."

"You're not serious."

"I don't know. Maybe I am."

"And if you *had* blown him away," she asked, "that would have made you feel better?"

"Damn right. Hicks doesn't deserve to live."

"So you believe in capital punishment?"

"You don't?"

"Killing Hicks?" She shook her head. "You would've been letting him off easy. Better he rot in a cell for the rest of his life."

"No. Better he die and rot in an alley with the rest of the garbage."

They rode in awkward silence for several blocks.

"Nice job with the door," Conor said, trying to break the tension. "One of your kicks and it looked like a pile of toothpicks."

"Which should tell you never to fuck with me."

"Believe me, I won't." The truth was, he felt as safe with Rosita next to him as he ever had felt with any other partner. Women can't handle the physical requirements of the job? Bullshit. He had just seen what a woman could do.

Conor dropped Rosita off at her apartment then drove back to Midtown totally wired. What the hell was he thinking? Was he really going to kill an unarmed man cowering in an alley? And then what? Get Rubio to lie for him? *I'm losing it. Jesus, I'm really losing it. I've got to get a grip.*

It was four thirty by the time Conor got home. He set the clock for eight thirty. Four hours' sleep would have to be enough. But before going to bed, there was one call he had to make. He dialed. It was ten fifteen in the morning in Albania. After two rings, a woman's voice.

"Alo?"

"Monica. It's Conor."

"Conor," she said softly. "How are you?"

"I wanted you to know, we caught John Hicks."

"Oh, my God."

"I'm sorry your father isn't here to get the news."

The last time Conor had seen Monica, she had rushed back to Albania to be at her father's bedside. Hicks had killed his daughter,

Monica's sister. Now the son of a bitch who killed Besa was behind bars for good. Too late for her father, though.

"Conor?"

"I've got to go, Monica."

"Conor . . . I . . ."

"I really have to go," he insisted, then hung up the phone.

Hearing Monica's voice made him profoundly sad. He had allowed himself to dream about a life with her. Kids, even. But it hadn't worked out that way. And even though he had put the fantasy of Monica behind him, it didn't make the hollow feeling in his gut any less real.

So Hicks was finished. And wasn't that the main reason he stayed on the job? To get Hicks. Conor had done that. Now what? With Alan Woodcliff on his side, he was in the batter's box as far as a record deal. *Fuck! Was that a sports analogy?* Which was one of his old partner's favorite ways to explain something—Ralph could turn any situation into a sports analogy. And now he was doing it. *Maybe it's some kind of senior partner thing.*

The question on the table was this: Could he afford to go after his music career part-time?

No. Definitely not. So the decision was simple. His cop days were almost over.

Chapter Seventy-two

Conor was jolted awake at eight thirty by his usual beginning-of-the-week iPod alarm selection—the Mamas & the Papas song "Monday, Monday."

Oh, Monday morning . . . you gave me no warning . . . of what was to be . . .

After a long, hot shower, Conor walked to the precinct. He was shocked to see Ralph sitting at his old desk, a tinfoil-covered dish in front of him.

"Ralph, what are you doing here?"

"I brought you some lasagna." Ralph tapped the tinfoil. "It's incredible." He pointed at a flower on the desk. "What is *this*?"

"That's a flower."

"I know what it is," Ralph groused. "Just never thought I'd see a flower on this desk."

"You don't like it? Lie about your age. Get yourself back here."

"You wish."

Ralph rubbed the top of the desk. "It's blue? I always thought it was brown."

Rosita walked up to them. "It *was* brown. Must've been an inch of grime."

"Rosita Rubio," Conor said. "Meet my old partner, Ralph Kurtz. And I *do* mean old."

Ralph shot out of the chair. "I'm sorry. I didn't mean—"

"It's all right," she said. "That was your desk for, what? Thirty years?"

"Yeah. Something like that."

"That explains why it was so hard to clean."

"Those were memories you wiped off this desk," Ralph said in mock horror.

"I know. Some of them were real stubborn. Didn't want to come off."

Ralph laughed, extended his hand to Rosita. "Nice to meet you."

"Nice to meet you too. Heard a lot about you."

"All bad, right?"

"No," Rosita replied, "there was *some* good. Not much, but definitely some."

"So what are you doing here?" Conor asked Ralph.

"I needed to tell you something but I didn't want to break the news over the phone."

Rosita started backing away. "I'll go get a coffee."

"No," Ralph said. "You need to hear this too."

Conor held up his hand to Ralph. "Wait. Let me tell *you* something. I got Hicks last night."

"Hicks?" Ralph searched his memory. "You mean the guy who killed the sister?"

"That's the one."

"Great news," Ralph said.

"So what did you want to tell me?" Conor asked.

Ralph hesitated.

"Come on, Ralph," Conor urged. "The suspense is killing me."

"I come in this morning," Ralph began, "and I start checking out the guy you arrested, Foley. And then I see he was picked up last Friday over on Avenue B. Acting crazy. Screaming at people on the street. But he wasn't arrested. He was taken to Bellevue and locked up in the psych ward."

"So Foley's a nut job," Conor said. "We know that."

"But I guess you didn't know *this*." Ralph handed Conor a sheet of paper.

Conor read a moment. "Fuck!"

"What?" Rosita wanted to know.

"Foley couldn't have killed Zivah Gavish." Conor looked up at Rosita. "The night she was murdered, Foley was bouncing around a padded cell."

Chapter Seventy-three

Conor threw the sheet of paper on his desk. A false confession. *I knew it*, Conor thought. And like anyone who *knew* something but didn't act, he had a sinking feeling in his gut. But after a week of nonstop investigation he had been too exhausted to really think it through. It can wait until Monday, Conor had told himself. Well, here was Monday. And here was the very reality he had feared.

"Look at it this way," Ralph said. "Foley's no different from any other suspect."

"How so?" Conor asked.

Ralph shrugged. "He's a liar."

Conor grimaced. "Very funny, Ralph."

Rosita picked up the sheet of paper. "What would cause somebody to confess to a murder he didn't commit?"

"Happens all the time," Ralph replied. "A suspect under duress. Diminished capacity. High or intoxicated in some way. With Foley, you probably had all of those factors in play."

"Maybe there was some mistake in the paperwork at Bellevue," Rosita said, unwilling to believe what was right there in black and white.

"Could be," Ralph allowed. "But I doubt it. He went in Friday night and wasn't released until Tuesday morning. I've seen hospitals log the incorrect time but not the day."

"Okay. So we go back over the case." Conor looked at Ralph. "Can you stick around?"

"Let's do it," Ralph said, pulling up a chair.

"We've got five possibilities," Conor began. "Another vagrant, not Foley, could have killed her. A deliveryman who saw an opportunity. Then there's Silberman."

"Silberman was in the middle of it," Ralph interjected. "Which means he knew a large transaction was about to go down."

"And what about his wrist?" Rosita asked. "Sprained it tripping on the street? Or while climbing onto the terrace?"

"But Silberman didn't know about the red diamond," Conor added. "So for now, we move him down the list. And we move Punjabi up. Punjabi was involved in cutting the rough stone and smuggling the finished red diamond into the country."

"You said five possibilities," Rosita reminded him.

"None of the above."

"I'm going to stick with an inside job," Ralph said. "This is all about the red diamond. It hasn't surfaced yet, has it?"

"No," Conor confirmed.

"A vagrant, delivery guy, doesn't know what he's got," Ralph pointed out. "He's heading straight to a pawnshop. You canvassed pawnshops in the area, right?"

Conor nodded.

"Whoever has the red diamond knows its value and knows there's too much heat to try to move it right now." Ralph pursed his lips, which he always did when he was onto something. "You'll find your killer on Forty-seventh Street. I'm sure of it. So I'd focus on the most likely suspect. Punjabi." He checked his watch. "Better get downtown."

Ralph started to walk away, then stopped, edged back to the desk, and looked down at the tinfoil-covered dish. "If you're not going to eat that . . ." Before Conor could say anything, Ralph scooped up the dish and walked away.

Conor and Rosita spent an hour amassing the now vast amount of evidence—crime scene photos, phone records, copies of documents, credit card statements.

"We need a bulletin board," Conor said. "Pin all this crap up."

They found an easel and a bulletin board in a storage room, dusted them off, set them up near his desk, and began tacking things onto it, grouping them by suspect.

Rosita looked at the items affixed to the board under an index card labeled PUNJABI. There was a photograph of the bidi. "When he told us about the bidi," she recalled, "he also let us know he was aware of the tenement next door."

Conor dropped into his chair. "You know what, Rubio? We've got Punjabi cold. Not for murder."

"For smuggling."

"Exactly. And Marwala's arrest was just what we needed. Immigration locked up Marwala based on what Kruger gave them—the same evidence we have that a valuable diamond entered the country illegally. And we have Silberman's statement. So we move on Punjabi for trafficking in illegal gems. Which might even shake things up in our homicide." Conor stood. "But first let's go see Madison. Zivah may have mentioned something about Punjabi that could help us. Besides, I think he deserves to find out from us that Foley wasn't the killer."

Madison's office was in the Empire State Building at Fifth Avenue and Thirty-fourth Street.

"My grandfather started his business here in the forties," Madison explained as he led them down a hall. "I decided to honor tradition and base Madison International Properties where my grandfather created his fortune."

So Madison was a trust-fund baby who inherited a bundle.

Somehow that made Conor feel better about his own meager bank account, every penny of which had been hard earned.

They entered a large corner office overlooking Fifth Avenue.

"Please," Madison said, "have a seat." He settled in behind his desk. "I really want to thank you for finding Zivah's killer so quickly."

"I'm afraid I have bad news," Conor said. "He wasn't the killer."

Madison frowned. "Wasn't the killer?"

"He was in custody at Bellevue Hospital during the time of the homicide," Conor explained.

"I can't believe this," Madison said, running his hands through his thick head of hair.

"Mr. Madison," Rosita began. "We're doing everything we can to find the person responsible for Ms. Gavish's death. But we also have another case. They may be connected, we don't know. So we'd like to ask you a few questions."

Madison was puzzled. "Another case?"

"It's likely that Zivah was involved in a diamond-smuggling operation," Conor said.

"That's impossible," Madison retorted.

"How do you know that?" Rosita asked.

"How do I know that?" Madison stood, paced behind his desk. "I just know. She was incapable of that kind of behavior."

"I understand why you might feel that way," Conor said. "But you had only known her a short time. So maybe—"

"I'm a very good judge of people," Madison interjected. "In my business, I have to be. Zivah would never do anything that blatantly illegal."

"We have a witness who indicates otherwise," Rosita said gently. "An extremely valuable diamond was smuggled into the U.S. and the witness has indicated that Ms. Gavish was the recipient."

"Then she was misled," Madison offered. "She didn't know the diamond was illegal."

"I'm afraid she did," Conor said.

Madison eased back into his chair. "What do you want to know?"

"Did you and Ms. Gavish ever discuss her business dealings?" Conor asked.

"I don't mix business with pleasure." Madison motioned out the window. "Besides, I've got hundreds of properties out there. I certainly don't have time to discuss diamonds. What? Ten, twenty, *hundred-thousand-dollar* transactions. My portfolio goes up and down more than that in a millisecond."

"We believe Ms. Gavish was involved in the operation with an Indian diamond cutter," Rosita said. "In the last few days before her death, did she happen to mention anyone who fits that description?"

"Aren't most diamond cutters Indian these days?" Madison asked as he turned and faced Conor.

"That seems to be the case," Conor replied.

"That Sunday, after brunch, we came back to the loft. Zivah mentioned she was having dinner with someone later that night. I remember the name sounded Indian."

"Punjabi?" Rosita asked.

Madison shook his head. "I don't know. It could have been. I guess I wasn't paying attention. I had a lot on my mind that day." He shrugged. "I wish I could be more help, but . . ."

"Well, Kenneth, thank you for your time." Conor stood. "We'll keep you posted."

Conor and Rosita exited the Empire State Building.

Rosita gave him a bemused look. "Kenneth?"

"Hey, you spend time in the backseat of a limousine with someone, you have a right to call them by their first name."

They climbed into the car, Rosita behind the wheel.

"Obviously he doesn't know about the red diamond," Conor said.

"If he'd been paying attention, he might have known a lot more about Zivah's life." Rosita started the engine. "When will men learn to listen?"

Chapter Seventy-four

Conor decided to stake out Punjabi's office building and catch him off guard.

"He probably takes bidi breaks," Conor said, "so we won't have to wait long."

They drove to Forty-seventh Street and parked across the street from Punjabi's office. Ten minutes later Punjabi emerged, lit a bidi, and paced back and forth.

"Let's go," Conor said as he opened the car door.

Conor and Rosita swept across the street and boxed Punjabi in against the building.

"Mr. Punjabi," Conor said. "How are you?"

Punjabi's eyes darted from Conor to Rosita. "What is this about?"

Rosita crowded Punjabi even more, her body inches from his. "Oh, come now, Mr. Punjabi. I think you know what this is about."

"The red diamond," Conor said. "How did you get it into the country?"

Punjabi puffed nervously on his bidi. "At this point, I think it best if you speak with my attorney."

"I think you're right," Conor agreed. "Now that Wouter Marwala has been arrested by Immigration and Customs Enforcement."

Punjabi reacted with a twitch of his facial muscles. "So? That has nothing to do with me."

"We hear Marwala may be looking to cut a deal," Rosita said.

Punjabi trembled slightly, clearly aware of the implications.

"And we have a statement," Conor began, "from Stanley Silberman that you—"

"Silberman's a liar," Punjabi countered, beginning to lose his cool.

"The point is, Mr. Punjabi, we have enough to charge you with trafficking in illegal contraband. Unless you have something to say that would change our mind."

"My attorney will call you." Punjabi flicked his bidi to the sidewalk.

"That's littering," Rosita said, feigning outrage. "We could take you in for that."

Punjabi hurried toward the entrance to his building.

"Mr. Punjabi," Conor called out. "I forgot to tell you something."

Punjabi stopped, turned toward Conor.

"Don't try to leave the country. You'll be stopped at the airport."

Punjabi spun around and disappeared into the building.

"We can stop him at the airport?" Rosita asked.

"Of course not. He hasn't been charged with anything. But if he believes there could be a problem, I don't think he'll make a run for it."

They headed back across the street.

"We've got Punjabi on the ropes," Conor noted. *Another sports analogy? What kind of legacy has Ralph left me?*

"So what now?" Rosita asked.

"We obtain a warrant for the arrest of Arun Punjabi. We need something to show for all our overtime."

Conor and Rosita had just begun the paperwork involved in seeking an arrest warrant when the phone on Conor's desk rang.

"Bard."

"Mr. Bard. This is Burt Judson. I've been retained by Arun Punjabi."

Judson, although only thirty-nine, had earned a reputation as a tenacious—and extremely well-paid—criminal attorney.

"We need to talk," Judson said.

"I agree. When?"

"I'm jammed today. How about tomorrow morning. Ten o'clock?"

Conor took down Judson's address then hung up and looked at Rosita. "Punjabi's attorney. Tomorrow morning, ten o'clock."

So the smuggling case against Punjabi was progressing. But what about his involvement in the homicide? If Punjabi killed Zivah Gavish, the question was, why? Did he get greedy and decide his commission in the transaction wasn't enough? That the whole seventy million was a better deal? Punjabi certainly was in a unique position when it came to moving a rare red diamond. After all, your average Joe wouldn't know where to begin with a piece of hot red ice like that. As Ralph had said, this was shaping up as a Diamond District death. But how to prove that Punjabi was the killer? Hopefully, arresting him for smuggling would be the first step.

Conor and Rosita spent the rest of the afternoon classifying evidence and completing the documentation for an arrest warrant. It was almost six and given Amanda's tirade about overtime, they decided to call it a day. Conor dropped Rosita off at her apartment then drove to the precinct to park the car. As he hung up the keys on a board, he saw Danny Hahn approaching.

"Hey, Conor. Got good news for you."

"I could use some good news right now."

"IAB's backing off. I made them understand it wasn't worth it to pursue any action against you."

"Thanks, Danny. I owe you dinner."

"Somewhere expensive, I hope."

"Only the best for you."

* * *

Conor went home, showered, pulled on a pair of jeans, T-shirt, and sports coat. He picked up the phone. No question about it, he was hooked like a heroin addict.

"Meet you there in fifteen minutes," Tasha cooed. "But this will have to be quick."

And it was. She was in and out in half an hour. Tasha was perfect. Sexy. Exotic. And not a permanent resident of New York.

Suddenly ravenous, Conor headed to Frankie & Johnnie's, his favorite steakhouse, on Forty-fifth Street between Eighth Avenue and Broadway. The eighty-year-old restaurant represented a bit of New York City history. Photographs of entertainment icons who had dined there over the years covered the walls.

Anna Maria, the hostess, led Conor to a corner table. Then Mario, a waiter from Cyprus who had been employed there for years, appeared.

"The usual?" Mario asked.

A martini arrived quickly. As Conor sipped the chilled vodka, he thought about the meeting with Sony the next day. How should he dress? Should he play it cool? What should he say? Nothing much made him nervous but thinking about Sony caused him a great deal of consternation. This was the big time, his break after all these years. Maybe his only opportunity ever. *No. Don't think that way. You're going to blow it if you show desperation.*

Conor finished dinner and ordered a martini nightcap. His cell phone rang. He checked the caller ID. Alan Woodcliff. *Shit. Don't tell me the meeting's been canceled.*

"Conor!" It was Anna, Woodcliff's cell phone girl. "Something terrible has happened."

"What?"

"Alan's been arrested."

Chapter Seventy-five

Conor tried to calm her down, get the details. Woodcliff was still at the precinct in Tribeca. Which meant he wasn't yet in the system. That was good. There was still a possibility that something could be done. Of course, it would depend on the charge.

"Why was he arrested?" Conor asked.

"I don't know," she sobbed. "He just asked me to call you."

"All right, I'm on my way."

Conor drove to the Tribeca precinct, where Alan Woodcliff had been taken. Anna was sitting in a chair by the front desk.

"This is so awful," she said through her tears. "Please! Do something!"

"What happened?"

"We were at Guva and—"

"Guva?"

"It's this new club. I was sitting at the table. Alan went to the bathroom. Next thing I know he's in handcuffs and some cop is pushing him out the door."

"Where is he now?"

"They took him upstairs somewhere."

Conor identified himself at the desk, then climbed a set of stairs to the Detective Bureau, where he located Giorgio, the arresting officer. *Does he know the script?* Conor wondered. Which meant: Was he willing to bend the rules or was he one of those cops who was as rigid as a steel beam?

"So what's the deal?" Conor asked.

"We got a call from Guva, a club just off Canal Street, saying there was a disturbance. When we responded, we found Mr. Woodcliff in a state of inebriation and possible drug intoxication. He had assaulted a woman in one of the bathrooms."

Depending on the degree of assault, Conor could probably arrange for Woodcliff to receive a desk appearance ticket rather than let him go through the system. Still, it would be tricky. Woodcliff's celebrity status was a dual-edged sword. There had been a lot of bad press lately about celebrities getting off easily. Worse yet, Conor was beginning to form the opinion that Giorgio was the kind of cop who wouldn't do anything even remotely sketchy.

"May I ask your interest in this case?" Giorgio asked pointedly.

Conor didn't know exactly how to put it. *I'm here because he's getting me a record deal and we have a meeting at Sony tomorrow.* No, that wouldn't sound right.

"I know him," Conor said simply. He looked around the room. "Is the complainant here?"

Conor was no fan of rescuing someone who would lay a hand on any woman. But considering what was at stake, he'd decided to at least speak with the woman involved.

"The complainant is over there." Giorgio pointed to a woman sitting on a bench.

Conor walked over to her. She had a swollen jaw and dried blood caked on her cheeks. He found it difficult to look at her.

"Excuse me," Conor said, "I'm Detective Bard."

"Gloria Parks." Her voice was muffled by her puffy face.

"Would you mind telling me what happened?"

"What happened?" She became agitated. "The bastard tried to rape me in the bathroom."

Although Conor had never been to Guva, he guessed it was one of these superhip joints with a fondness for coed restrooms.

"When I pushed him away, he did this." She pointed to her blackened eyes.

Conor studied her battered face, started to question her further, but then thought better of it and made his way to the holding cell to get Woodcliff's side of the story. There he was. Mr. Rock Star, Alan Woodcliff. His hair was wild. He was sweating. When he saw Conor, he jumped off the bunk and rushed to the bars.

"Hey, man, thank God you're here."

"So what happened, Alan?"

"What happened? The bitch went crazy. You know these crazy bitches. I'm a target, man. I'm famous. That makes me a fucking target." Woodcliff pressed his face between the bars. "Just get me out of here. We've got business, right? One hand washes the other. You can get me a desk appearance ticket, right?"

Conor looked at Woodcliff. Obviously he'd been in this position before. How else would he know what a desk appearance ticket even was?

"Listen, Alan. You have a problem. The woman's hurt pretty bad."

"Fuck her! She's just a fucking whore. That's all she is. She ought to be fucking happy I even touched her." He sneered. "You watch. Tomorrow she'll be telling her friends how Alan Woodcliff slapped the shit out of her." He grabbed the bars. "Remember that song by the Crystals?" Woodcliff started singing: "He hit me . . . it felt like a kiss."

Conor knew the song. *Not the best lyric to elicit sympathy*, Conor thought. It had been produced by pop legend Phil Spector in the sixties but was widely banned and played very little on the radio considering its seeming glorification of spousal abuse.

"Let me speak with the arresting officer," Conor said, suddenly desperate to get away from Woodcliff.

"Fuck the officer," Woodcliff spewed. "Talk to that fucking slut. Get her to forget about this shit. Tell her I'll get her tickets to my next show. Backstage passes. The whole fucking nine yards."

"I'll see what I can do, Alan."

"Hey!" Woodcliff slapped the bars. "You don't get me out of here tonight, ain't going to be no meeting at Sony tomorrow. What? You want to be a cop the rest of your life?"

Conor bristled. *That son of a bitch*. He started walking away.

"Hurry up, man!" Woodcliff shouted. "I need a fucking drink!"

Conor nodded, then walked back to Giorgio.

"What do you want me to do?" Giorgio asked.

Conor stared at the holding cell. "Put him through the system."

Chapter Seventy-six

Conor stopped downstairs, explained to Anna that there was nothing he could do, and suggested she call a lawyer.

"Don't you guys have a meeting at Sony tomorrow?" she asked, sniffling.

"Not anymore."

Conor climbed in the car and drove back uptown. There went his record deal. But what the hell? Woodcliff was an arrogant bastard who beat up women. Probably never got charged before. Now he'll spend some time thinking about what he's done.

Conor entered his apartment and dropped heavily on the couch. *Paul Simon was right,* he thought. *The nearer your destination, the more you're slip sliding away.*

Okay. Back to square one. Yeah, he probably could have done something for Alan Woodcliff; but after talking with the victim, seeing her swollen jaw, blackened eyes, he'd rather not make a record deal if it meant allowing Woodcliff to smash female faces. There was a line to be drawn. And he had drawn it.

I just flushed a record deal with Sony down the toilet. I'm an idiot. A total fucking idiot.

Conor got up, went into the kitchen, and poured a vodka. If ever there was a time to get plastered, this was it.

Conor walked up Eighth Avenue wrestling with one monster of a hangover. The rays of sun felt like tiny golden needles pricking his face, releasing beads of sweat on his forehead. He moved slowly, methodically—any quick motion made him nauseous—and stopped at a newsstand. The headline of the *New York Post* made him grimace: *Alan Woodcliff in Assault Rap.* By Lew Michaels. Woodcliff's wild-eyed mug shot filled the page.

Fuck! It wasn't a nightmare. It really happened.

He grabbed a copy, dug fifty cents out of his pocket. As he handed the coins to the vendor, he dropped one of them. It hit the metal counter with a ping, echoing like a gunshot inside Conor's dehydrated brain.

When Conor entered the precinct, he found Rosita standing at his desk adjusting the placement of a small clay flowerpot.

"Good morning, Bard." She looked up at him then went back to adjusting the position of the flowerpot on his desk.

Conor frowned. "What's that?"

"A cactus."

"Why do I need a cactus?"

She moved the flowerpot a couple of inches to the left. "What's the matter? Too much responsibility?" She shifted it a little to the right. "You don't have to water this very much, if that's what you're worried about." She stepped back and admired her interior decorating efforts. "You've got to have *something* on your desk."

He would have argued the point but his pulsating temples prevented him from doing so.

She looked at him. "Your eyes. Looks like you went twelve rounds with Muhammad Ali."

Conor dropped into his chair. "No. Just seven or eight rounds with a bottle of vodka."

"How come?"

"I just blew my chance at a recording contract with Sony Records."

He related the events of the previous night. Rosita was sympathetic.

"You did the right thing, Bard. There'll be other chances. Fuck Sony."

Fuck Sony? Conor almost laughed—but the truth was, he had just seen the best chance he would ever have evaporate.

Conor checked the wall clock. "It's nine thirty. Let's go see what Punjabi and his expensive lawyer have to say."

Chapter Seventy-seven

Conor and Rosita met Arun Punjabi and Burt Judson in Judson's Park Avenue office. Punjabi looked drained. Judson, wearing a dark gray suit with a neon blue tie, got right to the point.

"Detective Bard, Detective Rubio, I'm sure I don't have to tell you how important a reputation can be, especially in the diamond business. My client is a member of the Diamond Dealers Club, which is one of the most influential trade groups in the world. Any hint of impropriety on Mr. Punjabi's part would serve to get him expelled from the club and destroy his ability to practice his profession. That's a harsh penalty considering the fact that he is innocent and the accusations made by Mr. Silberman are categorically false. There has been no diamond smuggled into this country. In fact, my client is prepared to explain the situation regarding the diamond that was once in the possession of Ms. Gavish. And, as you will see, there has been no illegal activity whatsoever vis-à-vis Mr. Punjabi."

"I'm all ears," Conor said.

"We do have one request," Judson added.

"And what's that?" Conor wanted to know.

"That you keep our discussion confidential."

"We can't make any promises, Mr. Judson," Conor said.

Judson nodded. "But once you hear what my client has to say, please consider the fact that the information he is about to disclose will put his life in jeopardy."

Conor and Rosita exchanged a glance.

"Understood," Conor said.

Judson motioned toward Punjabi. "Go ahead, Mr. Punjabi."

"I delivered the diamond to Zivah myself," Punjabi said.

"A red diamond?" Rosita asked.

"Yes."

Conor expressed surprise. "You usually walk around with priceless diamonds in your pocket?"

"You don't understand," Punjabi said. "The diamond I gave to Zivah Gavish was worthless."

"What do you mean, worthless?" Conor wanted to know.

"Not exactly worthless," Judson cut in. "Perhaps a hundred thousand. No more than that."

"I thought red diamonds were worth millions," Conor said, confused.

"*Natural* red diamonds are indeed priceless," Punjabi confirmed. "But the diamond I gave Zivah Gavish was a yellow diamond of little value that had been irradiated."

Rosita cocked her head. "Irradiated?"

"Colored by radiation," Punjabi explained. "Irradiation is used to imbue diamonds with color. For years, it has been possible to make yellow and green diamonds through irradiation. Only recently have diamonds been colored red with any degree of success. The process involves high pressures, high temperatures, irradiation, and annealing, which is the precise control of the heating and cooling process. There are only a few labs around the world that can color a diamond red with convincing results."

"And where did you obtain this irradiated red diamond?" Conor asked.

"From a lab in Michigan."

"Which lab in Michigan?" Conor pressed.

"Vector Research," Punjabi replied. "In Ann Arbor. I purchased the stone through a holding company in the Canary Islands so it could not be traced to me. I can supply you with all the documents that support the transaction."

Contacting the lab where Punjabi had the irradiation done would confirm that he had, in fact, an irradiated red diamond in his possession at one time or another. It would not rule out the possibility that the diamond taken from Zivah's loft had been anything other than a smuggled gem. Still, Conor would confirm Punjabi's account with the lab. At least he would know that an irradiated diamond did exist.

"So you were running a bait and switch on Zivah Gavish," Conor said.

"Excuse me, Detective," Judson retorted. "Please limit the scope of this interview to the diamond, not any intention Mr. Punjabi may or may not have had regarding such diamond." He looked at Punjabi. "Go ahead."

"I was absolutely not doing any such thing," Punjabi insisted. "I was merely trying to save my life. Because the rough diamond my company received in India to be cut belonged to Wouter Marwala."

"According to everything I have been able to learn about Wouter Marwala," Judson interjected, "it is clear he is a ruthless criminal. Certainly not above causing harm to my client."

"But your client still tried to cheat him," Conor pointed out.

"No," Punjabi whined. "I did not."

"You were about to allow an irradiated diamond to be passed off as a natural one." Conor shook his head. "Sounds like cheating to me."

"Once again," Judson said, his tone emphatic, "I must ask you not to speculate about my client's intentions."

"So, was your client ever in possession of a rough red diamond?"

Punjabi and Judson exchanged a glance.

"You may answer that question," Judson finally said.

"Yes," Punjabi replied. "It happened that I received a rough red stone from Wouter Marwala." He grimaced, looked away. "I made a disastrous error when cutting it." He shook his head in disbelief. "I studied the stone for two weeks, until I was certain I had found the correct line. But when I struck it . . ." He could barely utter the words. "It fractured." His eyes misted. "I turned a priceless gem into a pile of red rubble."

Chapter Seventy-eight

Conor and Rosita exchanged an incredulous glance. Punjabi destroyed the red diamond? All this over a crimson impostor?

"Sure," Punjabi continued, "I suppose I could still cut the pieces into little pavé diamonds but they would not even remotely approximate the value of the intact stone."

"I don't suppose it was insured," Conor said, "since it was illegal."

"Whether it was illegal or not," Judson interjected, "you have no jurisdiction. Whatever transaction did or did not occur between my client and Mr. Marwala took place outside the United States and therefore, if there was in fact any transgression, it is subject to South African or Indian laws. Please, Detective, I will end this interview if you do not limit the questioning to the accusation that Mr. Silberman has made against Mr. Punjabi, which is that Mr. Punjabi illegally imported a diamond."

"Where did your client attempt to cut the diamond?" Conor asked. "In his office on Forty-seventh Street?"

Judson smiled. "Good try, Detective. But Mr. Punjabi never brought anything into this country without proper documentation. The 'disastrous error' Mr. Punjabi referred to occurred at his headquarters in Mumbai."

Conor smiled. "All right, Counselor. I get it. Whatever happens in India, stays in India." He looked at Punjabi. "You were afraid to tell Marwala the red diamond had been destroyed. So you irradiated another one. What the hell were you thinking?"

"I was in a state of panic. Marwala has killed people for far less than a rare red diamond."

"Can't someone tell the difference between a natural red diamond and an irradiated one?" Rosita wondered.

"I examined the diamond for days," Punjabi said, "and found no indication that it was anything other than naturally colored."

"But you must have known that the buyer would find out eventually," Rosita said.

"Perhaps not," Punjabi countered. "If the irradiation is done well, it can only be detected by a lab. In this case, it was virtually indiscernible."

"And if someone *did* take the diamond to a lab?" Rosita asked.

"Under intense scrutiny," Punjabi allowed, "it would have been discovered."

"And then what?" Conor pressed. "When Marwala came knocking on your door, what were you going to tell him?"

Punjabi looked down at the floor. "I am ashamed to say this."

"Say what?" Conor asked.

Punjabi raised his head. "My reputation is pristine. Zivah was young, just starting out."

"So Marwala would have blamed her for the switch," Conor surmised.

"Yes," Punjabi said softly.

"Counselor," Conor began, "you must realize your client has just given himself a motive. Now that the red diamond is missing and Ms. Gavish is deceased, he appears to be off the hook with Wouter Marwala."

"As long as it's not recovered," Rosita chimed in, looking at Punjabi, "no one will ever know the diamond was anything but natural red. And you're free of any threat."

Judson bristled. "Are you now accusing my client of murder?"

"Just stating a fact," Rosita said.

Punjabi grew agitated. "I will tell you a fact. I did not kill anyone and if I am arrested I will be known as Punjabi the smuggler. I will be ruined."

"In other words," Judson interjected, "we're engaging in a little preemptive damage control. The diamond stolen from Zivah Gavish's residence was irradiated at a laboratory in Michigan—a homegrown red diamond. Once you recover it—*if* you are able to find the killer of Zivah Gavish—you will see that all my client was doing, as far as you are concerned, was selling a legal diamond to a qualified buyer."

Rosita steered the car across town. "Boy, Punjabi's a real champ, huh? He basically murdered Zivah Gavish the day he gave her the irradiated diamond."

"That was Punjabi's plan," Conor agreed. "Let Zivah Gavish take the fall. But you know what I think? I think he changed his mind. What if Marwala *did* come after him? Punjabi didn't want to take that chance. So he came up with Plan B. Kill Zivah and retrieve irradiated diamond."

"Okay. But how did Punjabi know the safe would be open?"

"I thought about that. The day Punjabi delivered the red diamond to Zivah Gavish, let's assume she immediately put it in the safe. She was careless when she punched in the combination. Punjabi watched her, memorized the sequence."

"Punjabi waited for her to leave," Rosita said, picking up on the theory, "then gained access to the loft through the tenement and the terrace."

"But he didn't expect Zivah to come back," Conor added.

"So he had no choice but to kill her."

"Exactly."

"And he was forced to tell us about the irradiated diamond in order to avoid an arrest for smuggling that would destroy his career."

They rode in silence for a couple of blocks, contemplating the possible scenarios involving Punjabi.

"You know what I find totally bizarre?" Rosita asked.

"What?" Conor wanted to know.

"Okay. You've got a natural red diamond and one that's been irradiated. And based on what Punjabi said, it's impossible to tell the difference without some piece of lab equipment. But one is worth seventy million and the other is worth maybe a hundred grand. So if you can't tell which is which unless you send it to a lab, why spend seventy million?"

When Conor and Rosita got back to the precinct, they pulled up chairs in front of the bulletin board, which was now cluttered with crime scene photos, stills from security video, copies of phone records, receipts, anything even remotely related to the case. Nothing stood out.

"Let's assume the killer knew about the red diamond," Conor began, "and that was the target. Punjabi knew about both the tenement and, of course, the diamond. Since only *Punjabi* knew it was not a natural red diamond, his motive is clear and simple: keep the fact that the stone was irradiated a secret. And if not Punjabi, who else? Wouter Marwala knew about the diamond but offered a million-dollar bribe to gain possession of it. So scratch Marwala. Silberman knew there was a diamond but didn't know the value until we told him. Scratch Silberman too. Kruger? He did seem to have a motive at first—capture his Professor Moriarty 'by any means necessary'—but now I'm certain he does not have the red diamond and was not involved in the murder."

"Professor Moriarty?"

"Sherlock Holmes's archenemy." Conor looked at Rosita. "You never read Sherlock Holmes?"

"No."

"How can you be a cop and never have read Sherlock Holmes?"

"I'm younger than you are."

"What's that supposed to mean?"

"When I was in school, we had a different required reading list than you did way back then."

"So what was on your list? Harry Potter?"

"You said: by any means necessary."

Conor nodded.

"You realize who you're quoting?" she asked.

"I'm quoting Hendrik Kruger. Who was quoting Malcolm X."

"Kruger really said that?"

"With a straight face," Conor replied.

The phone on Conor's desk rang.

"Bard."

"Hey, Bard. It's Selzer."

"What've you got?"

"I hate to disappoint you, but the fine powder around the wound wasn't diamond dust."

"What was it?"

"Cocaine."

Chapter Seventy-nine

As Conor and Rosita drove to the medical examiner's office, both of them were wondering the same thing. *Were drugs involved?*

Rosita steered the car south down Seventh Avenue. "Nothing like a little cocaine to give you a jolt."

And this *was* a jolt. Any time drugs were involved, all bets were off. Anybody, sufficiently high, was capable of almost anything.

"You ever do coke?" Rosita asked.

"Never."

She was surprised. "You're a musician and you never did coke?"

"Never tried it."

"Are you sure?" she asked dubiously.

"Okay. Here's the thing. The first time I saw it, I was turned off. Sticking powder up your nose? Nasty. Plus, I liked to drink. Too much. I figured I had an addictive personality already, why throw another substance into the mix?"

"Come on, Bard. You were never tempted?"

"Honestly? Only once. Things weren't going so great with the band. Everybody was doing it."

"Why didn't you?"

"There was this piano player. Rudy. Saw him at a party one night. He picked up this girl, hot redhead. Took her home."

"I think I know where this is going," Rosita said.

"The next day I see him on the street," Conor continued, "and he's sweating like it's a hundred degrees with humidity to match. Only it's November and it's like around thirty-five, forty degrees. Rudy's shirt is drenched. So I ask him: Rudy, you okay? And he says he is. Of course, I really want to know how it went with the redhead. Rudy rubs his eyes, laughs. Says he did too much blow."

Rosita gave him a knowing look. "Couldn't get it up?"

"So right then and there I said to myself, 'Which would you rather do? Snort? Or get laid?'"

"Women can do both," she teased.

"Rubio, you don't . . ."

"Coke? Sure, I've tried it. Years ago, in my youth. But now? I'm not *that* stupid."

They parked the car in front of the ME's office and went inside. Selzer was waiting for them.

"Was our victim a user?" Rosita asked.

"I won't know for sure until I get the toxicology report," Selzer replied. "But here's the weird thing. The odd coagulation pattern I mentioned at the autopsy? That fine powder? Cocaine crystals in and around the wound."

"Did you say *in* the wound?" Conor wanted to make sure he'd heard Selzer correctly.

"Yes," Selzer replied. "I would say that the weapon used to inflict the wound across her neck likely contained a fair amount of cocaine residue."

Conor and Rosita exchanged a glance. *Some crackhead from the tenement?*

* * *

"There goes our diamond dust theory," Conor said as he climbed behind the wheel. "So now what are we looking at? Some addict from the abandoned tenement? A transient killer?"

Rosita pulled the driver's-side door shut. "Could be anybody. A lot of people use coke."

Cocaine had made a resurgence among the social set recently. *Guess nobody learned anything from the seventies*, Conor thought.

"And cocaine in the wound doesn't rule out Punjabi," Rosita added. "Those little bidis are really strong. I could picture a bidi smoker doing coke. Plus, a diamond-cutting disk is perfect for carving out a line of powder."

Conor steered the car into the flow of traffic. "Well, you're the expert on cocaine consumption."

"Expert?" She laughed. "Give me a break. I only did it a few times."

"How many?"

"Fuck, I don't remember."

"Which makes you an expert."

As Conor and Rosita walked toward their desks, Rooney waved at them from within his office. They walked over and stopped at the open door.

"Got a minute?" Rooney asked.

Conor and Rosita entered the office.

"Have a seat," Rooney said.

They sat across the desk from Rooney.

"I just spoke with the chief of detectives. He had lunch with the mayor. Anyway, the bottom line is that the chief wants to bring in the major case squad on the yarn factory homicide."

"Major Case?" Conor was incredulous. "They don't investigate homicides."

"They do on television," Rooney countered. "And too bad this *isn't* television. All our cases would be solved in an hour." He threw his hands in the air. "There's no fighting this, Bard. I told you before, the developer is the mayor's buddy. And an open homicide isn't good for the real estate business."

"But, Lu," Conor protested, "we've got a strong suspect. All we need—"

"What *you* need doesn't matter," Rooney interrupted. "It's what the chief needs. And he needs you off this case."

"What do you want me to do?" Conor asked, resigned.

"Get everything together. Major Case is coming by tomorrow morning at eight."

Conor and Rosita stood. They started out of the office.

"Bard," Rooney called out. "You stay here."

Rosita left the room.

"I just wanted to let you know," Rooney said, "I'm calling it a day. Taking retirement."

"Retirement?"

"Yeah. Things just aren't like they used to be in the city."

"What are you going to do?"

"I don't know. I got my pension."

"When?"

"Effective immediately."

Conor left Rooney's office depressed. *I've just seen my future. Retired. Living on a pension.*

Chapter Eighty

"What did Rooney want?" Rosita asked defensively.

"Nothing about you this time, Rubio. Don't be paranoid. He wanted to tell me he's retiring, that's all."

She looked away.

He could see she was bothered by something. "What?"

"Oh, I don't know." She spoke without looking at him. "Maybe it's my fault. Maybe if you had Ralph . . ."

"Then what? The case would have been solved?"

"Something like that."

"I was on the case too, Rubio. If the case wasn't solved, it's just as much my fault. And believe me, Ralph being here wouldn't have made a bit of difference."

Rosita glanced at the bulletin board. "Want to take this stuff down?"

"Leave it. I'll do it later." He looked at her. "We'll get 'em next time, Rubio."

"Yeah. Next time."

Rosita left. Conor reviewed the case in his mind. At some point, he thought of Kruger. *I'm miserable. Kruger's happy. Fuck that!*

*　　*　　*

"I know how you love these things." Conor held a hot dog out to Kruger. "That's why I asked you to meet me here. Because once you're back in Johannesburg you won't be able to get this cylinder-shaped New York filet mignon."

"Thank you." Kruger took the hot dog. "Look, Conor, I'm sorry about what happened with Customs. But I considered it my best play at the time."

"Hey, what can I say? You got Marwala, right?"

"Yes." Kruger took a bite of hot dog. "And this time there's no way out."

Conor wasn't by nature vindictive but Kruger had played him against ICE and now it was time for payback.

"Unfortunately, Marwala does have a way out."

Kruger almost choked on the hot dog. "What did you say?"

"I have reliable information that the diamond stolen from the loft was irradiated. You know what that is, right?"

Kruger's jaw dropped in disbelief. "I know what it is."

"Apparently, the diamond taken from Zivah Gavish's loft was artificially colored by a lab in Michigan. I've got documents to confirm that. Which means Marwala was attempting to retrieve a diamond made right here in the USA. A *legal* diamond. Which also means that ICE has nothing they can hold him on."

Kruger nodded, thinking. "But you don't have the irradiated diamond, do you?"

"Not yet, Hendrik. But I will. Believe me, I will."

"What happened to the natural stone?" Kruger wondered aloud.

Conor considered telling Kruger about Punjabi's unkindest cut but decided to let Kruger believe the rare red diamond still existed. "I have no idea. For all I know, the real red diamond never left Mumbai."

Kruger tossed his half-eaten hot dog in a trash can.

"Sorry, Hendrik. Looks like Marwala's head won't be mounted on your wall any time soon."

Conor returned to the precinct and took up a position in front of the bulletin board again. Where was the key that unlocked the case? It had to be there somewhere. But he couldn't find it. He called Ralph, explained the situation.

"Come on over to the house," Ralph said. "I'll throw a couple steaks on the grill."

Conor drove downtown, his mood somber. Okay, so the case was being taken away from him. What the hell? He did the best he could. *Let the major case squad figure it out.*

Conor entered the Brooklyn Battery Tunnel, cruised down the Gowanus Expressway and across the Verrazano-Narrows Bridge, and finally onto Staten Island. Ralph lived in a neighborhood called St. George, on the northeastern tip of the island overlooking Upper New York Bay with a postcard view of Manhattan just across the water. The Staten Island Ferry Terminal was nearby and the area was densely populated due to the easy commute to Manhattan.

Ralph greeted him at the door with a freshly made martini.

"Now *that's* service," Conor said.

"Maybe you'll take a ride over here more often."

As they walked inside, Ralph studied Conor.

"What's wrong?"

"I told you—I'm off the case. I'm supposed to turn everything over to Major Case tomorrow morning."

"That's tomorrow morning." Ralph picked up his own martini from a coffee table, took a sip, then motioned to Conor. "Come over here."

Conor followed Ralph to a painting on the wall. They stood very close to it.

"What do you see?" Ralph asked.

Conor stared at the painting for a moment. "Dots of paint."

"Right. Because this is pointillism. The artist uses dots instead of brushstrokes to create an image." Ralph looked at the painting, melancholy tinting his eyes. "When Laura and I first got married, we were out walking around the city, and we wandered into this art gallery, Arnot Galleries. On Fifty-seventh Street. She saw this painting and just had to have it. It was painted by an artist named Crépin—nobody famous or anything like that—who was a mailman in France. Once in a while Crépin would send him a piece and Herbert Arnot would sell it. So I asked how much and the guy said five hundred dollars." Ralph shook his head. "He might as well have said five million. Five hundred? That was a lot of money back then. Laura said that was way too much, that we couldn't afford it. But I could see how much she wanted it. So I pulled the guy aside, gave him twenty bucks to hold it. And I called a friend of mine, Bobby, an ex-cop who retired and had a security company. I asked him if he had any work. Bobby gave me a job as a night watchman at a parking lot across the bridge in Jersey. I lied to Laura. Told her Bobby needed me and I couldn't turn him down. Two weeks later I went back to Arnot Galleries, totally fucking exhausted from pounding the beat all day and sitting in a guardhouse all night, handed the guy four hundred and eighty dollars, and brought it home." He laughed sadly. "She was really upset with me. Said I shouldn't have done it. Thirty years later she would still bring it up." He looked at the painting. "But Laura loved it, enjoyed it all these years. That's what matters." He started walking across the room. "Come over here."

Conor followed him across the room.

"Now what do you see?"

Conor looked at the painting. There was a distinct image this time. "A cottage. Trees and bushes around it. A wooden fence. An open gate."

"There you go. Maybe you're too close to the case so it's nothing but pieces of evidence. Like the dots in a pointillist painting. Sometimes you've got to stand back to make sense of it all."

Conor was struck by the simplicity of Ralph's advice. What did the case consist of? Seemingly unrelated pieces of evidence. Like dots of paint. He needed to make them form a picture of the killer.

"Come on, kid," Ralph said. "Let's throw a couple steaks on the grill."

Chapter Eighty-one

After Ralph's speech about the painting, Conor was suddenly confident he could solve the case. But he wouldn't be given the time. Tomorrow it would all be under the jurisdiction of the major case squad.

Conor dropped off the car at the precinct then walked slowly toward his apartment. Was he giving up that easily? He thought of Rooney's decades-old proclamation: Never overestimate the criminal mind. Rooney was right. Whoever killed Zivah Gavish must have made a mistake. But what was it?

He turned and walked back to the precinct. It was eleven thirty. In eight hours the case wouldn't be his. But tonight it *was* his case. *His* case.

Conor began rearranging items on the bulletin board. Punjabi? He was in the loft, admitted being there. Knew about the tenement and its easy access. Had a motive: to keep his diamond-cutting disaster a secret. *It has to be Punjabi,* Conor thought. *But how do I prove it?*

Conor popped in the DVD of security video in the days leading up to Zivah's murder. He watched Zivah come and go. He turned his attention to the bulletin board, then rewatched the DVD.

What am I missing?

An hour became two. Then three. Then four.

"Tell me you didn't stay here all night."

It wasn't until Conor heard Rosita's voice that he looked up at the clock and realized it was morning, 7:42 to be exact.

Rosita, carrying a shopping bag, walked up to him. "Why didn't you call me? I would've come back in."

"Because this was an act of desperation. I've got a suspect, a strong motive, and no way to prove it."

Rosita opened the shopping bag and took out something wrapped in tissue paper.

Conor rolled his eyes. "What now?"

"This is for you." She handed it to him.

Conor tore off the tissue paper to reveal a mug with a guitar on it. "Thanks, Rubio. It's cool."

"Here, give it back to me. Let me wash it. And I'll bring you a coffee. Looks like you need one."

Conor handed the mug to Rosita and then went back to concentrating on the bulletin board. There had to be a way to unravel this.

A couple of minutes later, Rosita returned and handed Conor a steaming cup of coffee. "Here you are."

"Thanks."

Rosita looked at her watch. "We better take that stuff off the board. Major Case is due here in fifteen minutes."

"Yeah, I know. Just give me a second." As he sipped his coffee, something occurred to him. He pushed out of his chair, walked to the board, and carefully examined a time-stamped still photograph culled from the security video—Zivah walking in with a shopping bag. *She bought something. What did she buy?* The name of the store was printed on the bag, but because of the angle, only the first two letters were visible. Conor returned to his desk and sifted through the clutter until he found Zivah's credit card statements. He ran his finger down the list of purchases until he found a charge that matched the first two letters on the bag.

Could this be it? Could this be that one mistake Rooney always talked about?

Rosita noticed Conor's expression, which reflected a mixture of discovery and surprise.

"What?" she asked.

"I think I know who killed Zivah Gavish," he replied.

Chapter Eighty-two

Although Conor felt certain he knew who, he didn't know why. *Better than the other way around*, he told himself.

"You going to let me in on your little revelation?" Rosita asked.

Conor held up his hand and started typing on the computer keyboard. He stared intently at the screen.

Rosita looked over his shoulder. "What are you looking for?"

And suddenly there it was on the screen. The motive.

Conor stood. "Let's go."

"Where?"

"A little store on Seventh Avenue."

"Great! I love to shop."

"Bard!" Rooney bellowed as he spotted Conor and Rosita heading toward the door.

"Tell Major Case to come back later," Conor shouted as he quickened his pace.

"Bard! Wait!"

But Conor pretended not to hear.

* * *

Conor and Rosita approached the reception desk. Conor was carrying a soft leather briefcase.

"We're here to see Mr. Madison," Rosita said.

"Is he expecting you?"

"I don't think so," Conor replied.

"I'm sorry, but Mr. Madison is on a conference call."

Rosita pulled out her badge. "Don't get up. We know the way."

They walked briskly down the hall and stopped in front of Madison's office. Rosita opened the door and stepped inside. Conor followed.

Madison was on the phone. He looked up, surprised. "I'll have to call you back." He placed the receiver in the cradle. "Detective. What's going on?"

"Sorry to burst in like this, Kenneth, but I think I know who killed Zivah."

"That's great! Who?"

"Well, before we make an arrest, we want to be sure. And I was hoping you could help us."

"Of course, of course. Have a seat."

Madison motioned to two chairs in front of the desk then walked over and closed the door.

"We're having a little problem with the timeline." Conor eased into a chair and placed the leather briefcase on the desk in front of him.

Madison returned to his desk and sat facing them. "What timeline?"

"Yours," Rosita explained.

"Mine? What do you mean?"

"You had brunch with Zivah Gavish on the Sunday before she was killed," Conor pointed out.

"That's correct," Madison replied.

"Then you drove to the Hamptons." Conor reached into the leather briefcase and produced a sheet of paper. "Your E-ZPass account was charged at three forty-one when you left the city."

"That sounds right."

Conor looked down at the paper. "Your E-ZPass account was charged again on Tuesday morning at five thirty-two when you entered Manhattan."

"Again, that sounds about right."

"You go to the Hamptons often?"

"I have a house there."

"Is that a yes?" Rosita asked.

"Yes," Madison replied. "But I really don't see—"

"Do you ever use the Fifty-ninth Street Bridge?" Conor wanted to know.

Madison shrugged. "Sure. Sometimes there's traffic in the tunnel. So I use the bridge."

"The good thing about the bridge is that there's no toll like there is through the tunnel. And therefore no record when someone crosses the river. Of course, you can save a lot of money that way."

"Thanks for the explanation of toll laws and for the financial advice, Detective. But I hardly worry about things like that."

"You should. Tolls keep going up." Conor looked down at the piece of paper then up at Madison. "So, to make sure I've got this right, you're saying you left the city at three forty-one and did not return until five thirty-two Tuesday morning."

"If that's what the E-ZPass says."

"That's what it says."

Madison shifted in his chair. "Do you mind telling me why we're talking about bridges and tunnels?"

Conor stared at Madison for a long moment before answering. "Because I think you went through the tunnel on Sunday to register the time, then on Monday afternoon drove across the Fifty-ninth Street Bridge knowing there wouldn't be an E-ZPass record, killed Zivah Gavish, then drove back across the bridge to the Hamptons to complete your alibi."

Madison leaned back in his chair. "I would be offended by your accusation if it weren't so preposterous."

"So you're telling me that's not what happened?" Conor asked.

"Yes. That's what I'm telling you. Can you prove otherwise?"

"No," Conor admitted, "I can't."

"I must say," Madison huffed, disgusted, "I'm disappointed you're wasting your time hurling accusations at me. No wonder you haven't found the person who killed Zivah."

Conor pulled another sheet of paper from the leather briefcase. "Your cell phone records."

Madison frowned, annoyed. "And?"

"Based on the cellular tower closest to your phone," Conor began, "you were in Southampton on Monday between the hours of three thirty and eight thirty."

"Yeah . . . ?" Madison asked mockingly.

"So we know your cell phone was in the Hamptons," Conor said. "But I don't think *you* were." Conor held up the cell phone records. "You didn't make or answer any calls during that time because you left your phone in the Hamptons in an attempt to reinforce your alibi."

"And this is something you can verify?" Madison was smug.

"No," Conor replied, "I can't."

"This is ridiculous." Madison stood. "Is that all, Detective? I have a busy day."

"Actually," Conor said. "There *is* one more thing." He opened the leather briefcase again and this time produced a clear plastic evidence bag containing the hand-painted cocktail glass from the loft. "You recognize this glass?"

"Should I?"

"I think you should." Conor held up the evidence bag so Madison could see the glass. "It's from Zivah Gavish's kitchen."

"So?"

"Your fingerprints are on it," Rosita explained.

"I certainly would imagine my fingerprints are on Zivah's glasses," Madison said flatly. "I've spent quite a bit of time there."

"This glass had a little scotch in it," Conor said.

"I drink scotch," Madison acknowledged. "You know that. So what's your point?"

"You recall the last time you had a glass of scotch at Ms. Gavish's apartment?" Conor pressed.

Madison cleared his throat. "This is getting rather tiresome."

"Please answer the question," Conor insisted.

"I had a scotch on Sunday," Madison said, clearly miffed. "After brunch. Then I left for the Hamptons."

"You shouldn't drink and drive," Rosita offered.

Madison walked toward the door. "If you don't mind, I need to get back to work."

Conor cradled the evidence bag in both hands. "This is a beautiful glass. Hand-painted."

Madison rolled his eyes. "Why don't you keep it?"

"Oh, no. I couldn't do that." Conor placed the glass on the desk. "It's part of a set."

"Why don't you take them all?" Madison was losing patience. "I'm sure a set of glasses like that would be a great addition to your kitchen."

"You're right about that," Conor agreed. "I don't even have two glasses that match."

"Then it's settled. Now you can entertain in style." Madison opened the door. "If you'll excuse me, I really do have a full schedule today."

Conor stood, ranged toward Madison. "The problem is, Zivah bought the glasses from a place called American Craftsman over on Seventh Avenue. Fifty-first Street. I stopped by and spoke with the clerk. Pleasant young woman. And she remembered Zivah coming in."

"Of course she would remember Zivah," Madison said. "Zivah was unforgettable." He pulled the door open wider. "Please, Detective, perhaps you could come back another time and—"

"Anyway," Conor interrupted, "the clerk said Zivah was walking down the street and saw the glasses in the window. They had a nice conversation. Zivah told the clerk she was in the diamond business and the clerk said the artist who painted the glasses only does eight in each theme. This time the theme was diamonds. Zivah bought all eight. A one-of-a-kind set."

Madison was now totally exasperated. "Zivah loved unique things.

You found the glass in the loft. My fingerprints are on it, which, like I said, I would expect them to be. Am I missing something here?"

"Zivah purchased those glasses on Monday at two forty-seven." Conor stepped over to the desk and reached into the leather briefcase. "Here's a copy of the receipt."

Madison swallowed, his smugness suddenly gone. "The clock in the credit card terminal must have been wrong."

"No. I checked." Conor pulled a DVD from the briefcase. "Plus, I have security video of Zivah entering the lobby on Monday afternoon. And you know what she's carrying? A bag from American Craftsman." He placed the DVD on the desk and picked up the evidence bag containing the glass. "So the question is, *Kenneth* . . . how did your fingerprints wind up on a glass that Zivah Gavish bought *after* you left the city?"

Chapter Eighty-three

Madison didn't respond. His eyes darted as if his brain were spinning inside his skull.

"Here's what I think." Conor moved closer to Madison. "I think she told you about the red diamond. Maybe she even told you who the buyer was. Billionaire from Abu Dhabi with a penchant for collecting rare gems no matter where they came from. Guy like that, you just hand over the diamond, take the cash. He wouldn't ask questions."

Madison said nothing, apparently unable or unwilling to offer a rebuttal.

"But you're a billionaire, right?" Conor shrugged. "Why would a billionaire care enough about a diamond to kill for it?"

Conor walked to the desk, opened the leather bag, and removed a sheet of paper. "My old partner Ralph? Even though he had the best professional fee-based databases city taxpayers could buy at his fingertips, he loved surfing the Net. So that's what I did. I surfed." Conor waved the piece of paper. "I found this on the Yahoo Finance website." He looked down and began reading. "Madison International Properties faces debt service deadline. Lack of liquid assets may doom company." He looked up at Madison. "It says here that an eighty-two-million-dollar interest payment is due next month. And if you default on the loan, your company could collapse like a house of cards."

"That's ridiculous," Madison countered without much conviction.

"You saw the diamond as a way to fix your cash flow problems," Conor continued relentlessly, "so you planned to steal it. Planned it well, I've got to say. You knew she would be at the diamond dealers' dinner. You'd slip into the loft. But how would you know the safe would be open when you got inside the apartment? That bothered me from the beginning. Why was the safe wide open?" Conor rubbed his forehead. "So on the way over here I called a guy named Clifford Stevens. Works for the developer. I made Stevens wake up his boss. And you know what the developer told me? He told me you ordered the wall safe as an option. You were there when it was installed. So you knew the combination, didn't you? Which meant everything was in place. So you drove back into the city over the Fifty-ninth Street Bridge, made your way up the stairs of the tenement, climbed onto the terrace, into the loft, opened the safe . . ."

Madison's face reddened. Rivulets of sweat dripped from his forehead into his eyes.

"And just as you removed the red diamond from the safe, she walked in!" Conor's voice rose. "You saw her leave but now she was back." His voice lowered to almost a whisper. "And there you were, red diamond in your hand. How could you explain that? What did she say? Was there a confrontation? Did she suddenly realize you were there to steal the diamond? Is that why you killed her? To silence her?"

Madison stood motionless, staring into some void.

Conor drifted back to the desk. "On the way over here, I asked myself why you didn't just take the diamond when she was in the shower. Or why you didn't wait until she left for the diamond dealers' dinner and then walk right in through the lobby? But of course you couldn't do that. Zivah would figure out what happened to the diamond. The doorman would tell her: Mr. Madison was here. But if the diamond disappeared while you were in the Hamptons, she couldn't blame you, could she?" He frowned at Madison. "Or did you plan to kill her all along because you needed her buyer, Sulaiman Aziz? How could you call Mr. Aziz and offer him the diamond while Zivah was alive? Surely she would find out what you were doing. Better to slit her throat, wait a couple weeks, a month, call Aziz. He wouldn't care how you came to be in possession of the red diamond. A priceless gem to add to his collection. That's all that mattered to Aziz."

Conor glared at Madison. "When you saw her there lying on the floor, blood dripping from her neck, were you shaking? Were your legs wobbling? Was your head spinning? Is that why you needed a shot of whiskey? To steady your nerves?"

Brian and a team from the Crime Scene Unit burst into the office. Madison backed away, alarmed.

"We have a search warrant," Conor explained.

"I suppose I should call an attorney," Madison said softly.

"That would be a good idea," Conor said.

Madison rushed to his desk, reached for the phone.

"Oh," Conor added. "Before I read you your rights, there's something else you should know. That red diamond? It's a fake."

Madison paled. "What did you say?"

"You heard me," Conor fired back. "It's not a natural stone. It's been irradiated. Not worth more than a hundred grand. Which isn't bad. Unless you're staring at an eighty-million-dollar interest payment."

Chapter Eighty-four

The search of Madison's office turned up the red diamond, tucked away in the back of a wall safe next to several ounces of cocaine. Worse yet for Madison, when he was booked there was a small silver penknife among his possessions. It had a diamond embedded in it on one side and bore an inscription on the other: *Happy Birthday, Kenneth. Love, Zivah.* Brian had immediately noticed traces of what looked like blood in the hinge. Likely Zivah's blood. "They always forget the hinge," Brian had said as he examined the knife.

Conor and Rosita walked into the precinct.

"He killed her with a birthday gift?" She shook her head. "That's cold."

"Yeah, he's a cold son of a bitch all right."

They stopped at their desks.

"Congratulations," he said.

"For what?"

"For solving your first homicide."

"Thanks, Bard. But you're the one who figured it out."

"The record will show that Bard and Rubio solved a homicide. That's all that matters." He dropped in the chair behind his desk. "Besides, if it weren't for you, we would have handed the case over to Major Case by now."

"Me? What did I do?"

He held up the guitar mug. "I was drinking coffee, looking at this nice mug you bought me this morning, and it made me wonder when Zivah Gavish bought the cocktail glasses."

She raised her eyebrows. "Then why are you taking any credit?"

Lew Michaels rushed up to them. He slapped a *New York Post* onto the desk with the flourish of a card player tossing down an ace. "Page twenty-nine."

"What's on page twenty-nine?" Rosita asked.

"Take a look," Michaels replied.

Rosita picked up the newspaper, flipped to page 29. "One bright spot on the far West Side," she read aloud, "is the Rhythm Bar, which features live music. Last Saturday night singer Conor Bard took to the stage. His smoky voice offered a near perfect delivery for a solid selection of classic rock and R&B." She looked up. "Hey, Bard. You're famous."

"Is that the best you could do?" Conor teased. "Just two sentences about me and my extraordinary talent?"

"Come on, Conor," Michaels whined. "I got our music guy Dempsey there, didn't I? That's all I can do. I can't tell him what to write."

"Your timing is perfect," Conor told him. "We just made an arrest in the Zivah Gavish homicide. I'll give you something you can run with."

Conor spoke on the condition that what he said be "not for attribution." Although he divulged very little about the circumstances surrounding the arrest, he did provide enough fodder for Michaels to write an article that would make readers think he had an inside track.

Conor watched Michaels jog away. "We ought to go out and celebrate tonight."

"Where you want to go?" she asked.

"Why don't you meet me at the Rhythm Bar around seven? I've got to pick up a microphone I left backstage the other night."

"Yeah, you *were* in a hurry to get out of there," she said pointedly.

"So what do you say? Rhythm Bar. Seven o'clock. We'll have a drink then go to dinner somewhere."

"What about your girlfriend?"

"Tasha? She went back to India for a couple weeks. To visit her husband."

"Ouch."

"Hey, it is what it is." He looked at her. "Why don't you head home? Go get your nails done or your hair done or something."

"What's wrong with my hair?"

"Nothing. I was just saying—"

"See you at seven," she said icily as she walked away.

Wow, he thought. *I'm getting really good at pissing off women. And I wasn't even trying.*

Conor reached for the phone. There was one call he couldn't wait to make.

"Bailey."

"Hey, Jack. It's Conor Bard."

There would be some small consolation for Conor in telling Bailey about the irradiated diamond and that Immigration and Customs Enforcement would have to let Marwala go.

"How's it going?" Conor asked.

"Not so good," Bailey replied. "I'm afraid I have a little egg on my face."

"What happened?"

"Well, Hendrik Kruger called me early this morning and said the evidence against Wouter Marwala was somehow flawed and the South African government was withdrawing its extradition request. Next thing I know, a vice consul from the consulate was here pushing through Marwala's release."

"Marwala's no longer in custody?"

"No. He walked out of here a free man at two thirty this afternoon."

Conor hung up and stared at the phone for a moment before picking up the receiver again and placing another call, this one to a detective in Carlstadt, New Jersey.

"Did a South African government aircraft depart from Teterboro Airport in the last couple of hours?"

The detective placed Conor on hold for a few minutes, then: "Yes. An hour ago."

Conor leaned back in his chair. *Kruger isn't that diabolical, is he?* Was Professor Moriarty spirited out of the country, finally ending Kruger's quest "by any means necessary"? And if so, what were the odds that Marwala would actually reach a court of law alive?

Whatever happened, it was of no concern to Conor anymore. Kruger was a killer. Marwala was a killer. They deserved each other.

Conor straightened the mess on his desk, then stopped in to update Rooney on the arrest of Kenneth Madison.

"You were right, Lu. I finally found the one mistake you were always talking about."

"And hanging on to a murder weapon with your name on it isn't such a smart thing to do either," Rooney added.

Conor studied Rooney. "You sure you want to retire? We could use your experience."

"Use my experience?" Rooney's expression grew pained. "Don't you see, that's what I've become. Some encyclopedia tucked away on a shelf. People come in, flip through the pages, then go out into the arena and play the game. I haven't been in the game for over ten years." He shook his head. "With what I know, there are only two things I can do. Be a detective . . ."

"You were the best, sir."

"Thank you, Bard. But there's no going back now. My days as a detective are behind me."

Rooney's eyes fixed on a point somewhere beyond the room. Conor waited an appropriate amount of time before he asked, "And what's the second thing, Lu?"

Rooney snapped back to the confines of his office. "With what I know? I think I'd make a damn good criminal."

The line that separated cops from criminals was rather thin. Conor had run with a wild crowd growing up. Half the guys he knew had served time. The other half had become local cops. It almost didn't matter what side you were on. It was all about the action.

"Don't worry, Bard," Rooney continued, "I plan a big job, you're in for a cut."

Conor nodded. "Thank you, sir."

Chapter Eighty-five

Conor walked into the Rhythm Bar. The place was packed with the after-work crowd that had grown along with the tidal gentrification of the neighborhood. Rosita, cosmopolitan in hand, was at the bar waiting for him.

He looked at her. Something was different. "You had your hair done."

"Just a blow-dry," she said modestly.

Conor slid onto a stool. "Hey, Susie. Give me a—"

"Ketel One, straight up, twist, no vermouth." Susie already had a bottle of vodka in her hand.

"Am I that predictable?" he asked.

"Just a wild guess," Susie replied as she filled a shaker with ice.

Conor turned and faced Rosita. "You been here long?"

"Ten minutes. I was just talking to Ingrid."

"Ingrid?"

"We chatted when she came to the bar to pick up a drink. She waved at you. Didn't you see her?"

"No. Where is she?"

He swiveled around on the bar stool.

Rosita pointed to the side of the room. "She was over there. At that table. Guess she left."

He sang a line from the Joni Mitchell song "Big Yellow Taxi." "Don't it always seem to go . . . that you don't know what you've got till it's gone."

"That's true, Bard."

Susie placed a martini in front of him. He picked it up and raised the glass in a toast. "*Salud.*"

"*Salud,*" Rosita responded.

As he lowered the glass, he felt a twinge of pain in his shoulder. He grimaced noticeably.

"You really need to get that looked at," she said. "Maybe start physical therapy."

She got up, stood behind him, and began kneading his shoulder with both hands.

"Massage helps get the blood circulating in the area of the injury," she explained.

He felt himself relax as she worked her fingers into his aching joint.

"Feel better?" she asked.

"Yeah. Nothing like a woman's touch."

She gave his shoulder a final squeeze and sat next to him. "How many times I have to tell you, Bard. I'm just one of the guys."

"Thanks for reminding me, Rubio."

Esther Phillips's 1975 disco rendition of Dinah Washington's classic hit flowed out of the bar speakers.

"What a difference a day made . . . twenty-four little hours . . ."

Conor took a sip of martini. *Twenty-four little hours.* That's how close he was to a meeting at Sony. Okay, it didn't happen. But something good did come out of it. Validation. Alan Woodcliff liked what he heard. *That's not nothing, right?* So what now? Stay on the job? Retire and go after a music career with a vengeance? He'd figure all that out tomorrow.

Acknowledgments

My wife, Aida, for her unwavering support. My agent, David Vigliano, whose encouragement inspires my writing. My editor, Roz Lippel, who kept me on the right track throughout the process.

Detective Kevin Schroeder, who provided invaluable insight into the world of law enforcement. Diamond dealer Sam Lieberman, who gave me a crash course on New York's Diamond District.

My friends and family who are always there when I need them.

About the Author

CHARLES KIPPS is an award-winning screenwriter, producer, and author. His television credits include *Exiled: A Law & Order Movie, The Cosby Mysteries, Columbo,* and *Law & Order: Criminal Intent.* He is the author of the novel *Hell's Kitchen Homicide* and the nonfiction books *Out of Focus* and *Cop Without a Badge.* The recipient of an Emmy, a Peabody, and an Edgar Award, Kipps lives in New York City.